BLOOD ON THE BLADE

Haakon spun, knife in hand, just as the attacker leaped at him. He dodged the would-be assassin's long, thin blade, slashing frantically to try to keep the killer at bay. But the man moved like an eel, staying out of Haakon's reach—until, with one deft movement, he almost sliced Haakon's throat.

But Haakon was even quicker. He caught the man's knife hand as it flashed near his neck and snapped the assassin's wrist with a crack. Then he jerked the man upright and drove his own dagger into the killer's chest, up to the hilt. The man sagged and slid backward off the blade.

Haakon stood over him with a black look in his eyes that boded no good for whoever had unleashed this killer upon him. . . .

HAAKON'S IRON HAND

Eric Neilson

Created by the producers of
Wagons West, White Indian, and
Saga of the Southwest.

Chairman of the Board: Lyle Kenyon Engel

BANTAM BOOKS
TORONTO • NEW YORK • LONDON • SYDNEY • AUCKLAND

For all those whose love of adventure
marks them as true descendants, in blood
or spirit, of the viking folk.

HAAKON 3: HAAKON'S IRON HAND
*A Bantam Book / published by arrangement with
Book Creations Inc.*
Bantam edition / September 1984

*Produced by Book Creations Inc.
Chairman of the Board: Lyle Kenyon Engel*

ISBN 0-553-24368-3

Published simultaneously in the United States and Canada

PRINTED IN THE UNITED STATES OF AMERICA

O   0 9 8 7 6 5 4 3 2 1

Contents

HAAKON'S TRAVELS IN THE EAST

HAAKON'S ROUTE ·········

NORTH SEA

TRONDHEIMS FJORD

THE TRONDELAG

NORWAY

SWEDEN

BIRKA

HEDEBY

BALTIC SEA

GARDA

RUS

DVINA R.

GNEZDOVO

RUS

DNIEPER RIVER

Prologue: Harud Olafsson

The Slav woman backed against the kitchen wall, pale eyes wide and desperate. Harud Olafsson kicked a cookpot out of the way and came after her. She said something he didn't understand.

Harud reached out and grabbed her arm. He swayed on his feet, but when he was drunk he had the strength of an ungovernable temper. He caught her other arm and began pulling her after him by main force. She struggled, wailing at him, and he twisted her wrist. *I want her,* he thought drunkenly. *I should have her. She is only a thrall.*

Harud pinned her arm behind her and put his hand over her mouth, pushing her out the kitchen door into the corridor that led to the guestchamber. It was empty—Jarl Thjodulf and the rest of his men were still drinking Prince Oleg's ale and telling lies about old battles. Harud dropped the woman on a bed and began tearing at her gown. He had asked Oleg for her an hour ago, in the feast hall. Oleg had said he could have her only if she was willing, and she hadn't been. She had picked up her skirts to run, leaving Oleg's and Thjodulf's men to laugh at him and ask what was missing that the thrall-women didn't like his bed.

Oleg had offered him another woman, but Harud wanted this one, he thought stubbornly, drunkenly. She clawed and bit at him, and he raised a hand to hit her. She was pretty, but he didn't really care about that. He wanted someone to bend to his will, to be master over, because when he was master over someone else, it helped to still the fear that Haakon Olesson would come out of Norway and kill him. Harud had been running from that since the summer. It had driven him first to Sweden and now, in the service of a Swedish jarl, south to the Rus lands.

He hit the woman across the face to make her lie still, and she screamed and stuck her fingers in his eyes. Harud staggered back, fury rising up in him like a fire. He now had his dagger in his hand. The woman saw the gleam of the blade and tried to run. He caught her by the throat and stabbed up under her ribs.

Harud's eyes burned and streamed where she had jabbed at them. He wiped them with the back of his hand, raging, and looked at the dead woman on the bed. The ale was pounding in his blood, and his head had started to ache. She was only a thrall, he thought sullenly. He had enough money to pay Prince Oleg weregild. He pushed her off the bed and sat down so his head would stop aching. In the morning he would be gone anyway, south to Mikligard where Haakon Olesson couldn't find him, and he was safe enough until then. He was a guest. He looked at the dead woman angrily. Thralls didn't matter. She shouldn't have fought him.

I Ragnar the Noseless

"If Harald Halfdansson has a mind to speak with Haakon Olesson, then let him come to the Trondelag and speak." Haakon gave King Harald's messenger a look that plainly said he had other things on his mind and turned his attention back to the lowing stream of red cattle that were churning up the track from the high pasture down to Haakonstead. "We are somewhat busy just now," he added for politeness's sake. It might be a mistake to make himself unfriends just now with Harald Fairhair, who was king in Vestfold and who would be king in the Trondelag if they let him. But Harald wanted more bowing and scraping than Haakon considered proper for a free Norseman to give him.

"Tonight! We will talk tonight!" he shouted over his shoulder as King Harald's messenger stumped away downhill. Tonight he could get Harald's envoy drunk and give him a nice present, and with luck he might be on the road before he realized that Haakon hadn't committed himself to anything.

"He is right all the same, though." Knut One-Eye's voice spoke from behind his left ear, and Haakon jumped.

"Don't pop out at me like a troll. Who is?"

"King Harald's jarl."

"That is not a jarl. That is a lapdog. *I* am a jarl." Haakon hooked his thumbs in his belt and surveyed his domain benevolently. The red cattle coming down from the summer saeter were followed by a white ocean of baaing sheep and bouncing half-grown lambs, and the men on either side of the trackway were cutting notches in their tally sticks for each ten animals that passed. Small boys, barefoot in the last of the late summer warmth, were prodding the stragglers along. Downhill at the steading, the thralls would sort

3

them into the right pens and cut out any that didn't look fit to keep through the winter.

Haakon had spent some of the plunder from his Irish raid and his wife's stolen dowry on sheep and cattle and taken more land under the plow around Haakonstead this season. A hundred and fifty fighting men sworn to his service was a fine thing to claim, but a hundred and fifty mouths could eat a hold bare in a winter. There was really no reason why Haakon should oversee the autumn herding-in himself, but there was a certain satisfaction for him in watching his four-footed wealth trot by and knowing that he wouldn't have to buy outside the hold to keep his people fed through the winter. Also, he had no wish to talk to Harald Fairhair's envoy at a time when the man might pin him down to something.

"It'll be the treaty with Cadiz," Knut said. "King Harald likes to have a hand in foreign matters."

"King Harald likes to have a hand in my pocket," Haakon said. "The treaty with Cadiz is between Abdullah the Wise and me."

The treaty offered Haakon's name and protection in the Norse markets to any Arab merchant the wali of Cadiz should choose to send and the wali's protection in Cadiz to any Norseman who could claim himself a sworn friend of Haakon Olesson. That Haakon would be able to charge the Norse shipowners for that privilege would not have escaped King Harald Fairhair.

"I will talk with Harald next season when we have been to Mikligard and back," Haakon said. "I don't have time to tiptoe around a council table with him now."

Knut snorted. "You are still going to Mikligard? To chase a man who by now is probably dead and eaten by wolves in Sweden?"

"Harud Olafsson stole my wife," Haakon said.

"And you killed his father and burned his steading in Ireland, and his men left him in Sweden and stole his boats to go home in when they heard," Knut said. "Also you have your wife back, and she took no harm." Below the hillside, Knut could see a round figure in a blue gown come out of the dairy, with a jar of buttermilk. "Likely you will have a son in the winter."

"He stole my wife, and he stole that land from my father," Haakon said stubbornly. "That was a blood-debt for my father. And my brother and sisters. My mother would have given me no peace if I hadn't paid it. This is another matter, between Harud Olafsson and me. And Ragnar the Noseless says Harud has gone to Mikligard with a Swedish jarl."

"Birka market gossip."

"Likely enough to be true. Ragnar has a nose like a hound."

Knut knew when it was unwise to push Haakon further, but this was important. "Better than that hound," he said, grinning, to soften it. The great gray beast that was loping in and out of the trees beside the track saw them and sat down, fanning his tail happily in the grass.

"Wulf is a wolfhound," Haakon said indulgently. "He doesn't waste his time with rabbits."

A *man-hound*, Knut thought, looking at Wulf's gaping smile. The dog had torn the throat out of one of Harud Olafsson's spies. "It will take a whole season to get to the Black Sea and back," he said, working his way carefully to the subject of a vengeance trip to Mikligard as opposed to a proper trip for Norsemen, which was raiding. "The men are saying you will lose your luck if you turn trader in Mikligard." Trading was all right, but only to compensate for a viking trip that had ended empty-handed. "They talk of asking a seeress to tell them if they should demand you lead them viking instead. They want some sign that you're open to more than your own stubbornness in this."

Haakon grinned darkly. "Then we will go to Mikligard and drop Harud Olafsson into the Black Sea and see if he floats. If he does, we'll hang him up on a tree for Father Odin for good weather, and then go viking. Will that content you?"

Knut's one good eye had an exasperated look. When Haakon took a thing in his head, it couldn't be shaken out. "Ragnar aside, why are you so sure he has gone to Mikligard? Harud left a man on your ship to kill you. It was only good luck that he didn't. Why should he run to the Romans in Mikligard?"

"He wouldn't go home to Ireland," Haakon said. "He

won't sit in Sweden and wait for me, either. I know Harud.
He will run first, then find out if I'm dead. I will ask
Ragnar what sort of cargo to take to Mikligard, so you can
be telling the men they will be paid well enough. That
should take care of their signs and seeresses."

The last of the sheep bleated past, and Haakon shouldered
the ax that lay in the grass at his feet. It had a gold-washed
sheen to the blade and a haft of fine red wood, and it went
with him everywhere. No man who was not a fool went
unarmed, even on his own land. Haakon scrambled down
the hillside to the cattle track. "I should like to see
Mikligard," he said over his shoulder. "Ragnar the Noseless
says there is no place like it in the world."

Mikligard, the "Great City," sat on the Bosporus, and
the Romans called it Constantinople for their emperor
who had built it.

"Ragnar says their palaces are made of gold," Haakon
said, slithering down an outcrop of rock onto the trampled
grass.

Knut followed him. "Then why don't we raid there?"

"We haven't enough men," Haakon said wistfully. "But
it would be fine to see it."

What was the use of looking at it if they couldn't raid it,
Knut thought, but he followed Haakon down to the steading without asking.

There was a great deal of bustle in and around
Haakonstead and an overpowering smell of blood and
cookfires from the slaughter. The weakest of the herds
would be killed for winter meat and, what wasn't eaten
over the next few days, salted to last the season. Haakon
found his wife counting on her fingers by the door of the
main hall, an empty pitcher in her hand and her long pale
hair coming out of its heavy knot. "There will not be
enough beer," she said fatalistically as he came up. "There
never is."

"Ragnar sent three casks of mead," Haakon said. "They
can drink that, and if they are still standing, they can
drink the wine that Harald's envoy brought."

"Then they will all be sick," Rosamund said, but she
looked relieved. It was more important that there be

enough to drink at Harvest Festival than that they not be sick afterward. They would be anyway.

"Pour as much as you can into Harald's envoy," Haakon said. "And tell Gunnar I want a *long* poem."

"He won't go away until you talk to him, Haakon," Rosamund said.

"No, but the longer it takes him to get to the meat of his message, the harder it will be. I am *not* going to tie myself to Harald Fairhair, and I am not going to try to tie the Trondelag to him, either, which is what he wants."

"Haakon Grjotgardsson did, or so you said."

"Haakon Grjotgardsson was the greatest jarl in the Trondelag. He could afford to be friends with Harald Fairhair and still stick out a spear when Harald got his nose too close. I cannot—not yet. Certainly not while I'm in Mikligard."

"Mikligard." Rosamund sighed. "Haakon, can't you let that be? Let your gods have Harud. I doubt they'll deal very gently with him now."

"The gods expect a man to pay his own debts. So do I. And I have argued this already with Knut. And Gunnar. And Snorri Longfoot. And that mad Egyptian who keeps saying that *his* god has told him to build me a ship. I have had enough of the gods and enough of not going to Mikligard."

Rosamund, who was about to say that *she* was the one who had been stolen by Harud Olafsson's slavers, and that *her* God taught that punishment was to be left to Him, thought better of it. Haakon had the look of a man much tried just now, and when she had married him it had, after all, been by his own gods. She would have preferred a Christian marriage, but any marriage was better than none with a child on the way, and she doubted that any Christian priest would have been willing to come within a mile of Haakon's steading unless he had the stuff of martyrs in him, and certainly not to marry a Christian woman to the jarl.

She gave up and watched her husband stalk into the house. Prodding always made him irritable. His mother was an Irishwoman by birth, although she was Norse enough now, and Rosamund wondered if that had something to do with it. The Irish were a prideful, touchy lot. She smiled and set the pitcher down by the doorpost for a thrall to deal with. If Haakon had it under his skin to go to Constantinople in the spring, then she supposed he would go. She looked around the yard. The slaughter seemed to be well in hand, and the main hall was ready for the feasting, hung with pine boughs and with the fire new laid. And, in any case, Haakon's mother was here, and she was a woman who liked to take charge. Rosamund went in and pushed open the door to their bedchamber. The child was growing heavy. Better to be thought shirking her wifely duties now than to fall asleep at the feast.

Haakon was sitting on the edge of the bed with his ax across his knees and his dark beard jutting out stubbornly, even though there wasn't anyone in the room with him. Rosamund gave the ax a wary eye. There was something un—well, not unholy—but certainly un-Christian about it, and it seemed to her sometimes that it came to his hand like a hound. She curled up on the bed behind him and wiggled comfortably into the furs.

"Lazy thing." He smiled at her and put a hand to her cheek, and she kissed it.

"I've been up since dawn," she said, sleepily indignant. "What is the use in being a jarl's wife if I can't sleep in the afternoon?" She closed her eyes and then opened one again. "I forgot. Snorri Longfoot and your mad Egyptian were looking for you. They had a piece of wood with marks scratched all over it. They tried to explain it to me, to tell you, but it made as much sense as Arabic spells, and I said I would tell you to find them."

"Yazid says he can build me the greatest ship on the water," Haakon said, "and it seems that Snorri Longfoot doesn't think he's lying."

"That's a better payment than most men's gratitude," Rosamund said practically. Haakon had saved the Egyptian from a wrecked ship in the eye of a summer gale. "He's almost been living in the ship house since he was well enough to work. I told Guthrun to have one of the thralls take him and Snorri some food now and again, or I think he'd starve."

Haakon looked uncomfortable. It would be a fine thing

to sail a ship like that, but just now there was the matter of where he would sail it. A large, deep ship would ground itself in the shallow rivers of Rus that were the traders' route to Mikligard. He stood up. "Sleep. I'll have someone send Guthrun to you in a while, or you will sleep through the feast. I know you."

Outside, there was no sign of Snorri Longfoot, the ship's carpenter, or Yazid and his mysterious scribblings, or anyone else who might demand the jarl's attention, and Haakon trotted guiltily through the open yard and back up the cattle trail. He felt foolish hiding from his wife and his shipwright, but he had no mind to be caught talking to the empty air, or, worse yet, to anything that might appear to be talked *to*.

The land above the steading rose sharply, and he found a clear spot among the trees that clung to the slope, and a rock to sit on, and sat. He laid the ax in the pine needles at his feet and looked at it thoughtfully. It was a god's gift. It had been given to him in a night of dark magic on an island that, for all Haakon knew, might have risen from the sea for that purpose only and disappeared again by now. Certainly he hadn't tried to go back to look for it again. But the ax was real enough, and it had come from Thor Odinsson. Haakon was as sure of that as he was of most things. But no man who makes himself friends with a god is ever entirely free of the god afterward. The ax was an accepted part of him now, but there were times when he felt the need to assert himself, lest he become the thing's thrall.

"I am going to Mikligard," he said experimentally. The golden head of the ax seemed to glow slightly in the fading light. Haakon picked it up again and felt it tug at his hands until he turned it to point to the west. It seemed satisfied with that and glowed a little more brightly. Haakon had always wondered if anyone besides him could see that. So far no one had seemed to find the ax odd, except for the men he had killed with it in combat and the wali of Cadiz when he had asked for it as a treaty gift. The ax had made its wishes plain enough then. Just now it seemed inclined to be cryptic. Haakon glared at it. The ax had pointed at things before—it had found Yazid of Alexandria, for in-

stance, clinging to a reef amid drowned men and the
shattered timbers of his ship. And in a roundabout way it
had sent him to the Ram's Head Cape on the west coast of
England to get Rosamund. But those were tangible things
that a man could put his hands on or people that the
Norns had marked to cross his path. Lately, wherever
Haakon was, the ax had begun to swing to the
west . . . sometimes a little northwest or southwest, but
always west. And there was not, so far as Haakon knew,
anything in that direction but Iceland and maybe the edge
of the world.

"I am going to Mikligard," he said again, firmly. And
then he thought that through the wind in the trees and
the noise of the gulls on the fjord and the far, muffled
noises of the steading, a voice in his head said quite
plainly, *That is not my wish*.

He put the ax down gingerly. Voices in his head un-
nerved him. He didn't care for the idea that there should
be anyone in there but himself. "You gave her to me," he
said aloud. "You sent me to England to steal her out of her
father's hold, and you sent me Gunnar Thorsten, who
used to be her father's thrall, to show me how to do it
because her father was going to give her to Harud Olafsson,
who has already had two wives and beat one of them to
death. And Harud Olafsson took her and Gunnar Thorsten
out of my hold while I was gone and sold her to an Arab
slaver for spite, because I took her to wife."

You also took her dowry. The voice sounded amused.
Three chests of coin, was it not?

"I am going to Mikligard." He seemed to have been
saying that to someone or other all day. "When I have sent
Harud Olafsson down Hel-Road, then I will go west."

Is that a bargain, Haakon Olesson? The voice was
serious now.

One didn't make a bargain with a god if one might have
to go back on it. Haakon took a deep breath and picked up
the ax. "That is a bargain."

The glow began to fade from the axhead, and he remembered the question that he hadn't asked. "Wait! Why
west?"

The gulls' mewing voices were sharp in the clear air, but

there was nothing else save the ring of a hammer on metal down below in the steading and the voices of the herdsmen. The ax shone dully in his hand. It was only an ax now, a fine, well-balanced weapon, oddly colored, but with the life-feel gone out of it. It might not be a good idea to cross Thor Odinsson, he thought. The gods were not above playing jokes on men, and Haakon had just made a promise to this god that he couldn't break. He hoped Thor wasn't going to let him sail west with no notion of why— and have the amusement of watching Haakon trying to find a crew to go with him.

"Eat." One of Jarl Thjodulf's men prodded Harud Olafsson in the ribs with his dagger hilt. "And keep your sour temper to yourself," he added as Harud glared at him and put a hand on his own knife.

"This is swill for pigs." Harud poked a finger in the dung-colored mush in his bowl.

"You'll get used to it—" Thjodulf's man said, "or you'll offend them, and the jarl won't like it." He turned back to watch the Magyar horsemen galloping in a cloud of dust on the flat plain. He didn't like Harud and thought it would be no great sadness to anyone if the Magyar chief took offense and killed him. Jarl Thjodulf had been trading with the Magyars for twenty years, and the old man would be furious if Harud picked a quarrel.

Harud took a mouthful and spat it out, glowering, but he didn't say anything else. The Magyars were savages, ferocious as wolves. Jarl Thjodulf was the only outsider ever to set foot in their camps and come away with his head still attached to the rest of him. For Thjodulf the Magyars sent mounted warriors every year to guard his trade ships through the wild lands south of Koenugard, so Thjodulf traveled when he pleased. The other Swedish jarls had to wait at Prince Oleg's city in Koenugard until there were enough of them to make a convoy.

Every year Thjodulf brought cloth, furs, and cooking pots to the Magyars before he went on to trade the rest of his goods in Mikligard. He was sitting with the Magyar chieftain, Arpad, now, perched cross-legged on a flat stone spread with horsehides, while Arpad's warriors played

some mounted game in the meadow for the chief's amusement. Stuck in the ground were flags, which the horsemen
tried to pull free; but the flags were tied to spears, and the
man who held one could turn it around and use it on those
who pursued him. Two men and a horse had been killed
already, and Arpad appeared to be enjoying himself hugely.
He bellowed with laughter as two horses crashed into each
other and their riders fell under the thrashing hooves. Jarl
Thjodulf sat beside him, his white beard wagging as he
jabbered to the chieftain in some unintelligible tongue. A
girl in red and green skirts, layered one over the other,
poured a drink into a bowl, and Jarl Thjodulf gulped it
appreciatively.

Harud spat again. He knew what was in the bowl. They
had given him some, and it tasted like horse's piss.
Thjodulf was an old fool. These people were like vicious
dogs, but they would come to Thjodulf's hand, and they
could be useful. A jarl who made an army out of these
people could take all the land between here and Koenugard
and control the trade himself instead of paying Prince
Oleg ship-tax just to pass through Koenugard. But no,
Thjoduld paid the tax and brought cooking pots and
watched them play silly games with horses. Thjodulf was
old and soft—too soft to go viking anymore.

Three men had caught up all the flags among them.
They reined in their horses up in front of Arpad and stuck
the flags spearhead-end first into the ground. The losers
limped after them. One grabbed a man who had carried
the flags and twisted him around in the saddle. The first
man lashed out with a knife, and the horses reared. In a
moment both men were thrashing on the ground.

Arpad got up off his horse skins and pushed his way to
them. He was a mountain of a man. He caught each man
by his hair and flung them apart. Harud watched with his
mouth open as Arpad drew his own knife and cut the first
man's hand off. He flung it at him, grunted, and walked
back to his seat while the man howled and someone tied a
thong around his wrist. Jarl Thjodulf sat unmoving. Harud
shuddered in spite of himself. He picked up his bowl and
ate. If he angered Arpad, Thjodulf wouldn't save him; the
jarl was still angry about the thrall-girl Harud had killed in

Koenugard. Harud watched as the Magyars carried the screaming man into a tent. Arpad was a savage; he believed that his soul was in a little gold box that he kept in his tent. But these people would be like a Hel-Wind if they were ever loosed on the country to the south. There might be something in that. Harud stuck his fingers in the bowl again, ignoring the taste. Arpad and Thjodulf stood up. Harud caught Arpad's eye and nodded to show that it was good. Arpad grinned at him, showing blackened teeth. He strode by with Thjodulf, and Harud gagged and swallowed the mouthful. He surreptitiously tipped the rest into another man's bowl and followed Arpad.

The orange glow of the Harvest Fire dimmed the pale light from the iron lamps and made a nearly overpowering heat in the crowded hall at Haakonstead, but no one seemed to care. Most of the men had thrown their shaggy wool or fur cloaks behind them, back over the benches, where they trailed in the straw and the gnawed bones or were slept on by the hounds that lounged at their masters' feet. Thralls with beer crocks threaded their way between the tables, while Haakon's men held their beer horns with one hand and roasted meat with the other and told each other tales of old fights. Most of them grew somewhat with the telling.

At the high table, King Harald Fairhair's envoy sat cutting strips off a piece of meat with his dagger, scowling impatiently at Haakon. The jarl was head to head with Ragnar the Noseless, flipping a silver coin to settle some dispute, the start of which neither of them seemed to remember. Haakon looked very fine, in a russet-colored shirt and breeches, embroidered in gold, and a dark green cloak stuck through with a massive gold and amber pin that made his broad-shouldered form look heavier than usual. His dark hair and beard were freshly washed and contrasted interestingly with the other, fair, heads around him. Ragnar gave a yelp of triumph and snatched the coin off the table as it came down head-side-up. Ragnar the Noseless had a reputation as the shrewdest trader in Norse waters, and it was not undeserved. He was a short, bowlegged man, with pale hair beginning to fade gray, and

was wearing a bright purple cloak and breeches, colored
with what must have been a fortune in dye. Half his nose
was a twist of old scars and the other half was gone,
souvenir of a knife fight that had happened so long ago
that no one really remembered it, save to mark Ragnar as
a man to be cautious with.

Rosamund sat between Haakon and King Harald's envoy, with the envoy glaring across her at Haakon. Guthrun
had awakened her at twilight and brought out a fresh gown
of pale green linen and an overgown of purple-blue,
pinned at the shoulders in Norse fashion with great circu-
lar brooches of gold, like round, entwining beasts. A
necklace of gold and carnelian and white quartz beads was
strung between them. Her pale hair was combed back into
a heavy knot under her kerchief, as befitted a married
woman.

She watched the envoy out of the corner of her eye and
waved a hand behind her for a thrall to come and fill his
beer horn. The envoy bowed his head to her politely, but
he didn't leave off scowling. If Haakon didn't talk to the
man, he was going to explode, Rosamund thought. She
raised her eyebrows at Haakon's dark-haired mother, sitting with her second husband across the long table from
them, but Sigrid just shrugged and gave Haakon an exasperated look. She had spent thirty years trying to get
Haakon to do things that she wanted him to, without
much success.

Gunnar, Rosamund thought. It was time for Gunnar. He
was sitting with Guthrun on the far side of Sigrid's husband, Erik, with his long hands wrapped around his beer
horn and staring with an abstracted gaze into its depths.
Composing tonight's feast-poem, no doubt. Or maybe only
mooning over Guthrun, who had a will-she-won't-she atti-
tude about marrying him, which was enough to drive even
a poet mad—all poets quite possibly being mad to start
with. The black-haired slave girl whom the wali of Cadiz
had given Gunnar was standing behind him, keeping his
beer horn full and offering him bites of the spiced fruit,
nuts, and fine, white wheat bread that were the feast fare
at the jarl's table. Guthrun, Rosamund noted, had slid as
far away down the bench as she could get from Gunnar's

thrall-girl, with the air of someone avoiding a contagious disease.

The only people who are enjoying themselves are Haakon and Ragnar, Rosamund thought. And maybe Sigrid and Erik, who were both getting drunk and beginning to fondle each other. And Haakon's men, of course. She saw Knut One-Eye with a full horn in one hand, arm wrestling with Donal MacRae with the other. At least they would remember this Harvest Feast as a proper one, befitting a jarl, if they remembered anything at all tomorrow.

It was her first feast since she had been married— properly married, before priests—to Haakon except for her wedding feast, and Sigrid had taken charge of that. This one was all Rosamund's doing, and she was determined that no one would say that the Englishwoman that Jarl Haakon had wedded wasn't openhanded. The walls were hung with her best tapestries and decked with twisted ropes of pine boughs and autumn foliage. There had been guest-gifts for every man, and new clothes for all the thralls. Every table in the hall was covered with white linen, and the high table had silver dishes. Besides the freshly killed beef and mutton, there were wild and tame pigs; ducks and hares roasted whole; apples, hazelnuts, peas, plums, and even strawberries shipped in baskets from Hedeby; mead and the beer that was brewed on the steading; and fruit wines and King Harald's hopeful gift of red wine from the Rhine. The red wine was a rarity and for the high table only unless the beer ran out. Haakon's men wouldn't think much of it anyway, except for the expense of it.

Ragnar had no such prejudice. He took an appreciative gulp and beamed at King Harald's envoy. Haakon sat, looking jovial, and the envoy bent slightly forward and opened his mouth.

"Hah! That is fine wine," Ragnar said. He bit into a duck's leg. "Where is my dog?"

"In the dairy with her dam, where she won't frighten the Harvest Spirits," Haakon said before the envoy could speak, and they were off again. Haakon let out a bellow of laughter, and the envoy sat back and snapped his mouth shut. Ragnar had brought Haakon a wolfhound bitch to

mate with Wulf, and a puppy from the first litter was to be
the price of her passage. Wulf thought she was fine
enough, but everyone else thought she looked like a troll's
changeling. Ragnar wanted a bitch to breed pups of his
own, and the only one in the litter favored her mother
with unfortunate faithfulness. "Maybe you'd best wait for
the next litter."

"Go and get her!" Ragnar shouted at the thralls in
general, and someone went. "We'll see." He counted on
his fingers. "If you take Wulf with you in the spring, we
can mate her back to him and have pups to sell in
Mikligard. I think." He counted again and got a different
sum.

"You are drunk," Haakon said. "It is simple enough. She
is two months old, and it takes two months to make pups,
and big dogs come late in season mostly, so call it ten
months to breed her . . . and that is—ten months!" he said
triumphantly.

"That is twelve months," Rosamund said, vexed that he
was talking about dogs and being rude to the envoy. "You
can't sell the pups the day they are born."

Haakon counted again and looked sorrowful. "She is
right."

The thrall brought the puppy and set her down on the
table in front of Ragnar. She was a dark slate color, with
ears that stuck out in different directions and a fat stumpy
tail that hadn't grown any of its feathering yet. Her eyes
were set at slightly different levels. She sat down on her
haunches and put a foot in the salt dish.

"Mother of God," Rosamund said. The envoy looked
mad enough to ride for Vestfold now and tell Harald
Fairhair a thing or two about Haakon Olesson that would
start a war. She looked desperately at Gunnar and prodded him with her shoe under the table, and he took his
nose out of his beer horn and stood up.

He jumped up on the bench and stood there, swaying
slightly, until the men in the hall took notice of him and
started pounding their knife hilts on the tables. Haakon
and Ragnar were feeding the puppy pieces of mutton on
the table linen, but they had the grace to stop talking and
listen.

> "Seed-giver, sun-bringer,
> Husband of harvest—"

Gunnar closed his eyes and stopped swaying on the
bench. He was very nearly as drunk as Haakon, but it
never changed his poetry. Drunk or sober, he could pull
men's attention around him like a cloak, so that they
ceased their quarrels and forgot their grievances and listened,
caught in the sound of it.

> "Gold-headed, horse-lord,
> Life-sower—"

It was a praise-poem to Frey, who was lord of the
harvest and, with his twin, Freya, giver of fertility to
fields, herds, and man. They came of an older stock than
the other Norse gods, Haakon had told Rosamund. They
were among gods that went back to the world's beginning.
It was also said, she noted wryly, that King Harald Fairhair
in Vestfold gave his first worship to Frey. Gunnar was
being particularly diplomatic. He painted a bright picture
of lively Frey, who had danced in the cornfields at the
world's start, so that the guests, if they cared to look,
could almost see the god's face, gold in the glow of the
Harvest Fire; then Gunnar shifted carefully into a praise of
the men who worshipped Frey, Harald Halfdansson the
Fairhaired presumably among them. From there it was
easy to shift again, into praise of other men who would
bring good to Norway and word-fame to Harald, even if
indirectly: Haakon Olesson, for instance, who had raided
the Arabs to take back his lost wife, and had come away
with wife and a treaty to make Norsemen rich with goods
from southern markets. Great was the fame that Haakon
Olesson had brought to Norway. Gunnar's implication was
that any king who could not be content with that and
wanted instead a share in a free jarl's rightful reward was
not the just man he claimed to be.

The men in the hall were swaying on their benches in
rhythm to Gunnar's words, spell-caught, by the time he

finished. Harald's envoy looked less impressed, but he
knew when he was cornered. Haakon grinned broadly at
him and asked if King Harald in Vestfold could boast a
finer poet than Gunnar Thorsten. Gunnar got down off his
bench before he fell down, and the envoy looked as if he
would like to see Haakon Olesson and his poet both dead
and howe-laid. There was very little pressure he could put
on Haakon now that would accord with Harald Fairhair's
dignity.

Haakon swung his legs over the bench and patted
Rosamund's shoulder, and she knew to move down beside
Ragnar. Haakon sat down again next to Harald's envoy and
held out his beer horn for someone to fill. He wiped his
moustache on the back of his hand and gave the envoy a
jovial smile. "Now we will talk."

"He has gone," Haakon said. "He was not in a good
mood and his head hurt, but he has gone away home to
Vestfold, and I didn't have to make any promises."

"Not this season," Ragnar said, "but you will. Or fight.
You grow too powerful, my friend."

They were sitting at the high table, amid the mess from
last night's feasting, while the thralls cleaned and the men
who hadn't yet awakened snored from the benches and the
floor.

"Maybe. But by then I will have thought of something.
I do not wish to be King Harald's friend in the Trondelag,
and I can't afford to be unfriends, either. But it will keep
for a while now, I think. I gave the envoy a fine present
and one for King Harald, better than Harald gave me.
Now tell me about the ship-roads through Gardariki."

Gardariki was the "Land of Towns," the country between the Baltic—Norse waters—and the Black Sea.
Gardariki had no central rule, only the scattered villages
of the Slavs and the trade-built towns of the Rus along its
rivers. The Rus were Swedish jarls, raiders who had
settled in, as the Norse had done in Ireland. Some had
their home steadings in Gardariki; some came only for the
trading season.

"You will want smaller boats," Ragnar said. "There are
dry-land crossings and rapids—bad ones. You need shallow

ships that can be carried when they're loaded. And it's a wild road—you'll need fighting men. The tribes south of Koenugard are raiders. The Pechenegs are the worst, but the jarls of the Rus aren't above raiding, either, if you look like easy pickings. Oleg, who is jarl in Koenugard, is honest enough, if you watch him."

Haakon pulled at his beard and thought it over. There was beer on the table in front of them, in clay pots instead of horns so they could set them down, and they drank it carefully. The wolfhound pup was snoring on Ragnar's foot. "How many traders make this passage?"

"You'd be surprised. One good trip can keep a man two, maybe three years, if he makes it. I've been once or twice. As I told you, it's a wild road. This may be my last trip. But there are always other men with a mind to try. They flock to Koenugard in the spring like geese going south and then sit there and mend sail and get drunk until the floods go down. In the fall they come back the same way."

"What is good cargo?"

"Anything from the north country is good trade in Mikligard. Furs, amber, walrus ivory. And slaves. There is always a market for slaves. And in Mikligard there are silks, fruit, spices, and wine to come home with."

Haakon whistled. Riches indeed. And spices and silk took little hold space for their value. "What about raiding?" He laughed. "Knut says we should raid Mikligard if it is as fine as all that."

"It has been done, but it took an army of all the Rus jarls to do it, and it was only to make the emperor open his harbor to trade with us. You might find something on the way back." Ragnar scratched the scarred remains of his nose and gave Haakon a shrewd look. "If they don't raid you first. They were snapping at my heels like Loki's wolf all the way. I grow old, Haakon, and I will make a bargain with you."

"When you are old, I will be bones in a green howe," Haakon said.

"Maybe. But I will make a bargain. I have been to Mikligard, and I have even spoken with their emperor there, whose name is Leo and who is not an unreasonable man. If Harud Olafsson is in Mikligard, he will be trying to hide under Leo's wing. We'll sail together, your ships and mine, and I will talk to Leo for you."

"Why?" Ragnar was a friend, but he would have to have a good reason to mix in something that might spoil his trading.

"Because if it comes to fighting there, I want your men at my back. I have heard there is trouble between the emperor in Mikligard and the Bulgars, who live along the Danube. And a country with a war going on is a chancy country to travel in. Also because I like your lady."

Haakon decided that both reasons were probably true. There was no one who had met her who did not love Rosamund, he was finding. "Done, then." He swept the empty beer horns on the table out of the way and got a piece of half-burned wood from the ashes in the hearth. "Now show me." He folded the cloth back. Rosamund wouldn't like it if they spoiled it any more than it already had been.

A thrall came and piled the things into the cloth and took it all away, and Ragnar drew a wavy line on the wood with the charcoal. "Here is the coast, see—the Baltic. The best route from Norway is here, up the Dvina River. Then we will have to carry the ships here, to Gnezdovo, then down the Dnieper River to Koenugard. Then we sit in Koenugard until the water level on the river is such that we can make the lower rapids with the least men killed. I am not joking, Haakon—they are bad. Then through the land of the Pechenegs to Berezany Island here, then hug the Black Sea coast past Bulgar country, and then, if we are still afloat, through the Bosporus to Mikligard here. That Arab shipwright of yours speaks Greek. Have him teach you over the winter. It will help." He sat back while Haakon traced his finger along the charcoal marks.

"And back the same way?"

"In the fall, yes. Some of these rivers freeze in winter. If you are late, you'll sit in Koenugard till thaw. As it is, there's very little turnaround time."

Haakon sat squinting at the charcoal marks, trying to see them as the rivers and steppeland of Gardariki.

"It's a long way for a blood-feud," Ragnar said quietly.

"I have a large grievance," Haakon said. "Besides, I

shall grow rich in Mikligard and come home and wear
purple trousers like Ragnar the Noseless."

Ragner snorted.

II Midwinter

"If you are going to pace like a penned wolf, go out and
check the cattle pens," Sigrid said. She gave Haakon a
push. "That child has bitten nearly through her lip trying
not to make noise because she knows you are out here."

"She told me her family's women have an easy time
with their babies."

"Undoubtedly," Sigrid said dryly. "*I* had an easy time
with my babies, but it is not something I would do after
breakfast to amuse myself. Also, it is her first. Go away,
Haakon."

Guthrun and a thrall-woman darted by with an armload
of bedding and a kettle, and Haakon eyed them nervously.
Sigrid gave him another push toward the door.

In the bedchamber, Rosamund heard the murmur of
their voices, and she looked up as Sigrid came in.

"He has gone to count his cows," Sigrid said, "and also
no doubt to curse me. Now try to relax. If you fight against
the pain, you will fight against the labor too, and that is
not good."

Rosamund nodded. Her face was pale, and she was
drenched in sweat. Red-haired Fann, who was betrothed
to Donal, sat beside the bed, holding her hand. A little
silver image of the Virgin, who was God's Holy Mother,
was wrapped in Rosamund's fingers, and her knuckles
were white from clamping down on it. Sigrid and Guthrun
had put a gold ring for Freya and a spindle for Frigg, who
was Odin's wife and queen in Asgard, under the straw of
the mattress, and Fann crossed herself when they weren't
looking, but Rosamund hadn't protested. She thought she
could happily pray to anyone who could speed this child
on its way.

"Not long now, I think," Sigrid said. "Take a deep breath with the next pain and push." A sharp knife and a thong for tying off the cord were ready on a table by the bed. The thrall-woman had a blanket in her arms. It was midwinter, and the wind howled icily under all the doors and found chinks in the timber walls and roof thatch. Another pain began on her left side and ground its way across to the right. Rosamund yelled, and all the women began to bustle importantly.

She was propped on pillows, and they lifted her under her arms until she was nearly sitting, and Sigrid pushed the covers back from her knees. There was another tearing pain that made Rosamund want to twist into a ball, but Guthrun held her by the shoulders and wouldn't let her, and then there was a high, thin cry like the gulls that swirled around her father's hold on the Ram's Head, and Sigrid was holding something that was wet and screaming and still tied by the cord to herself.

She only saw it for a moment before the thrall-woman had it bundled in her blanket, and then there were more pains and Sigrid was pushing down hard on Rosamund's stomach. She batted wearily at Sigrid's hands with her own, which felt like lead.

"The afterbirth has to come," Sigrid said. "Push."

Afterward Rosamund lay exhausted and watched while they washed her and changed the bed linens with her still in them and pushed a roll of bandages between her legs. The baby had quit crying, and the thrall-woman was cooing to it.

"Let me see him."

The thrall-woman looked frightened, and another old woman sniffed dolefully. "I knew no good would come of it, with all that happened while she was carrying."

"What's wrong?" Rosamund struggled to sit up, panicked.

Sigrid snatched the baby from the thrall-woman and gave it to her. "It's a girl, that's all," she said briskly, glaring at the women.

Rosamund cradled the baby, which opened its mouth and sucked at the air. She put it to her breast. "A girl. I was sure. . . ."

The old woman shook her head and clucked. "Foreign lands are always unhealthy."

"And that potion that the evil one gave to her," the thrall-woman said—Rosamund's brother had tried to have the child aborted when he still thought he could marry her to Harud Olafsson.

Sigrid raised her hand and cuffed both the women. "I never heard that a potion could change the sex of a child in a womb. Go and wash the linens and keep your tongues between your teeth. Fann, go and find Jarl Haakon and tell him his child is born. And stop crossing yourself; we are not demons. I was born a Christian, so I should know." Guthrun was cradling Rosamund's head against her shoulder, and Sigrid sat down on the other side. "She's a fine, healthy babe. Look how she sucks."

The baby's face was a mottled purple, and she had black hair like an ape's nearly to the bridge of her nose. Rosamund touched it gingerly with one finger. "Haakon—"

"Haakon will be happy to have her. He is not an oaf like some men, who think that they are not men at all if their first is not a son." She brushed her finger across the baby's cheek. "Haakon's father loved my Asa better than his sons, I thought sometimes." Sigrid's face looked younger than usual but etched with an old misery in the fitful lamplight. Asa had been only five when she was killed, and Sigrid's next youngest, Gwyntie, had died a few days later. Sigrid's arms had been empty very suddenly. She watched the baby hungrily.

"Asa," Rosamund said. She had thought of calling her Jeannot just now, for her own mother, but she couldn't bear to, not with Sigrid sitting there with that old, sad hunger in her eyes. It should be Asa, for the baby that Sigrid had lost when Olaf Haraldsson's men had come.

"Haakon will love her," Sigrid said, "you'll see. He will want to name her for you, I expect."

"Her name is Asa," Rosamund said, "and Haakon will have to like it." She put out her free hand and wrapped it around Sigrid, who was crying.

"A few minutes, no more. She is tired." The women's voices twittered outside the door, and Haakon's bulk loomed in the doorway.

"Am I to sleep in the byre with the cows? Go away." He

grinned at her proudly in the lamplight, with relief in the depths of his eyes, and shut the door in their faces. "You are clever," he whispered and kissed her, careful not to lean on the baby, asleep in the crook of her arm. "Mother told me what you named her. That was kind."

"You don't mind that she's a girl?" Rosamund's arm curved protectively around the baby. She had had it by her now for nearly an hour, long enough to make it hers. She would have hit him if he had said he did mind, he thought, laughing.

"She is a fine girl. Better to look like you than me, anyway."

Rosamund chuckled. "Only for a girl." Haakon was better looking than most men, and he knew it.

"Besides, we can always make a son if I feel the need for one."

Rosamund winced. *The second baby was always easier, they said. Please, Mother Mary, that "they" were right.* But the memory of pain was already fading against the satisfaction of the warm child in the crook of her arm. Asa did look healthy. So many babies never lived past infancy. She wouldn't think of that, Rosamund told herself firmly; it was ill luck. And this one had been through so much already—she must be strong. Rosamund giggled suddenly. "Old Bergthora thinks the climate in Cadiz is responsible for her sex."

Haakon let out a whoop of laughter, and the baby flung her arms wide, startled.

"Be quiet!"

"I'm sorry. And I don't care what sex she is, my heart, as long as we have her. Bergthora's a silly hen, but she's right in one thing. What happened in Cadiz can't have been good for either of you."

"Cadiz, no . . . Cadiz was not that bad," Rosamund said tiredly. "But Birka . . . I thought myself lucky when we got to Cadiz."

"What?" Haakon said sharply. "You told me he didn't ill treat you." The things that Harud Olafsson might have done to Rosamund between the Trondelag and the slave markets at Birka had been a nightmare in his mind until he had got her back.

Rosamund cursed herself under her breath. She hadn't told him any more than she could help because she had still been hoping that Haakon would decide against chasing Harud any farther. And in truth Harud hadn't laid a hand on her. But it was a forlorn hope, likely, that Haakon would let that change his mind for him.

"He didn't touch me," she said wearily. "Not once. I don't know why. Prideful, maybe. But he used to sit on an oar bench and tell me what would happen to me in the slave caravans. He paid Red Ali money to sell Gunnar and me to someone who would use us badly, and he used to sit for hours and tell me how it would be and what would happen to the child."

Haakon was sitting in the rushes on the floor by the bed, and now he sat up straight with a dark, wolf-look in his eyes and his teeth half-bared. "Go on."

"I don't want to," Rosamund said. "You can imagine. He wanted me sold for a kitchen drudge or a whore. He made Ali swear it, and then he would come and tell me again. But Harud was afraid of the Moors in Cadiz, and Red Ali knew he could get more money if he took us to the wali. Ali was a thief—we were lucky."

"That is another score to settle with Harud Olafsson," Haakon said. "Rosamund, I want to know what he said. I am going to do every one of those things to him before I kill him."

"No!" Rosamund's eyes were drooping closed, but they snapped open again. "You are not. That is an evil man, Haakon. I will not help you make yourself like him. Now go and send Guthrun to me. I'm so tired."

Haakon gritted his teeth, but he stood up. "You pick a fine time to tell me this, when you know I don't dare quarrel with you. That isn't fair."

Rosamund smiled up at him sleepily, her pale hair still damp against the pillows. He pulled the furs up around her and the baby. "No," she said. "I know it's not. I love you."

He kissed her and stalked out, and she heard him in the hall outside, swearing at the thralls.

The ship house seemed to be very full of people shifting new-cut oak timbers about, to the danger of the unwary, and setting out coils of hair rope and pots of caulking pitch for someone to inadvertently step in. Haakon supposed there was order in it somewhere. Yazid of Alexandria was clambering over a new-laid keel and muttering approval or displeasure at the workmanship; Haakon couldn't tell which. Snorri Longfoot stood with one enormous boot up on the base of a ship frame, waving a boat ell and shouting at a thrall for some unknown error. Most Norse ships were built in the open, as close to the water as they could be got, but not in midwinter. And these were being made to be carried, anyway.

Haakon stuck his head through the doorway and thought about taking it right back out again. His new ships seemed to be giving some trouble in the making, and Snorri Longfoot was an artist, not a man to be trifled with. He hadn't been pleased when he had had to haul the new ship he and Yazid had just started into its own ship house, with only the forestem fixed to the keel and all the planking to be stored in water through the winter and somehow kept from freezing, and all because Jarl Haakon had decided he wanted three riverboats instead. Haakon suspected that Yazid was not overly happy about it either, but he was an Arab, and it seemed that Arabs did not argue with their chieftains in the way that Norsemen felt privileged to do.

Yazid looked up from his calculations, saw Haakon in the doorway, and threaded his way to him through the confusion. He bowed solemnly and straightened up again, and Haakon thought there was a certain amount of amusement in the Arab's dark eyes. "We progress, lord. As you can see."

Snorri was still shaking his boat ell at the thrall, but Yazid seemed oblivious to the chaos, and he stood out like a wild, exotic plant among the tall, fair Norsemen in the ship house. He had a beaked nose and watchful hawk's eyes under a red and white head scarf held with a twisted cord around his brow. For the rest, he had adopted Norse dress in deference to the climate, and his Norse speech was good, if accented, but there was no one who would ever take him for a Norseman, even without the head scarf.

"You will have your fleet by spring, lord."

"I'm grateful," Haakon said. After all, Yazid could have simply thanked him for the kindness of his rescue and taken himself off to wherever he had come from, and Snorri couldn't have done all this work alone.

"It is the will of Allah," Yazid said solemnly. "Not these"—with a flick of his hand he dismissed the three half-built ships as lesser craft—"but the great ship that Snorri, your shipwright, and I have begun. I told you, lord, I saw it and you in a dream the night before you came to save me. One does not argue with a dream from Allah." The hint of a smile touched his hawk's eyes again. "Especially not when one has nearly drowned."

"No." Haakon suspected uncomfortably that the will of Thor might have had something to do with it, too. It was the golden ax that had directed him to a broken ship in the mist. In any case, Thor and the Arab's god could both wait one season. The gods were too thick about his head for his liking just now. "Do you have enough help?" He spoke Greek for the practice. Getting these three small longships built was what was important now, a plain task with no gods in it.

"Yes, lord." Hagar the Simple's substantial form lumbered by with four freshly trimmed strakes for the second ship's hull, and the Arab ducked. "Somewhat too much at times. We work by ourselves, Snorri and I, when your men have gone to eat, if there is delicate work to be done."

"I see. And when do *you* eat?" It occurred to Haakon that he had seen neither of his ship's carpenters at his table lately. Either they were living on sawdust or someone was feeding them.

"Your lady sends someone with a basket when she thinks we are in danger of starving," Yazid said.

"Ah? Good." Haakon turned his attention back to the hulls forming in the ship house: One was nearly finished, and the men were cutting the floor timbers for it. The second was half-built, and Snorri was tightening the clamps on the last strake laid on and checking its angle with the boat ell. The third was only a bare keel and stems, skeletal on its ship frame. They would be finished by sailing weather, but barely. Haakon leaned in the doorframe of the ship house and watched Hagar the Simple hoisting a wedge-shaped oaken strake into place. Meanwhile, the steading life revolved around the ships.

Nothing was more important than ships. Haakon remembered telling that to the wali of Cadiz when they had grown friendly. He chuckled: He had in the end given the wali a longship as a hearth-gift, but it would be worth it. Already two Norse shipowners had come to pay for Haakon Olesson's safe-conduct into Cadiz harbor. If he'd a mind to, he could grow as fat as his stepfather just on the trade with Cadiz. Erik the Bald had been putting on some girth since he had married Sigrid; she had swept his household into order with a new broom. It did Sigrid good to have someone besides himself to manage, Haakon thought, and he suspected that Rosamund thought so, too. They got on well together, Rosamund and Sigrid, but they were two strong-minded women and agreed best when each had her own house to rule and neither one's fingers poked into the other's pies.

The door swung inward, and Haakon dodged out of the way, stepping around a bucket of iron nails and roves for fastening the clinker-laid strakes, and a jumble of forked timbers marked for cutting as ribs or keelsons. Yazid and Snorri had chosen every tree themselves and stood by like overseers while they were cut. Haakon backed around a half-cut keelson, expecting another load of timbers to march by and very likely hit him in the head, and blinked as a muffled figure with a basket came through instead.

Guthrun shook the hood back from her face in a flurry of snow and pushed the basket at Yazid. "It is time that these men come and eat. If you wish to stay, this is for you."

Yazid put his hand over hers on the basket, but he didn't seem inclined to take it from her. "You are very kind. Also most beautiful in the snow."

It appeared to be an established routine, and Guthrun saw Haakon out of the corner of her eye and looked a little embarrassed. The men began laying down their work, and Yazid took Guthrun by the hand. "Come, Most Beautiful, I will show you what we have done today."

"I thought you told me you told Guthrun to send a thrall to the ship house with food when they wanted it."

"I did." Rosamund was sitting up in bed with the baby at her breast.

Haakon chuckled. "There would appear to be a great scarcity of thralls then. Or maybe it is only her fine blue eyes. Although not as fine as yours." He kissed her and put one hand on the breast that was free, and she pushed him away indignantly.

"What do you mean?"

"I am told that the Arabs like fair women," Haakon said, laughing. He stretched out beside her and put his hands under his head. "Yazid would appear to have an eye for Guthrun. He addresses her as 'Most Beautiful' and tells her how ships are built."

Rosamund looked appalled. "And where is Gunnar?"

"Having his feet rubbed by the wali's gift, no doubt. I want to see his face when he stops being an emir in a *hareem* and notices what Guthrun is doing."

"That is not funny, Haakon." Rosamund put the baby up on her shoulder and patted. "I have kept to my bed long enough. I will get up this afternoon and talk to Guthrun. And *you* will talk to Gunnar."

"No, I won't. I'm not his nurse. And a little competition will do them both good. Guthrun should have married him by now, and Gunnar should have taken his mind off his poems long enough to insist. He got her into bed with him, and he could have got her to a priest if he'd put his mind to it."

Haakon didn't look particularly worried, and Rosamund gave him an exasperated look. *He* wouldn't have to deal with a pair of squabbling lovers. *He* was going to sail to Mikligard in the spring and leave her here with Gunnar as steward and most likely a blood-feud when Gunnar woke up and probably tried to put a knife in Yazid. "The wali made an ill-chosen gift," she said, glaring at him. "And *you* should have stopped him."

"Gunnar can always give her away," Haakon said. "To me, for instance." There was a light in the back of his eyes, and the corners of his mouth twitched.

Rosamund put the baby in her cradle, very carefully, and got back on the bed. She sat next to Haakon and leaned over him. "Don't even think it."

"What would you do to me?"

Her pale hair hung down over her shoulders on either
side, like a curtain, enclosing them both. She smiled
sweetly. "It would be a surprise. You wouldn't ride a horse
for a while. Or anything else."

He let out a bellow of laughter and grabbed her and
pulled her down on top of him, and she yipped because
she was still sore from the baby, and they wrestled for a
while until she tore her night shift.

She sat up, holding it with one hand and trying to
straighten the furs on the bed with the other. "All right, I
will leave Guthrun and Gunnar alone. But if someone puts
a knife in your poet or your shipwright, don't blame me."

Haakon shook his head. "They won't go that far. I know
Gunnar."

"Well, you don't know Yazid." She gave him an innocent
look, purple blue eyes veiled in lashes. "If he is that fond
of blond women, maybe I will take his mind off Guthrun
for him while you are gone."

He grabbed for her again, but she rolled off the bed and
scooped the baby up out of the cradle to put her over her
shoulder. The baby belched, loudly, and Haakon fell back
laughing. "Hah! That is a Norseman's daughter!"

It was snowing again, a white flutter of powder through
the black trees, like lace against the glow from the open
door of the hall, and the yard glittered with a white,
unbroken crust. A drift of torches at the far end meant
that the thralls were shutting up the cattle byres for the
night. Most of the men who had farms of their own had
gone home to them for the winter, to be ready for the
spring sowing that would have to be made before sailing
weather. The rest had stayed in Haakonstead, and most of
them were gathered in the hall now to hear Gunnar sing
and to tell lies about old fights and to get drunk and chase
the thrall-women. Snorri and Yazid were still in the ship
house. Heaven knew what they were doing, Rosamund
thought—it was too dark to work by lamplight. Just talking
about ships, maybe. And maybe a good thing, too. Gunnar
was singing to a spot on the bare wall above Guthrun's
head, and Guthrun was sewing a shirt from the new cloth

they'd dyed yesterday and glaring at Gunnar over the needle.

Rosamund wasn't sure whether Yazid was oblivious to the trouble he had started or didn't care what Gunnar liked. She looked dubiously across the white yard, and then pulled the door closed against the snow and wrapped her shawl more tightly. It was cold in Norway, colder than England. But in her father's hold on the Ram's Head, she remembered always being cold in the dank stone keep, with only Wulf to curl up against, and the weight of trying to feed a threadbare household on the few pennies her father hadn't taken to pay his soldiers. Here she had Haakon for a bulwark against her cold. He was sitting beside Gunnar with a horn full of mead, getting very drunk and amiable. He had a strap for his ax sheath in his lap and had been punching new holes in it, but Rosamund thought that he probably couldn't see them anymore. He had put the awl down before he punched it through his knee.

Knut One-Eye was beside him, in much the same condition, and between Gunnar's songs they were arguing about whether it was possible to hatch a gull's egg with a hen. Rosamund had no idea why either of them would want to. Hagar the Simple sat with his broad back against a house beam, fletching a lapful of new arrows, and Thorfinn Solvisson was carving a new bone comb from a piece of deer antler. Neither time nor materials was wasted over the winter. There were always things to be built and mended, spun and dyed and sewn. And there was Haakon and the music for warmth—Gunnar's tales of Norse heroes and giants and trolls and great fights; and Donal's songs, a softer, wilder music that came, he said, from the old Britons who had held England before the Saxons.

Donal and Fann sat a little to one side, Donal with one arm around her shoulders, his dark head leaning on her red one, and his other hand fiddling with the white bronze strings of the harp he'd bought from Ragnar over the summer. In the protective circle of his arm, Fann looked a little less nervous than usual. They were Scots, a people who were kin in a roundabout way to the Irish, and

Haakon had bought them both out of a Birka slave market a year ago—Danish raiders had caught them too far from their hold and sold them into slavery. In anyone's household but Haakon's they would be thralls still. But Haakon had some bee in his helmet that Donal was one marked by the Norns to shape Haakon's fate in some way, and Donal would plainly have gone oath-sworn to Haakon if Haakon had been the devil himself. It was equally plain that Fann thought he might be. She was young, no more than fifteen, a little, plain thing with a church-mouse expression, her one great beauty in her flaming hair. When she was married, Rosamund thought, even that would be hidden under her headrail.

Rosamund gave her an encouraging smile as she threaded her way through the men sprawled on the benches around the hearth fire, to squeeze herself in by Haakon's other side. Donal thought Fann was a beauty, and even if she clung like glue to Rosamund's skirts when Donal was out of sight, at least she was courting no feud. A little of Fann's mousiness would do Guthrun no harm.

Guthrun sat very straight on her bench, in a cluster of other women, and sewed on her shirt. Not for Gunnar, Rosamund suspected. The lamplight and the hearth fire turned her butter-colored hair to bright gold and danced on the gilt and bronze pins at her shoulders. Gunnar's black-eyed thrall-girl was not in evidence, but if that was a peacemaking gesture, it was a tardy one.

> "Giant's cold daughter, wolf's companion,
> Look you how you're husband-finding.
> Foolish maiden, marriage-making
> To a face you've never seen."

Guthrun's eyes snapped up from the shirt and blazed at Gunnar, and there were red splotches of pure fury on her cheeks. He continued to address himself to the wall above her head.

> "Mountain's daughter, seacoast wedding,
> Mourning for the wolf-kind's howling,

> Seafowl mewling, salt waves lapping,
> Ill content the marriage breeding."

It was beginning to dawn on anyone not too drunk to take notice that there was more to Gunnar's choice of story than a fine tale to show off his talents. Skadi, a giant's daughter, when offered a husband from among the gods in Asgard, accepted—even though she had to make her choice after seeing no more than her prospective husbands' legs. She made her selection on beauty alone, hoping for Baldur the Shining, and got the hoary sea god Njord instead. They married, but neither was ever happy in the other's land. Ill-fated from the start, that marriage, Gunnar finished piously, and Guthrun jabbed her needle into the shirt and stood up. The women behind her were beginning to giggle, and there was a ripple of bass laughter from the men. It was a dull winter, hearth bound, and Gunnar was providing more excitement than had come their way since the summer raiding. Even Haakon and Knut had forgotten about their hen and were grinning broadly, waiting to see if Guthrun stuck the needle in Gunnar.

"Guthrun, go and see if the babe is waking yet," Rosamund said, wishing she could strangle Gunnar with his own beard. "Send Bergthora for me if she is, please."

Guthrun stalked across the hall to the door that led to the jarl's chambers at the end, not much minding whom she stepped on, and disappeared in an aura of flame and sulfur.

Gunnar sat down with a tight, drawn look around his mouth and held out his hand for his beer horn. Donal stood up and began to make a music on his harp, very quickly, and Rosamund gave her husband a look that said as plainly as any woman could with her silence, *I told you so*.

She could have saved her look. Behind his grin, Haakon was trying to think of a way to take either Gunnar or Yazid with him in the spring because a blood-feud was no joke, and they had a way of spreading. But he couldn't take Gunnar and leave Yazid behind to steal Gunnar's woman, and he couldn't take Yazid if he wanted a ship to go west in

the spring. He added it three ways and came out with the
same sum.

There was another matter that made Gunnar's woes
seem less pressing. The golden ax lay beside Haakon as it
always did, more an extension of himself than a weapon to
be picked up or laid aside. But it was only an ax now, as it
had been since the autumn herding, with none of the
sense of power, the feel of something living at the heart of
it, that had come when he laid his hand across the head.
Had Thor gone out of it, intending to keep his bargain and
return when Haakon sailed back from Mikligard? Or had
he gone away entirely to find another man more willing to
serve him? *I never swore to be your thrall,* Haakon
thought, looking at the ax blade and the light of the hearth
fire running red down the haft. He concentrated, trying to
call the power back again, and for a moment there was a
flicker, brief as a bird's wing. The god returning? Or was
the glint only something residual, left behind and fading?

Donal was singing, his black head bent low over the
harp, the firelight running down the scar on his cheek—
the scar that Haakon had seen in a dream before he had
met Donal and before the scar had been inflicted, Donal
under the golden roof of Valhalla where he sat and beckoned
to Haakon, and there was something wrong there, too,
because Donal was a Christian, and that he should go to
Valhalla made no sense.

The men had settled in again to listen to the wild harp
sound that was so different from the crashing voice of the
ocean, the whale's road, that was the music of their own
kind. Donal's songs came from the earth, from an old
land, up out of the low green hills where the faerie folk
lived and where the god Midir loved a mortal woman who
had once been his queen in the long ago. So he stole her
out of her new king's hall and turned her to a swan, and
together they flew into the green hills.

That was not a Christian song either, and it made Fann
look cross, but Donal seemed to find no conflict between
the silver medallion of the Christ around his neck and the
wild swan-wooing of the god in his song. And oddly,
Haakon had thought that the ax had gone warm under his
hand, although Midir of the hollow hills was no god of

Norway—nor even a god in his own land since the words of the White Christ had come there. Maybe it was the music that called up something older than gods. Or newer. Haakon found this line of thought confusing and tried to push it from his mind, but it sat there, insistent, riding on the ebb of the harp song.

He looked around for Rosamund and found that she had gone, probably to feed the baby or maybe to see that Guthrun wasn't angry enough to go out to the ship house and Yazid. The bench was still warm where she had sat. He would think of Rosamund, and that would take care of gods and old magic and any other thoughts but Mikligard. But Thor Odinsson had sent him Rosamund, too, hadn't he?

Haakon found that his head was beginning to ache, and for once he got up from the hall while he was still half-sober and went into the bedchamber. Rosamund was curled up under the furs with the baby, and he got in beside her and buried his beard in her shoulder.

III The Wild Swans

Spring comes late to Norway, but when it does, there is a green and watery beauty to the fjords. Haakon stood at the top of the footpath that ran from the steading yard down to the narrow shore and watched his men loading crates of soapstone pots into the little *Curlew* drawn up in shallow water. There were whetstones and pigs of Trondelag iron in the hold of *Gull Wing*. Homely goods, but useful trading at Hedeby and Birka. Packed in *Gray Goose's* hold, carefully baled in hides, were goods that would make the full trip to Mikligard—red fox and beaver furs and bundles of walrus ivory. Fighting shields, newly painted over the winter, were slung between the oar ports, and the men milled on the shore, kissing their women good-bye, counting weapons and gear, and watching the woolen tufts of clouds that sat fatly in a blue sky.

"There is an itch in your foot, Husband. It shows from here."

Haakon swung around to find Rosamund watching him, with the baby wide-eyed on her hip. "That is an itch all Norsemen have. We are sailors. You knew that when we wed."

"Not all Norsemen." There were Norse farmers and millers and hunters and all the other things that men did. She looked at him thoughtfully. "You are bandits."

Haakon was indignant. "We are rovers."

"It is the same thing."

He laughed. "Well, you were knowing that, too. But not this trip. We'll sell the pots and the iron at Hedeby for amber and probably at Birka for slaves and better furs. And this time you will please be here when I get back." It was a joke, but not entirely. The last time he had sailed from home waters, Harud Olafsson's men had come like thieves behind him, and Haakon still hadn't forgotten the way his heart had stopped in his chest when he had learned she was gone.

"Here. For a parting gift. You may be needing it." Rosamund slipped a blue leather scabbard with a thin English dagger in it into his hand.

He kissed her for a thank-you and stuck it in his belt, laughing. "You were a practical woman from the start."

Rosamund set Asa in her blanket on the ground. There was a silver cross at Rosamund's throat, and she pulled it over her head and touched it gently to his forehead. "I know he is not your god, so I won't ask you to wear it. But maybe he will bring you back safe to me."

She slipped an arm through his, and her blue-purple eyes were clouded like a lake in the rain, and Haakon blinked in surprise. "You aren't afraid to be left here now, are you? Not after all this time? My people love you now."

"God save me from fools," Rosamund said, "and you are one of them! I'm afraid for *you*! What good are your people to me if I lose *you*?"

He stood staring at her. No one but his mother had ever been afraid for *him* before. Afraid *of* him or dependent on him for their own safety, but never afraid *for* him. He caught her to him in a bearlike embrace that knocked the breath from her and lifted her feet off the ground, and he danced her in a tight little circle, remembering to be careful of the baby.

"Haakon! Put me down!"

"Never!" He danced her around again and kissed her.

"Jarl! We are loaded!" Thorfinn Solvisson called from the shore.

He took her by the hand, giving her just enough time to scoop up Asa. "Come on!"

The sacrifice had been made that morning: three white horses for Father Odin, whom it was always wise to placate, and three red goats for Thor Hammerer, for luck and good wind. The carcasses had been hung up in the trees above the shore, and the weather had come up fair afterward, which was accounted a good omen. Now all the folk of Haakonstead were filing down to the shore, thralls and free men, and a ragtag herd of children running and shrieking in the shallows and being swatted off the ships by Knut One-Eye and the other helmsmen.

Gunnar was standing with his arms crossed on his chest, gloomily watching the green water in the fjord. Not to sail with Haakon was a matter touching on honor. But the men staying behind needed a firm hand kept on them, and a clear head, and Gunnar's were the best. Seventy-five men was all that the jarl's new ships could carry, and the rest were not overly pleased to bide at home, either, even for a share in the summer's profit. There had been a great deal of arguing before Haakon had sorted out who should go and who should stay to keep King Harald Fairhair from getting any large ideas while the jarl was elsewhere. Guthrun stood a pointed three feet away from Gunnar, with her gold head turned in the other direction. She and Gunnar were still lovers, but in between they squabbled.

Donal MacRae stood, sword in sheath and spare shirt and helmet slung from his back, with Fann clinging dolefully to him. Yazid of Alexandria was giving the new ships a professional eye, and Wulf sat waiting expectantly on the shore with his tail in the water.

As Haakon came down the path, everyone scrambled more or less to attention, and the men began to wade out to the ships and pull themselves over the side. Wulf came up and stuck his nose in Rosamund's hand for a good-bye. He was wet.

The wind picked up as they stood there, a bright spring breeze with the smell of new leaves in it, mingled with the salt scent of the fjord. Haakon kissed Rosamund one more time, and a thrall handed him his helmet and sword belt. The helmet was iron, pointed at the top, with only a nasal for a face guard. He settled it on his head.

"Mikligard! We will send Harud Olafsson down Hel-Road and come back rich!"

They cheered that with a noise that would have waked the dead already in Hel, and *Curlew* and *Gull Wing* ran out their oars and began to swing about in the fjord. Knut One-Eye lifted *Gray Goose*'s anchor stone as Haakon pulled himself over the stern and hauled Wulf in after him. Wulf was Rosamund's dog on dry land, but when Haakon sailed, Wulf sailed, and no one had ever been able to stop him.

"Make sail!"

The bright cloth billowed in the wind, red and green, red and black, black and green. *A Norse wind*. Haakon put his foot up on an oar bench and crossed his arms on his thigh while the narrow beach of Haakonstead slipped past and was gone. *A viking wind*.

At the mouth of Trondheimsfjord lay two of the great sea routes of the Norsemen—south and west to the Frisian coast and England, or south and east to the wild fur lands of the Baltic. And in between, the market towns of Hedeby and Birka, where the trappers' skins and the loot of the sea rovers' ships came to be sold: gold crosses and carved ivory, the loot of Irish lords; the luckless from the slave ships; knots of amber, tin from England, and stolen wine from France.

It was for amber that they put into Hedeby, treasure washed onto the Baltic shores, a gift from who knew where, sometimes with an insect trapped inside, perfect, frozen, transfixed across the ages. A rarity to dress an emperor's concubine in Mikligard.

The merchants at Hedeby had cut their teeth on balance weights, or so Ragnar the Noseless said, and they clucked and muttered at the soapstone pots and hefted the iron pigs, while Haakon stood by and said flatly what he would take. They threw up their hands and said that they were poor men, jarl, and then it all began again. Finally agreement was made, and Haakon came away with two-thirds of the price in raw amber and one-third in English jet and drawn glass beads from a Hedeby bead maker.

Haakon posted five men on each ship to discourage thieves and let the rest go into town to waste their money on beer and women—if a Norseman ever really consid-ered those wasteful—or pick up cargo of their own if they'd a mind to.

The ships were anchored in the nearby *nor*, an inlet off the Schleifjord, which was Hedeby's harbor, and Haakon settled himself on an oar bench to watch the conglomera-tion of trading craft that jammed the harbor and to think of the things he would do to Harud Olafsson when he caught him. In truth, he knew that he would do none of them because Rosamund had said that that would make him like Harud, and somewhere behind his fury was the knowl-edge that that was truth. He would kill him, and see him howe-laid himself if there was no one else to do it, and that would be an end of the thing, with honor. A man became the things he did, maybe, Haakon thought. Thor had said so, and if that was true, then there was much tragedy in it.

"Are you all right, jarl?" Donal came and peered at him through the fading light. He had volunteered to be among the shipguard in Hedeby for the chance to go ashore at Birka. He had a score to settle at Birka. "Are you ill?"

Haakon stood up and stuck his ax through his belt. "No, but I grow philosophical, which is a thing for poets. I've a mind to go and drink it away, I think."

Donal MacRae grinned after him. There was more of the Gael in Jarl Haakon than showed from the outside. It was the wild stream flowing in practical Norse blood. It made a man thoughtful unexpectedly.

The jarl managed to drink away his thoughtfulness in a tavern next to the fur dealers' sheds in Hedeby, and the next morning Haakon's three boats were away again into the sea channels that wove through the tangle of Danish islands at the Baltic's mouth, and then north to Birka.

Birka was not so big as Hedeby, but it was closer to the best fur-trapping country and accessible over the ice in winter to the trappers who came on skates and sledges with their catch. The wild lands of the north were the best hunting for the slave dealers, too, and everything was cheaper before it had been shipped to Hedeby.

In Birka, Haakon traded the whetstones and the iron pigs from *Gull Wing's* hold for ten slaves, all broad-faced Lapps, and more furs. The fur dealers bought from the trappers all winter and sold to the merchants in summer at much higher prices after the trappers had gone back to their forest. There was sable, glossy and black as a piece of warm jet, and spotted lynx, ermine, beaver, and ruby-colored fox. They hung from hooks on poles to mark the fur dealers' houses, and inside they were tied in bales stacked to the roof beams.

Haakon ordered the bales opened, and the fur dealer complied, grumbling. Then Haakon picked each skin himself, while the fur dealer, in oily breeches and a fox hat, sat on a bale of ermines and watched him suspiciously.

"I am not a thief," Haakon informed him. "A thief is a man who puts bad skins at the center of a bale." He slung a fox with the scars of an old fight into a corner and continued to rummage in the bale.

"Jarl, the bales are as they come to me from the trappers." The fur dealer was plaintive. "I am a trusting man."

Haakon pulled out another bad skin. "And I am the king of Alfheim." When he was done he shouted for Donal and Thorfinn Solvisson, who was *Curlew's* helmsman, to come and carry the bales, while the merchant glowered and weighed out Haakon's silver in a bronze balance that unfolded from a case on the merchant's belt.

"These can go in *Curlew* with the Hedeby goods. There won't be room in *Gull Wing* for anything but the Lapps. And where is Donal?"

"He said he was going to buy a comb," Thorfinn said. "I can get Hagar to carry these."

"Trolls take him!" Haakon said. "Yes, go and get Hagar

to help. And tell this thief in a fox hat"—he eyed the merchant—"that if the furs I bought are not the furs that are loaded onto *Curlew*, I will skin him and bale him with the water rat he is selling to honest men for beaver."

Thorfinn grinned, and the fur dealer scowled and began to bale up Haakon's skins. "Where are you going, jarl?"

"After that Scot," Haakon said. "I know where he has gone to buy his comb, and I've no mind to be barred from Birka." Birka was an island in Lake Mälar, accessible only by its own pilots. It was easy enough to keep a shipowner out simply by refusing to send a pilot to guide him through the entrance channels. And the merchants of Birka did not look kindly on troublemakers.

Haakon left Thorfinn to intimidate the fur dealer, and set out across the town at as fast a pace as accorded with his dignity. Birka was crisscrossed with wooden walkways linking the merchants' houses, and the streets were full of traffic. The merchants and their families lived year round at Birka, and the population was swollen now by the start of the spring trading season. At the southern end of the town was a small hilltop fort built to house the guard that the merchants paid to keep the peace in Birka. Past the town the island was thickly wooded with birch trees, and beyond them, ringed by ditches and other discouragements to escape, was the slave camp.

It teemed with humankind, sold back and forth across Europe and the East to satisfy the world's hunger for labor. There was always a market for slaves—captured, sold, bartered, some lawfully, some not—to build roads and cities, to weave and dye and spin, and to do all the things for which it was cheaper to buy a slave than pay a free man. It was in the Birka slave market that Haakon had found Donal—being lashed for some transgression and cursing his tormentors—and it was at a combmaker's house in the town that they had eventually tracked down Fann.

Haakon dodged around a craftsman's wife with a fortune in gold around her neck and a basket of onions on her arm, her broad beam blocking the walkway as she inspected a bolt of tablet-woven braiding. He quickened his step. He should have known better than to let Donal loose in

Birka. He had been fooled because Donal hadn't acted like
a Norseman. A Norseman would have proclaimed loudly
to anyone who would listen that he had a blood-debt to
pay, and then gone and done it. Donal had merely kept
himself to himself and waited until they got to Birka. And
now if Haakon didn't catch him, he was undoubtedly going
to put a knife in the unfortunate combmaker—who had
presumably done something or other to Fann, but that
would not be taken as an excuse by the combmaker's
neighbors in Birka.

I ought to tie him up in the hold with the Lapps,
Haakon thought furiously. He pulled open the combmaker's
door and with one hand lifted Donal off his prey. Haakon
had his ax in the other hand in case either of them was
inclined to argue with him.

"Get back to the ships!"

The spluttering combmaker fell back against his counter, and Donal twisted out of Haakon's grasp. The floor
was littered with bits of antler, and Donal had a scratch
down one arm where the combmaker had defended himself
with a tooth saw. He was middle-aged, short and balding,
with a fringe of gray hair, and he looked aggrieved.

"I will send for the guards," he said when he had got his
breath back.

"No, you won't," Haakon said. He swung around to face
Donal. "Back away."

"I owe him a debt," Donal said through his teeth. "For
Fann."

"Sit down." Haakon glared at them both, ax in hand,
and they picked up an overturned bench and sat on it, at
opposite ends. "Now we will sort this out. Fann looked
well enough to me when we bought her out of here."

"The son of a whore bedded with her," Donal said.

"She was my thrall," the combmaker growled. "Bought
and paid for." He rubbed his neck. Donal had apparently
been trying to strangle him with his bare hands.

That might be hard for Donal to live with, but that was
the way of the world. "Did he ill-use her? Truthfully,
Donal, on your god."

"I don't know what he did," Donal said. "But she is
afraid now, afraid of men. Afraid of me," he added miserably.

"I did nothing but bed the girl," the combmaker said, retrieving some of his dignity. "In the usual fashion. And if she is afraid of you, it is likely because you are a madman."

Haakon thought that Fann had probably been born afraid, but he didn't say so. On the other hand, the combmaker was no beauty, and Fann had likely been a virgin. "This man was within his rights," he said to Donal, and Donal bristled. "If I let you kill him, will that make anything any different with Fann?"

The combmaker opened his mouth, and then closed it again. The jarl didn't appear to be *going* to let the madman kill him. And if he shouted for the guards, all they would do would be lock the madman up and tell a good story over the soup pot that night, which would make him look a fool. He studied Haakon. The jarl's trousers and tunic were good blue wool with gold tablet-braid around the hem. He wore a gold cloak pin and twisted gold neck and arm rings. And he had had enough money a year ago to pay a good price for the girl whom the combmaker wished he had never seen. There was also the matter of the broken combs.

"You don't understand," Donal said stubbornly.

Haakon thought about Rosamund. "By all the gods in Asgard, don't tell *me* I don't understand!" he roared. "Now get back to the ships, or I will tie you up until we get to Dvina Mouth!"

Donal went, with his mouth compressed into a tight line, and Haakon watched him with relief. He would have to make his peace with Donal later, but Donal wouldn't hold a grudge against Haakon, only the combmaker, and tomorrow the combmaker would be out of reach. Haakon put his ax back in its sheath. The combmaker collected a handful of toothy fragments and held them out.

"And I have had to buy forty combs to keep my good name in Birka," Haakon said. "If you get off ship again in Birka, I will saw your ears off with them."

Donal pulled on his oar and looked up at Haakon over his shoulder. "You can give them to your stepfather for a present," he said, "when you wish to annoy him." Erik the Bald had very little use for a comb.

"Pull," Haakon said, and that was the end of the matter.

Gray Goose nosed her way out of the channel, with *Curlew* and *Gull Wing* behind, and Knut One-Eye raised a hand to the Birkan pilot bobbing in his boat in the channel mouth. Heading into open water, they reattached the dragon heads, to which the land spirits might have taken affront, on the forestems, and Wulf got up off his bed on the baled fox skins in the hold to bark at the painted heads.

Haakon looked at the wind arrow. "Make sail!"

"Ship ahead, jarl."

Haakon narrowed his eyes and squinted at it. It was coming at them out of the sun. They were to meet Ragnar the Noseless at Dvina Mouth, but that was a day's sail away, and this was no ship of Ragnar's. It was lateen rigged, the way the Greeks and Arabs built their ships. It might belong to the wali of Cadiz, who had sent men to trade at Hedeby and Birka under Haakon's name, but Haakon doubted it. The wali's ships had orders to stay strictly within the established sea-lanes, and the wali wouldn't risk his treaty by letting them go raiding.

"That one means no good, jarl," Knut said softly.

"I begin to think you're right," Haakon said. The ship was also far bigger than Haakon's boats, and the decks were thick with men.

Donal came up to stand at his elbow. "A slaver?"

"I think so." There was nothing else for which to come raiding in this quarter of the Baltic. "We're going to give them a surprise. Get most of the men down out of sight."

"They'd back off most likely, if they saw how well armed we are," Knut said, but it wasn't an argument. He would as soon fight instead.

Haakon shook his head and grinned. "I'll teach them to come poaching in Norse waters and disrupting honest men's trade." The Norse sold slaves from the Baltic to the Arabs of the Mediterranean. There would be no profit in that if the Arabs began to come north and take them for themselves.

Knut shouted across the water and waved his hand at the helmsmen of *Curlew* and *Gull Wing*, and two-thirds of their crews ducked down behind the shields and vanished. They lay on the deck and wriggled into their armor.

"Now turn about and run, for the look of it."

The three ships slowed and turned in the water, somewhat unhandily because there weren't very many men on the oars. The lateen-rigged ship sped after them. It had a favorable wind and more oars. The ship glided on the water like a hound after prey. If Haakon's boats had looked like warships, the Arabs would have run, but the little riverboats were inviting: There might be cargo worth looting, and the crews offered the chance to fill the Arab hold with slaves without the bother of chasing them down on land. Haakon chuckled. The Arab captain would be praising Allah for an easy catch.

When the Arab was nearly within firing range, Haakon ordered the sails furled. It might make the Arabs more wary, but the one thing he didn't want was a fire arrow in the sail.

The Arabs were too close to their prey to be wary. They took it for a sign of surrender and for a further argument sent a hail of arrows down onto *Gray Goose*'s deck. Haakon's men put their shields up over their heads and waited. The Arab captain shouted at them in bad Norse to halt and be boarded. Haakon shouted back to come ahead. The Arab ship edged closer, and *Gray Goose*'s deck was suddenly thick with fighting men. Hagar the Simple climbed up out of the hold with his bow in his hand, and the Arab captain swore. He tried to put his ship about, but *Curlew* and *Gull Wing* had also sprouted more men on the decks and the oar benches, and they were coming around at his rear.

Haakon's men pulled in their oars on the starboard side as little *Gray Goose* bobbed closer to the Arab; a few more strokes of the port oars brought her alongside. Hjalmar Sitricsson and three others pushed a boarding ladder up against the Arab's side while the Arab's crew shot down at them furiously. Hagar the Simple sent a stream of arrows into the Arab archers, and Haakon went up the ladder, with Donal and Wulf behind him. The Arab captain knew he had been trapped, but he was determined to make a fight of it. He could expect very little from the Norsemen

but the slavery he had intended for them. The Norse were
infidels and unholy; it was better to kill as many of them as
he could—and die in doing it—than to go tamely.

Gray Goose's crew poured up the ladder behind Haakon.
This was better than trading, and proper work for Norsemen.
That they could have intimidated the Arab into backing off
without fighting never occurred to most of them. There
was no fame in that. *Curlew* had got up against the Arab
ship's other side, and Thorfinn Solvisson, his ax swinging,
dropped down into the Arab crew. "You must make a song
for us, Scotsman," he shouted cheerfully to Donal, across
the chaos on the deck, "since we haven't Gunnar Thorsten
with us!" There was always a song to be made from a
battle—that was how a man's sword-fame spread.

Donal fought beside Haakon, cursing steadily in Gaelic,
something Haakon had discovered was the Scot's invari-
able behavior in a fight. There was more than his usual
temper in it this time, though. He gave the Arabs what
Haakon hadn't let him give the combmaker in Birka, with
his grudge against slave raiders added in for good mea-
sure. Haakon decided that Donal had the makings of a
berserker in him if he got mad enough, and then Haakon
hastily turned his attention back to the Arab captain.

The captain's long curved sword slashed down and
skidded along the links of Haakon's mail as Haakon twisted
out of the way. He swung his ax, bracing his feet against
the pitching of the ship. The Arab dodged and backed
away into the shadow of the sail, leaving Haakon with the
sun in his eyes. Haakon squinted and came after him, ax
raised. There was no sign of the god in the ax, but it felt a
part of him as it always did. "You came too far from
home," he said in rough Arabic.

The Arab captain eyed him with hatred over his shield
rim. "Dog of a Norseman!" he spat at him.

Haakon thought of several Arabic words he had learned
in Cadiz, all of them foul. He tried one, and the Arab
captain shrieked with fury and swung his sword. Haakon
sidestepped, pushed with his shield to knock the blow
wider, and caught the Arab in the neck with his ax. The
Arab fell in a shower of blood, and Haakon looked around
him for someone else to fight.

There was none. Donal was pulling his sword out of a dead archer, and there were only three Arabs left, unarmed, being held in a group in the bow by Hjalmar Sitricsson. Haakon wiped his ax blade and stuck it back in its sheath.

"What about those?" Knut jerked his head at Hjalmar's prisoners. "Kill them?" They would be more trouble than they were worth to bring along, and anyway there wasn't room in the hold for them with the Lapps.

Haakon thought. "No, there's no lesson in that. I've a mind to teach their kind not to poach in our waters." That these waters were Swedish and not, strictly speaking, Norse didn't matter. All the viking folk regarded the northern sea-lanes as common ground between them, and interlopers were unwelcome. Haakon pointed at the ship's boat, a small craft with two oars and a bench and very little else. "Put them in that. If they make shore, they can go home and tell their master not to send his hounds hunting here again. Are there any slaves on board?"

"No, we looked. They must not have been here long."

"There is some silver though, jarl." Thorfinn came up out of the hold.

"Fine. We will take that. Snorri!"

"Aye, jarl?"

"This ship—is it any use to us?"

Snorri Longfoot put his hands on his hips and surveyed it. "A ship is always useful—at home, with time to refit. But here, to say truth, jarl, no. It's no good for Gardariki, too big, and to send it home you would have to send men back too."

"Then put a hole in it," Haakon said. He looked at the prisoners. "I don't want these coming back for it."

The Arab ship tipped up its prow and slid under the water. The three prisoners bobbed disconsolately in their small boat and watched it disappear. As it sank, they put their oars out and began to paddle. Haakon watched with satisfaction; the Arabs would tell their kinsmen to think twice before they came raiding here again.

Haakon felt pleased with himself. It had been a good fight, and only two of his men were wounded, neither of them badly enough to be taken ashore. And Wulf had a toy: an Arab's shoe, which he had proudly brought back onto *Gray Goose* and taken into the hold to chew on. Haakon had gingerly inspected it first to make sure there wasn't a foot still in it. With Wulf you never knew.

If Thor Odinsson wouldn't help, it certainly seemed he would send no hindrance. Haakon's men had some extra silver for their trouble, and it had sweetened their tempers greatly. Haakon whistled cheerily to himself as they set sail for the mouth of the Dvina and the unknown lands beyond it.

Ragnar was waiting for them at Dvina Mouth, his own three ships beached and their tents set up on the shore. When they saw Haakon's sails, Ragnar's men came scrambling out of the tents in their mail, and Haakon raised the peace shields on all three masts because his ships were new and Ragnar wouldn't recognize them.

There was a jumble of squat huts along the shore behind Ragnar's camp, but no sign of the fisherfolk who probably lived there. They would be back in the forest, hiding, until the dragon ships, lean and predatory as hunting wolves, moved on.

"There is nothing there worth taking," Ragnar said. "We looked."

Haakon nodded. His men chased the Lapp slaves out of the hold to set up their own tents and began off-loading tubs of salt-meat and beer. Haakon took a deep breath of alien air and watched the silver loop of the river flow toward them. He had never been here before because, as Ragnar said, there was nothing along this edge of the Baltic shore worth taking unless a man was a trapper or a slave hunter. There were reputed to be sea monsters in the Dvina. *I will see one, maybe*, he thought. It would be a fine thing to bring a sea monster's head back to Norway.

Rosamund pushed the stray tendrils of hair back from her face and rubbed at her nose. They were shearing the sheep today, and the air was full of the thick, oily smell of the wool. The hair got into everything and made everyone itch. Asa was sleeping in Bergthora's lap while the old

woman spun. The baby's bare feet turned outward like a
duck's, and one starfish hand was flung across her eyes.
Every child on the steading old enough to walk was
helping with the shearing. The younger ones sacked the
wool and carried jugs of buttermilk to the shearers, and
the older ones chased the sheep, one by one, out of the
pens and sat on the heads of the ones that gave trouble.
The air was full of the baaing of sheep and the bleating of
ewes for their lambs and the occasional curses of the
shearers when a sheep kicked out and made someone nick
his fingers.

The women were already cleaning the wool and carding
it, with the long, iron-toothed carding combs. When that
was done it would be spun on hand spindles, and then
wrapped on skein reels to be dyed. Then there would be
hours spent over the boiling dye vats, and everyone's
hands would be blue or red, with dark lines under the
nails that wouldn't come clean but had to grow out. Then
the wool would be woven on the heavy warp-weighted
looms, some in plain twill or tabby for the thralls and
everyday wear, some in geometric patterns or with borders of fanciful entwining beasts, depending upon the skill
of the weaver. It would take nearly a year until the last of
the wool was woven, and then the shearing would begin
again. The sheep were the cycle of the women's lives on
the steading, Rosamund thought, sneezing as she picked
burrs from the new-sheared wool. It was not proper for a
jarl's wife to think herself too fine to help with the
shearing.

Guthrun and Fann were cleaning wool beside her, and
Gunnar's dark-eyed slave girl, Riziya, was some distance
away, carding what they had cleaned. She wasn't doing
very much work, Rosamund noticed. Likely she would do
better with the jarl's wife's eye on her, but likely it was
also better not to stick her under Guthrun's nose. Rosamund
had told Gunnar that Riziya would have to help, less
because they needed her than because it wouldn't be fair
for Riziya, who was a thrall, to spend the day keeping
clean and bringing beer to Gunnar while free women
cleaned dirty wool. No one was talking very much because
no one could hear anyone else over the bleating of the

sheep. The man who rode along the inland track to the steading gates was nearly through them before anyone noticed him.

Gunnar got up off the sheep he was shearing and went and talked to the newcomer, and then brought him to Rosamund. He was very fine, in a blue cloak with red braiding and a mail shirt that was nearly as shiny as silver and not dark and rusted the way mail got when a man had worn it to fight in. He took off his helmet and bowed grandly to the jarl's wife, and the jarl's wife sneezed and brushed a lapful of burrs out of her apron.

"You are welcome at Haakonstead, Jarl Sigurd." She recognized him, a Trondelag jarl from upfjord, not so powerful as Haakon, but known as a man with an eye to the main chance. What was he doing in Haakonstead?

"I have been in Vestfold," Sigurd said. "At King Harald's court there. I have messages from King Harald to his friend Jarl Haakon and the king's thanks for the jarl's gifts last winter."

"Jarl Haakon is not here," Rosamund said firmly. "But he will be happy to hear your messages in the fall. Will you stop at Haakonstead for a few days nonetheless?" There was no way out of that—hospitality demanded an open hand. "We would be glad to hear news, and you and your men must be weary." She glanced at the knot of riders and the wagon full of baggage that had rumbled through the gate while they talked. Jarl Sigurd hadn't waited to be invited.

Sigurd beamed. "My thanks, lady. We would be grateful." He was a tall, rangy man, with a sandy beard carefully combed into two forks, and the beginnings of a potbelly under his mail. "I will give King Harald's messages to you, instead."

Rosamund tried to think of a polite way to say she didn't want them, and couldn't. "Certainly. But the jarl must understand that I can do nothing without my husband's knowledge."

Jarl Sigurd raised his bushy eyebrows in surprise. "I had understood that Jarl Haakon's lady and his steward"—he gave Gunnar a friendly glance—"held authority in Jarl Haakon's absence."

"Not entirely," Rosamund said. She looked quickly at Gunnar, who had put his hand very quietly on his knife hilt. The fact that Jarl Sigurd had known that Haakon wasn't here hadn't been lost on either of them.

"It is not so grave a matter, my lady," Sigurd was saying. She wondered if he had seen Gunnar make a move toward his knife. "But King Harald is wishful to make a visit of state in the Trondelag, and certain things must be arranged beforehand, of course."

"Of course," Rosamund said. "But is this wise of King Harald? Might there not be—difficulties?"

"Surely not." Sigurd tugged at his beard, smiling. "You might not be knowing, my lady—being English and new to Norway—but our local folk have a great love for King Harald. The Tronds have always been stout friends to Harald's line."

Even Rosamund knew better than that. The Tronds had always spat in the eye of any outsider seeking to take them under his rule. Even Haakon Grjotgardsson had kept his alliance with the king between himself and Harald only. "No doubt," she said. "But I cannot speak for my husband's people—being English and new to Norway. I am sure that you must be thirsty, jarl. Come you in and rest now."

Gunnar sent a thrall scurrying for beer, and Rosamund took off her apron and smiled at her unwelcome guest. Fann looked as if she thought Jarl Sigurd might bite her, so Rosamund took Guthrun with her instead, to show them to the guesthouse.

They found no sea monsters on the Dvina River, only trees. The endless forest stretched away on either bank, broken by occasional clearings and native huts, where roughly dressed men and women ran away into the forest as the ships approached. Haakon ordered his men into their mail, and they put it on grumbling, but they wore it. A mail shirt was no light thing for a man to carry on his back all day; but he was helpless for the time it took to get it on over his head, and the forest might hide more than frightened peasants. Those who had no mail wore leather cuirasses boiled in whale oil.

They found a fair wind on the river, but it was upstream going. Haakon thought about putting the Lapps on the oars, but there weren't enough of them to go around, and it was easy to tangle one man's oar with the next and break them all, deliberately or only from lack of skill. He took his own turn on the oar bench for fairness—and because rowing in mail was the best way he knew to work out a winter's softness. The first night in camp they changed the shipguard every two hours because, after all that rowing, no one could stay awake longer than that, and in the morning they were all as stiff as old men.

"Bah, I am too old for this," Ragnar said, creaking over to the fire where Donal was turning barley bread in a skillet. "Next season I will stay home and go to fat and hire a captain."

"Who will cheat you," Haakon said, stretching and laughing. "Or so you've always said."

Ragnar eyed the mail shirt at his feet as if looking at it made his shoulders ache.

"My share of the bargain is to protect your fine hide," Haakon said. "So you will have to wrap it in mail when I tell you to." He was amusing himself with the opportunity to order Ragnar about.

Ragnar bit into the barley cake. "I was raiding in Frisia when you were a puppy in Ireland. I have slept in mail. There was a time when we didn't take it off for a seven-day at a time. Go and see to your fox skins."

Haakon laughed and went off to see that the bales in the open hold were properly covered with canvas. The sky was ash gray, and everything felt damp. Wulf wriggled out of the tent and followed him. The Lapps eyed the animal with watchful curiosity. Wulf was big enough to be a cub of Otava the Bear God, but he was fashioned like a dog. Maybe he was magic.

In the camp, Haakon's men and Ragnar's smaller crew were striking the tents and rolling up the skin sleeping bags, one man at each end. The bags were big enough for two men each, two bodies being warmer than one. They refilled the water bags from the river and rolled the tubs of meal and meat and beer back on board. As they heaved the ships off the sand it began to rain. Cursing, they

pulled their cloaks of fur or shaggy home-woven wool
around them. The Lapps sat miserably in the hold under a
leather awning until someone handed them a bailing pot.

It rained for two weeks, not hard, but steadily, dappling
the river in a shimmering beauty. They bailed constantly,
and everyone had blisters where wet clothing had rubbed
their skin raw. It was still raining when they came to the
place in the river that Ragnar the Noseless said marked
the start of the overland portage to Gnezdovo on the
Dnieper River.

A clearing had been cut in the right-hand bank. Wet
stumps stood up jaggedly with new saplings growing in
between, and there were marks of old fires. There was no
sign of human habitation now, but Ragnar said the place
was used for a camp by the ships that made the Dvina-
Gnezdovo portage. It was almost marshland here. The
men climbed out of the ships like drowned water rats, and
found enough dry ground to build three fires. Haakon
shook the rain out of his beard and squelched across to
one of the fires, where he stood trying to dry the damp
wool of his shirt and breeches, and smelling of wet sheep.

The rain had stopped temporarily, and Ragnar sat fanning the fire with his hat, while smoke billowed up from
the wet wood. Nobody had bothered to get out the tents;
the ground was too wet to sleep on. They would spend the
night under the oar benches or under the awning in the
hold.

"This is land for bog trolls!" Thorfinn said. He squinted
and coughed when the smoke rolled his way.

"It isn't generally this wet," Ragnar said. He looked at
his wet hat, trying to decide if it would be colder to put it
back on or not. "For truth, I've never seen it like this."

"What is wrong?" Haakon said.

Ragnar shrugged. "Maybe Thorfinn is in the right of it,
and we should put out meat for the trolls tonight." He
hunched himself under his hat and held his wet gloves up
to the fire.

There were nearly a hundred men trying to find a place
around three sputtering fires, and it was then that the
words "ill luck" began to run through them, like a current
just under the surface. Haakon the Dark was accounted a

lucky man to follow, but this trip had been cursed with foul weather from Dvina Mouth, and the sullen, lowering sky and the alien river gave much credence to the prospect of some darker force at work. The goats and horses sacrificed at Trondheimsfjord might not have been enough.

No one said anything to Haakon directly, but he could feel the unease. He put a wooden bowl of meat for Ragnar's bog trolls on the edge of the clearing, but he doubted that trolls entered into it.

In the morning the sky was still bleak, and it stayed that way for three days as they slogged their way through marshland that sucked at their feet and made Ragnar cautious in his directions. The small, loamy rivers turned too shallow even for the smallest of the dragon ships almost as soon as they were launched on them. At night the marsh had a sickening phosphorescent glow. Haakon knew he was going to have open rebellion on his hands by Gnezdovo if he didn't do something.

A life for Father Odin: That was the obvious thing. Two years ago Haakon wouldn't have questioned it. They had slaves with them, so it wasn't even a question of having to hope that one of their own would consent to go to the gods and an assured place in the next world to give his brothers fair wind. And a slave who was sent to the gods died with honor and a better hope for the next world than he would have had with a straw death in bed. So they said.

Haakon looked at the sky. Nothing evil had actually happened yet; it was only the grayness and the wet that gave a foreboding feel to the country. No one had sickened, so maybe there was no disease in the sucking marsh—but only great inconvenience. Maybe his men would see it that way when they reached Gnezdovo—tomorrow, so Ragnar said. And maybe the ships would sprout wings and fly. The Lapps watched him with bright, dark eyes, and he wrapped his hands around the towrope and shouted at them to heave.

Ragnar was right about one thing: With larger ships they never would have made it. He had best come back with lightweight cargo or something that could walk on its own feet. The towrope bit into his shoulder, and he gritted

his teeth and tried to emulate Hagar the Simple, who, like
an ox, simply leaned into the rope and pulled.

Gnezdovo was a dirty sprawl of one-room huts such as
the Slavs built, log houses built by Swedes, tents, shacks,
beached ships, and fenced-in camps in wild confusion
along the Dnieper bank. Gnezdovo was the end point of
the portage from the Dvina River and the equally arduous
trek by land from the upper reaches of the Lovat River.
Many trade routes crossed here from the Gulf of Finland
in the west and along the great Volga River from the Arabs
in the east. It was not a town, but rather a jumping-off
place of shifting population and little law, where a man
slept with his knife by his hand.

The sky was still somber, gray like a dead hearth. They
lost Orm Persson there, and matters came to a head.

A rain-rutted slope ran down to the huts on the riverbank, and at the top of it a woman came out of the forest
almost under their noses. She was a Slav, in a coarse dress
and fur boots, with pale, frightened eyes, and she backed
away when she saw them and spilled her basket of wild
berries in the road. They had stopped to shift the rollers
on *Gull Wing*, the crew pulling back on the towropes to
steady her while Snorri fiddled with the jammed place.
Orm Persson was *Gull Wing*'s helmsman, and he was
walking at the front of the boat with nothing to do but find
trouble. He darted in front of *Gull Wing* to catch at the
woman's skirt just as Snorri knocked the roller loose.

Gull Wing lurched and slid on the hill, and the forestem
careened forward, dragging the towing crew with it before
they could get their footing in the mud. The woman
lashed out in fright at Orm. Then she was stumbling away
down the muddy slope, her brown hair flying, and Orm
was pinned under the keel. By the time they pulled the
ship off him, he was dead.

"This is bad." Knut One-Eye looked at the fresh mud of
Orm Persson's howe.

"Bad enough for Orm," Haakon said. He was furious. To
lose a man in a fight was bad enough, but to lose him in a
fool's mischance under the keel of his own ship—that had

the look of some god's hand about it. The muttering around Orm's howe had grown too loud to be ignored.

"There should be a sacrifice," Knut said, and Haakon saw that there were eight or ten other men at his shoulder now, "before Father Odin feeds another man to the ships!"

"Orm Persson gave himself to death," Haakon said. "From chasing a woman he could very likely have bought and playing the fool in front of a ship on rollers."

"There should be a sacrifice," Knut said doggedly.

"Is this your idea, Knut?"

Knut shrugged. "No, but I am the spokesman."

The Lapps stood a little way away, watching Haakon, silently, like wild things in a cage. They weren't sure what was happening, but he was the leader. Whatever it was, he would decide. Haakon could feel their bright, dark eyes on his back.

Two years ago he would have thought like his men— these tall, big-boned, fair men in mail shirts and helmets who pushed around him stubbornly.

"There will be no sacrifice." As he said it he realized that he didn't know why, only that he wouldn't do it.

"It is ill luck to cheat Gallows Lord," Hjalmar Sitricsson said, and the others edged closer, muttering agreement. That was one of the many names of Odin, who was a dark and double-faced god, and it was always unwise to withhold his due.

"There will be no sacrifice," Haakon repeated. Most of his sworn warriors were taller than he was, and he hooked his thumbs in his belt and glared at them, and they halted uneasily. Wulf came and sat at his heel. Haakon could see Donal at the back, not pushing forward, but keeping out of the matter because he was a Christian and it would not help to have him interfere in a matter for the Norse gods. Ragnar was beside Donal, waiting, Haakon thought, to see if Haakon could master them, but Ragnar's crew was with Haakon's men.

More of them were beginning to crowd around him now, and he thought that if he didn't do something quickly, they would take one of the Lapps anyway, and then Haakon's hold on the leadership would be gone for good.

He unslung the ax from his back to give a weight to his arguments.

The haft was warm when it should have been cold, like everything else in Gnezdovo, from the ash gray sky to the mud on Orm's howe. But it wasn't—it was warm to the touch, as if with some unspoken approval. Haakon eyed it dubiously. It would appear that the god was not entirely gone away from it after all. Was it Thor's doing that had put that reluctance to make the sacrifice into his head? Haakon liked that as well as he liked voices in his head, but a man who makes a pact with a god does not have the ordering of when the god may speak his mind.

"There will be no sacrifice," he said again. He hefted the ax. And if that was Thor's wish, then Thor could lend some weight to his words. "You are Norsemen, not field mice to run scuttling because you think you have seen a hawk! Orm Persson brought his own ill luck on him, and as for the rest, what has happened? It has rained, and you are wet, that is all! I made a proper sacrifice on Trondheimsfjord, and if there is any man who wishes to convince me that I should make another because he is wet, then let him come and do it."

Knut One-Eye looked over his shoulder at the rest. He was spokesman because he was first helmsman, but he wasn't going to fight the jarl for them. Hagar the Simple just leaned on his bow and waited, and Hjalmar Sitricsson looked stubborn, but not enough to step forward either, not alone. Haakon gripped the ax two-handed, his feet braced, and the Lapps looked frightened and backed away behind him.

"The rain is no joke, jarl," Thorfinn Solvisson said quietly. "It is unnatural, and that is the bad omen, not that we are wet."

"It is not raining now," Haakon pointed out. He risked a quick glance at the sky, hoping it wouldn't make a liar of him. The clouds looked thinner, wispy against a lightening sky behind them. The ax was still warm under his hand, and a pale light shimmered on the blade. *Blow it away, or I will have to give in.*

They mumbled among themselves as they realized that the rain had stopped while they had stood arguing the

matter. Haakon saw Donal on the edge of the crowd and
caught his eye, and Donal lifted an eyebrow in clear
inquiry: *What will you do if you can't turn them?*

The cloud cover wavered, and there was a flash of light
that might have come from a break in the sky or from the
ax blade itself. Donal's voice said softly, "Look you there
for the jarl's weather-luck."

The sky had parted to let down light as quickly as it had
given rain. As they watched, it washed the green mounds
of older graves and the brown of Orm Persson's howe and
flooded down the riverbank to turn the Dnieper golden.
Then there was a whirring in the air, a rush and beating of
wings, and they came across the sky like a tumble of
blown leaves—wild swans, black against the sun, their
great wings beating the air. They flew from who knew
where, low over the tumbled camp, and then out across
the broad river, south in the sunlight. Their wings were
gilded like the axhead.

After that there was no more talk of omens or sacrifices,
but Haakon sat for a long time on a rock on the wet
riverbank and looked at Thor Odinsson's ax. In Cadiz it
had put the notion in his head to save a frightened rabble
of Christian villagers from their neighbors, who had been
armed with rocks. On the homeward voyage it had bade
him rescue the Muhammadan Yazid. Now it seemed that
the ax had spoken against the tribute of human life, which
was the rightful due of the lords of Asgard. Odd conduct
indeed from a gift of Thor. He sat and waited for the god
to speak, but no word came, until he wondered if he had
spoken at all, even in the swans.

Finally he got up and went back to where the fires were
burning low in the camp. Judging by the noise down the
riverbank, some of the trader folk were still awake, drunk
and singing, but the shabby huts of the village were closed
tight, silent, dark, and wary. It might be that the villagers
were staying out of sight for fear that the Norsemen would
wish to take out their temper over the loss of Orm
Persson. The Slav woman's husband had run away upriver
with her before they had even pulled Orm's body out from
under the keel.

Haakon counted the silent sleeping bags in his camp and decided that no one had disobeyed him and gone to find more trouble. Like the other traders, they had ringed the camp with brushwood and a rough-cut fence to make it hard to get in quietly. He could see Wulf, like a gaunt gray shadow, pacing the perimeter. The men of the shipguard raised their spears to him from the dragon shadows of the ships. Donal was asleep and snoring in his half of the bag he shared with Haakon, his harp bag under his hand, as always. Haakon wriggled in beside him and wadded his cloak up for a pillow. The night was wild, moon-shot, and a mist grew up on the river and rolled over the low ground of the camp. Haakon had always slept with the gold ax beside him or under his hand, and it had been like another presence there, irksome at times, but grown familiar. He had not realized how alone he would feel without it.

Have you gone, lord? he thought, putting his hand on the haft, prodding it, trying to make it speak. Was there anything there or not? *Have you left me?*

The mist seemed to thicken, but also to grow paler, as if from some reflected light. There was music, and Haakon grinned suddenly and touched the axhead.

It burned. He jerked his hand back, bewildered, and the music changed to distant laughter. He sat up, looking wildly at the mist. The voices that mocked him were in his head, and they hurt. A voice, old, familiar, terrible, roared: *I do not break bargains! Does Haakon Olesson doubt ME?* The ax spat sparks. *I have been here, but now I go! Thor does not come like a servant when Haakon Olesson wants assurances! Since you doubt me, you can go your road alone and see what that is like!*

Flame ran along the axhead, burning blue, and there was a face in the flame, a face with an old and fearful beauty that burned brighter than the fire. And then the flame was gone, the golden head lay tarnished, and the handle was scarred and age-worn.

Haakon pulled himself out of the sleeping bag, shaking, with the pain still in his head and a cold fear running through him. He had waked the fires of Thor, and there was no knowing what they would consume before they had burned out again. A god bent on vengeance could blacken the land with a touch—cattle gone dry, fields seared and withered, children stillborn. And himself—lamed, drowned, killed at Mikligard? All for stubbornness and one too many questions asked. He sat hunched miserably over the ax, and gradually the terror drained away, and fury came to take its place. A free man had the *right* to question; it was what made him free. He picked up the ax and started for the river.

At the bank he stopped. The cold water whispered by, and he raised the ax and shouted at the empty sky, "*I am not your thrall!*" He swung his arm back to throw.

"No!" Something hit him from behind, and he staggered and turned to fight. "No!" Donal said. He ducked as Haakon swung the ax at him. "Damn you, put that away!"

"What are you doing here?" Haakon lowered the ax.

"I might be asking you," Donal said. "Charging at nothing like Cuchulain fighting the Shape-Changer and bellowing like a bull." He looked at the ax, still in Haakon's hand. "You were going to throw it in the river."

"I still am."

"I don't know what that thing is," Donal said, "and if it were mine, I might have thrown it in a river straight off. But that's your fighting ax, and you can't buy another in this hole. Were you thinking you mightn't be needing it?"

Haakon looked at the ax and Donal and the river, and then the fury drained out of him, and there was nothing. He was tired. He turned the ax in his hand. It was only an ax—sharp enough to fight with.

IV Koenugard

In the morning the Dnieper was blue in the sunlight and gold-dappled where the current rushed past, full of melting snow. Thorfinn Solvisson had carved a rune-stick for Orm Persson, and they hammered it into the mud above his howe. It was not the only Norse grave in

Gnezdovo: Men died here of new fights, old wounds, or the diseases of a strange land. There was a larger colony in the green mounds than there was in the village, Haakon thought. He bought a cock from a Swede who kept an inn for travelers too fine to sleep in the camps and killed the bird over Orm's howe. Then he swore Orm's share in the venture over to his widow, with Thorfinn and Hjalmar for witnesses, and gave the helm of *Gull Wing* to Kalki Estridsson, and they pushed the ships out into the river.

Haakon let out his breath as he felt the current catch them. The air was cold, with a clean, washed smell to it once they were clear of Gnezdovo. Gnezdovo stank of old refuse pits. There were other ships on the river, small dragon ships like Haakon's and Ragnar's, and Slav-made craft hollowed from a single giant tree. The traders appeared to know each other and shouted threats or greetings across the water, according to the nature of their acquaintance.

Below Gnezdovo, the river changed its face again and again through wild, uninhabited lands, at one moment running swift and dangerous through a narrow channel, then suddenly spreading wide through ancient forests, like a water labyrinth. The trees were the old giants of a younger world, tall, majestic, with gnarled roots curving above the water. Here and there the water had toppled them, and they lay, blocking the channel, with twisted roots clutching the air. The shallow-draft dragon ships and dugouts picked their way through the green maze, and then the river shot them out again into sunlight and fast-running water between low, empty banks.

It was two weeks to Koenugard, and there the river flowed calm and graceful, past the city that clung to the bluffs above the west bank. Koenugard was a traders' city, not an outpost like Gnezdovo. There were orderly paths between the sunken houses of the Slavs, which were dug into the ground so that only the steep-pitched roofs showed above the street. The square, log houses of the Swedes had a quarter of their own, clustered around the great hall that Ragnar said was Jarl Oleg's, who was great prince in Koenugard and a man to be reckoned with.

The rooftree of the hall was a ship's keel, smoke-blackened with age, with the dragon's head snarling above the doorposts. Oleg had come six years ago to rule in Koenugard—which the Slavs called Kiev—from Holmgard in the north, but the hall was older than that, built by the first jarl to take a holding here and to set his ship's keel for the rooftree as a token that he meant to stay.

Oleg himself came down to the riverbank while they were beaching the ships at the large, well-ordered merchants' camp below the city. He was a tall, fair man with red-gold hair nearly the color of his fox-skin cloak. His shirt and breeches were of fine green and blue woolen, and his cloak pin was a great silver ring with a prong the length of a man's finger stuck through it. Eight or ten of his house carls stood around him, spears in hand, and he looked at Haakon's crew and at Haakon. Haakon dropped over the line of shields slung along *Gray Goose*'s hull and looked back, and Ragnar came up from the jumble of tents and bales on the shore and presented himself and Jarl Haakon and his best wishes for the great prince's health.

"That is a lot of men for a merchant voyage, Ragnar," Oleg said. His speech had the accent of the Swedes, overlaid with some unfamiliar dialect.

"These are dangerous waters, Prince," Ragnar said. "To the south," he added politely. A man who was wise would watch himself in Oleg's camps, too.

"Also I am looking for someone," Haakon said. "It may be I will need some men." They were gathering behind him, looking over his shoulder at Oleg's carls.

Oleg grinned. "Most certainly, if it is one of mine you are hunting."

Wulf erupted out of the hold behind them, drawn by the streak of menace in Oleg's voice. "*No!*" Haakon snapped. "Heel!" Wulf bristled and halted at Haakon's heel. Haakon grinned back at Oleg, a dark grin, with his teeth showing a little like the dog's. "None of yours, Prince. I have no reason to quarrel in Koenugard."

"So?" Oleg rocked back on his heels a little. "That is good. I do not allow men to quarrel in Koenugard."

"It is a Norseman I look for," Haakon said. "An Irish jarl, but he will have come from Sweden. His name is Harud Olafsson, and I have heard that he passed this way last season, to go to ground in Mikligard. I want him."

Oleg laughed suddenly, white teeth splitting his red beard and mustache. "I thought last fall that that one had someone on his trail. He scuttled like a weasel."

"He was here?"

"He came with Thjodulf Ottarsson, and Thjodulf said that he left him in Mikligard. No one was much grieved," Oleg said. "He made trouble, that one."

"He has always made trouble," Haakon said. "He made enough trouble to hang himself. Where is Thjodulf Ottarsson?"

"Gone home to Uppsala a week ago," Oleg said. "He is old, and he said that would be his last trip. This Harud made some grievances here—he was a quarrelsome, bad lot. What did he do to you, for you to come out of Norway with three ships full of men to get him?"

"Enough," Haakon said shortly, and his mouth tightened, but he went on. "He came like a thief and stole my wife and my poet and sold them onto a slave ship, south to the Arabs. Now I have them back, and I am going to kill Harud. Also he tried to kill me, but that is not why I want him. He was betrothed to my wife, and when she took me instead, he took that way to settle the score."

Oleg rubbed his beard and thought. He had no love for Harud Olafsson, and this dark jarl out of Norway might be of use to him one day. Also it looked easier not to quarrel with him. "Come you up to the hall when you have unloaded," he said finally. "If you go chasing him down to Mikligard sword in hand, you won't get farther than the harbor gates. They are touchy there." He grinned. "But I will give you a letter for their emperor. Also they are a little afraid of me."

"If Oleg calls him a bad lot, Harud Olafsson did more than brawl in the taverns here," Ragnar said. "Oleg is a thief himself."

"Harud leaves enemies behind him like spilled grain out of a sack," Haakon said. "If I have ill luck, someone will kill him before me."

"And save the jarl his trouble," Knut said gruffly, but he was only grumbling because there was enough wealth in Koenugard to fill all six ships, and it couldn't be got at because Oleg's fortress bristled with guards. Even the city itself was ringed with fortified camps. Haakon had taken Ragnar, Knut, and Donal with him, with Hagar the Simple's mountainous bulk walking behind for a rear guard, but they went decorously down the wooden street to Jarl Oleg's hall, where he held his court with his *druzhina*, his council lords, and called himself great prince in Koenugard, after the manner of the Slavs.

Oleg's hall was built much like Norse halls at home, with a hearth at the center, tables and benches for eating and sleeping, and a clear space for the high seat and the important folk of the jarl's household. Haakon saw that unlike the traders, who came only for the season, Jarl Oleg and his lords had their women with them. The great prince's wife was a tall, fair woman with a strong-boned face and a red gown of native cloth, caught at the shoulders with gold brooches in the fashion of her homeland. Ragnar had said that Oleg had married a Swedish princess, Haakon remembered. It was her dowry that had paid the men he had brought with him to Koenugard to fight for the rule here. That had been six years ago, and now Oleg was jarl over the Slavs and the Rus both and made the emperor at Mikligard nervous. In the winter he collected tribute in the form of furs and wax and honey from the Slavs in the district. In the summer he taxed the river traffic going south to trade.

There was a fire burning on the hearth, and a great many men and women gathered around it. Some of the women were Slavs rather than Swedes, and most of the thralls, male and female, were Slavs.

One of Oleg's *druzhina* met them at the door. "The great prince wishes to speak to the jarl Haakon and Ragnar, the merchant, in his chambers." He looked at Knut and Donal and Hagar the Simple looming in the doorway. "These others will stay here."

Haakon nodded. Oleg had no reason to do him an evil. Hagar would sit and drink beer and eat anything that was offered him, but he would not get drunk, and he would keep his eyes open. Donal, no doubt, would talk and set other men to talking. Knut would sit and glower at everyone and try to figure out a way to come raiding here, but they would be polite to him because there was always the chance that a one-eyed man was Father Odin in disguise.

Haakon and Ragnar followed Oleg's man through the hall to a door at the end that led into the private chambers at the back. Oleg was sitting on a chair covered with marten skins and drinking honey mead out of a silver pot. A smaller fire burned in a stone hearth, and his hair reflected the flames. A Slav woman in a quilted jacket handed them mead in pots not so fine as Oleg's, and then scuttled out when he looked at her. Oleg leaned back in his chair and stuck his boots to the fire.

"You are settled in the camps with no trouble?"

"Yes, Prince. You've made improvements since I was here last," Ragnar said.

"I was new to Koenugard then. Now we are an orderly city. No trader is robbed in my camps."

Ragnar drank his mead. "No, we are robbed at your customhouse instead. I have heard that the ship-tax has gone up."

Oleg chuckled. "Better that I steal from you a little when you are expecting it, than other men when you are not."

"Better for whom, Prince?"

"Better for me," Oleg said frankly. "Also better for you. In return for the ship-tax, which you complain so greatly of, you get safety in the camps." With that he dismissed the ship-tax and now he looked at Haakon. "This Harud Olafsson went south with Thjodulf Ottarsson late last season, to trade some in the Magyar villages, and then in Mikligard."

"Magyars?" Ragnar whistled. "Likely he would trade his head there."

"Thjodulf Ottarsson has been trading with them for a while and a while, and they pay mostly in silver for what he brings them. Also they give him an escort through Pecheneg lands, so he goes when he pleases. Thjodulf wintered with them this last season." Oleg looked thoughtful. "True, I had hoped this Harud might run afoul of them—the Magyars are bad tempered. But Thjodulf told me that he left Harud in Mikligard, so likely he is there still, mixing in the emperor's war with the Bulgars."

"Why is the emperor in Mikligard fighting the Bulgars?"
Haakon drank his mead and watched Oleg, who was
taking a great deal of trouble in a matter that didn't
concern him. Haakon decided that Oleg also wanted Harud
dead, for some reason that he wasn't telling.

"Because the emperor of the Romans has annoyed the
Bulgars' king enough to attack him," Oleg said. He drank
some mead and settled back with a storyteller's air. "It is
all for trade. Mikligard is the heart of trade. The only
greater place is Baghdad. And if you get to the heart of
them, all of Mikligard's wars are for trade.

"The emperor now is Leo, who is supposed to be, or to
not be, the son of Basil the Macedonian. Basil thought he
wasn't, but Basil would suspect his own mother, let alone a
wife. Likely enough Leo is Basil's all right, and he's a fair
enough ruler. But he's always had an eye for a woman, and
in a roundabout way, that got him a war. He made his
mistress's father chief minister, and then *he* gave the
Bulgarian trade monopoly to two jackals of his own, and
they raised all the taxes and shifted the customhouse out
of Mikligard to Thessalonica."

Oleg's lesson was making Haakon's head ache. He put
his mead pot down and tried to pay attention because
anything this complicated was usually important.

"As I said—it is all trade. Trade is more important than
anything, and the Bulgars' carrying trade from the Black
Sea down the Bosporus is gone now. Now the Bulgars have
to go overland, and it is a very bad route. And the taxes
are higher. So Symeon, who is khan of the Bulgars,
complained to Leo, and Leo may have seen the justice of
that, but he is too proud to reverse his policies for a khan
in Bulgaria. So Symeon took his warriors and marched on
the empire, and now they are fighting."

Oleg seemed uninclined to care who won, except maybe
as the war might weaken one side or the other enough to
make it vulnerable to his own raids. But Haakon thought
that Oleg was right about one thing: If there was trouble
in Mikligard, then Harud Olafsson would have managed to
get his fingers in it, very likely to no one's advantage but
his own. Also it might be that someone *had* killed him by
now. Haakon thought that he would give another horse to

Father Odin that Harud was still alive. It didn't seem much use asking Thor. He picked up his mead pot again and studied Oleg over it. The pot was cast bronze, with a hound chasing reindeer around it, and the mead was winter mead, very strong. It made the fire and the room and Oleg's face flicker redly. What had Harud Olafsson done in Koenugard that had made Oleg want him dead and not care greatly by whose hand?

Oleg caught Haakon watching him and stood up. "Come you back to the fire in the hall. I have told you everything I know."

In the hall a thrall brought them more mead and a platter of goat's meat. They found the others much as Haakon had expected. Donal was talking, half in sign language, to a woman whose clothes and brooches were in the Swedish style, but who looked as if she might be a Slav. Every minute or so she would look over her shoulder at a stocky blond man in a squirrel hat, as if to be sure that he permitted her to speak to the stranger. Hagar sat methodically polishing a rib bone bare, and Knut had regained his good humor and had begun throwing dice with a Swede with baggy blue breeches and a nick in his ear. Haakon hoped the Swede hadn't got the nick cheating in a dice game; he had drunk too much mead to sort out a quarrel.

Some of the other men in the hall were traders too, Haakon thought, but most were Oleg's *druzhina*—tall and fair like all the Swedes, but with an indefinable foreign look to their clothes: Swedish styles adapted to native materials or with an odd overlay of native pattern. Their speech, too, had the same accent as Oleg's and was peppered with Slavic words. There was no comparable term for *druzhina* among the Swedes, and they spoke of going on *poludie*—which meant "visiting" but was really a tax-gathering excursion—every winter to collect the *dan* from the Slavic tribes. *Dan* was furs, or sometimes silver, or anything paid in tax and tribute. Then with the merchants who came from upriver, Oleg's men would go south in June to trade it in Mikligard. The ships would go in convoy down the Dnieper, like a floating marketplace, to brave together the rapids and hostile tribes along the way.

Until June, they sat in Koenugard and refitted their
boats and renewed old friendships—or old feuds that
could be settled later, away from the guard that Oleg
employed to keep the peace. Many of the Rus merchants
used the hollowed-out boats, which the Slavs built for
them. In the winter, while the Rus made *poludie*, the
villagers felled trees and hollowed them with fire and
hatchets, then floated them to Koenugard. There they sold
them to the Rus, who would take the oars and thole pins
and other fittings from their old boats and refit them to
the new. And then the Rus would wait in Koenugard for
the river to go down, and mostly they got drunk while
they waited, which was why Oleg kept a guard to patrol
the city and the camps.

Much rode on setting out on the right day. They did not
wait for any good or ill omens in the stars, but for the river
itself. In April the ice melted and the spring runoff began,
and the Dnieper ran high and cold and strong enough to
break boats in the rapids below Koenugard. The river
could be ridden only in early summer, when the greatest
force of the high water had eased and the drought had not
yet begun. There were seven falls to be gotten over, which
broke ships and men if a crew was unlucky. When the
water was low, the rocks were worse—in some years, on
the return journey in the autumn, it was necessary to
carry the ships for forty miles, clear of the falls where the
river ran compressed between walls of granite. It was little
wonder that the hollow log boats were only good for a
season.

The danger of attack was worst along the rapids, too.
The Pechenegs held the land along the falls, and they
were a savage tribe, half-wild. They made their drinking
cups from human skulls, it was said, cleaning them and
mounting rims and bases in silver. It was one of the most
dangerous trade routes in the world, and it was only the
gold in Mikligard that brought the traders back year after
year to try it.

They sat and drank mead with Oleg's *druzhina* and the
other traders until Haakon decided that he and Ragnar
were as drunk as they ought to be in a strange city.
Outside Haakon took a deep breath of cold air and stead-

ied himself on his feet. The sky was clear and black, lit
with stars.

"Colder than a sea goddess's kiss," Knut said. He beat
his hands on his sleeves.

"You didn't drink enough," Hagar said.

"And I won't fall in the river on the way home, either."
Knut looked at Hagar. "Block the channel, likely."

Hagar lumbered on, unperturbed. He wasn't drunk. He
never got drunk. It took too much mead.

"Oleg is a thief," Ragnar said thoughtfully, "but an
openhanded one. That is good mead. He promised a cask
of it, for a guest-gift."

A guest-gift meant that a like gesture was necessary. "I
will send him six sable skins in the morning," Haakon
said. He looked at Ragnar. "Three of mine and three of
yours."

"You have more men, who will drink more mead,"
Ragnar protested.

"I will also pay your openhanded thief a bigger ship-
tax," Haakon said. "Does the great prince tax ships on the
upriver journey?"

"The great prince taxes anything that will sit still,"
Ragnar said.

"Maybe not, if we catch Harud Olafsson," Donal said.

Haakon swung around to look at him. "How so?" He
stopped in the middle of the wooden street so that Donal
bumped into him.

Donal grinned. "You are blocking the road, jarl." Oleg's
guards, making their midnight rounds, had come up with
them and were glaring at them to move on.

Haakon glared back, and the guards went around. "I
thought there was more than a little grievance for the
trouble he was taking. What is it?"

"It was a woman," Donal said. "A Slav woman, who was
a thrall in his house. The Slavs here are some free, some
thralls, but never quite equal to the Rus even when
they're free. The women have a better time—a lot of the
Rus didn't bring women with them, and so they marry
Slavs. Or sometimes they just pick one and live with her,
without a marriage. The woman I was talking to is married
to a man from Oleg's *druzhina*, and she told me because

she doesn't like the lady Ingrid, who is the prince's wife
out of Sweden and proud in her ways."

This was as complicated as the emperor's war with the
Bulgars, Haakon thought. Everything that happened on
this trip was twisted inside out, like a decorative chain.
"What about the other woman?"

"You have to understand the rest, or you won't be
understanding about her," Donal said.

The Gaels never told a story from beginning to end,
Haakon thought. They went at it sideways or began in the
middle and explained things until you had forgotten what
they were talking about.

"Well, walk while you explain it," Ragnar said, "or we'll
freeze to the road."

"The other woman was a thrall," Donal said, "and she
was the prince's favorite. The lady Ingrid's beauty is in her
dowry, I'm thinking. Anyway, this one was still a thrall
because the prince wasn't wanting to offend his wife, and
risking her maybe going home again to Sweden with her
dowry if he did. So then Harud Olafsson came, and he was
a guest in the hall because he was with old Jarl Thjodulf.
He asked the prince for the woman Ana for the night, and
the prince couldn't be refusing because she was only a
thrall, so he said only if the woman was willing, which was
the best he could do.

"The woman *wasn't* willing, and she said so, but Harud
Olafsson found her when he was drunk and dragged her
off to his bed anyway, when the prince wasn't there. She
fought him, and he killed her for spite." Donal paused and
looked somber. "I am thinking that Harud Olafsson would
wither the grass he walked on."

It was a stark story and horrible in the silence it left
behind it. "What happened then?" Haakon said finally.

"Harud Olafsson paid the prince blood-money," Donal
said. "There wasn't much else that could be done. The
woman was a thrall, and the prince's wife is reasonably
proud. He couldn't offend her by making a scandal and
killing a man who had already paid blood-money, just
because the woman was one he'd been keeping in his bed.
And the *druzhina* wouldn't have liked it, either. Slavs
don't matter."

They walked on in silence for a moment.

"I'm thinking you'll have a friend in Prince Oleg if he hears you've put a knife in Harud Olafsson," Donal said quietly.

"The emperor is willing to give an audience to the Rus." The minister Stylian Zautzes gave Harud Olafsson a smile gently tinged with menace. He folded his dark arms across his gold and green gown. "But let the Rus remember that he is in the city illegally and can still be deported."

"I am not a Rus. I have told you, I am Norse. And I paid a fee for leave to stay here."

"That was a bribe." Zautzes gave him a look of mock horror. "It cannot be imagined that the emperor would countenance a bribe. All Rus are to leave the city in the autumn. It is law."

"I am not a Rus!" Harud studied the minister warily. He was a dark man, of Armenian blood mixed with blackamoor, it was said. Mahogany skin glowed against his court robes, and his face was framed with a crisp black beard. He was the father of the emperor's mistress, Zoe, and accounted a dangerous man to cross. "I have sent the emperor a gift," Harud said, "to make my friendship known." It had cost nearly the last of his money.

Zautzes raised his eyebrows. "The emperor of Rome receives many gifts."

"No doubt!" Harud snapped. "I have been asking for an audience since the fall."

Zautzes shrugged. "It is necessary to be patient." This man didn't look patient, he thought. There was a faint wash of sweat on his face. And his clothes were good ones, but old: tunic and breeches such as the Rus wore, with very fine embroidery that was beginning to show ragged in places. *He needs something*, Zautzes thought. *And he is afraid of something.* "The emperor has been occupied," he said.

Harud Olafsson ran a hand over his beard. "With the war, yes. I have told you—I have told everyone in the emperor's palace, by now!—that that is the reason I wish for audience. I can tell the emperor how he can win this war."

His Greek was vilely accented, but understandable.

Zautzes said, "The emperor has many generals who are paid for the purpose of telling him that," but he looked thoughtful. Leo was fighting with Symeon because it was not for an emperor of Rome in the East to bow down before a mere khan of the Bulgars and reverse an imperial minister's policies because the Bulgars were shouting threats. But he would not be in a good temper over it if he should *lose* the war. And Symeon was not some barbarian princeling polishing his spear in the mountains and making challenge to an empire whose vastness he could not even understand. Symeon was a Christian king, educated in Constantinople with Leo in their boyhood, whose court at Preslav had been said to rival the emperor's own. He was a modern king, capable of making a modern war, and he was very dangerous.

Stylian Zautzes looked at Harud and was not impressed. His pale skin was shiny with sweat now, and his long face had an expression that alternated between bad temper and fear. He looked like something that was cornered and had turned with its teeth out. It occurred to Zautzes that he was not very clean. But still . . . "What is this so-great plan you talk of that will win the emperor's war?"

Harud's jaw tightened. "I will tell it to the emperor."

Zautzes grinned. "Lest I present it as my own? And maybe deport you? What are you so afraid of, outside the city?"

"I will speak to the emperor," Harud said again, stubbornly. He folded his arms like the minister and stared back at him. Again Zautzes thought of something in a corner.

He shrugged. "As you wish."

Beyond the golden doors of the golden palace, the emperor sat on a golden throne, guarded by golden lions. Golden trees sprouted beyond the lions, their branches alive with jeweled birds that sang as sweetly as the live ones in the emperor's garden. Harud stopped, gaping, and Stylian Zautzes put a heavy hand on his back and pushed. Harud sprawled on the floor with his nose against the porphyry steps that mounted to the emperor's throne.

"Prostrate yourself before the emperor, Rus," Zautzes said, unnecessarily.

Harud began to rise.

"Three times," Zautzes said. The golden lions roared suddenly, an ear-splitting sound, and Harud flung himself back, startled. The emperor's eunuchs giggled, and the courtiers and guardsmen behind the emperor looked bland. Harud gritted his teeth and bent his face twice more to the laurel and rosemary that strewed the floor. When he looked up again, the emperor and his throne had risen nearly to the gold dome of the ceiling. They hovered there, before a glass mosaic of the Christ, leaving Harud to address himself to the emperor's red boots.

Zautzes stroked his black beard and hid a grin behind his hand. This reception was generally kept to overawe ambassadors, not for petition-bringers and supplicants. The emperor was amusing himself, he thought. "This is the Rus, O Basileus, who has words to speak of the renegade Symeon."

Leo VI considered Harud and remained where he was. Leo had a mild, pleasant face, made imposing by the stiff purple and gold of his gown and the imperial diadem that sat above it, hung with pearls. He flicked a hand at someone below him, and the jeweled birds ceased their song. "The Rus may speak."

"I am not a Rus, Basileus," Harud said for what felt like the fiftieth time. They seemed to feel that anyone who came through the Dnieper lands must be a Rus. "I am a Norseman, from the Norse holdings in Ireland."

"Then why are you here?"

"I lost my holding in Ireland most unfairly and came here—"

Leo looked bored. "That is very little to us. If you wish to speak of our war with the renegade who calls himself a king of the Bulgars, you may speak."

"Yes, Basileus." He arranged the Greek words in his mind first, carefully. "I came with a trader of the Rus, through Magyar lands, Basileus. They are very fierce, but they know this man. He has traded with them a great while. Now they know me. They are also greedy, and there is much plunder in Bulgaria. If the khan of the Bulgars were fighting with the Magyars, could he fight also with you, Basileus?"

Leo's hand moved again, and the great throne dropped

slowly down to rest upon the cloth of gold between the golden lions. "You may come before the throne, Norseman." He looked at Stylian Zautzes, and their eyes met. "You will stay. The rest have our leave to go."

V Danegeld

Rosamund wiped her hands on her apron and gave Gunnar a hunted look. "He won't leave. He dogs my footsteps like a hound or a man courting. I have told him a hundred times I cannot make an agreement with King Harald without Haakon, but it is like talking to the bucket in the well."

Gunnar stuck his head around the dairy door for a look at the yard. He, too, had begun to look like a horse with Sigurd Njalsson hitched like a cart to his tail. "That was what I came to tell you," he said. "He *is* leaving—"

"Mary be thanked!"

"—today. And King Harald is coming."

"Holy Mother, no!"

"With his hounds and his falconer and his court—all of whom can drink a beer barrel dry in one gulp—and his lords of state and his poet and his herald and Thor knows who else. It will be very expensive," he added gloomily.

Rosamund sat down on a milk bucket. "It will be very dangerous if he traps us into *any* agreement. And it will be harder to say no to King Harald. It is almost impossible to say no to kings. King Alfred used to visit my father, with his retinue, and when they had gone we had nothing left to eat, and my father had promised a hundred extra men for the king's army. We will have to give him a present, too. What on earth?"

Gunnar thought. "Give him one of Gerd's pups." He nodded at the two half-grown hounds sprawled in an empty stall. "Haakon may not like it, but—"

"Then Haakon should have stayed home!" Rosamund said. "And dealt with this king himself." She tucked her hair back under her kerchief and looked up at Gunnar. "I am telling you, Gunnar, I wish I could bide in the dairy with the cows until this king has gone home again." An infuriated shriek from the direction of the hall announced that Asa wished to be fed, and Rosamund stood up again wearily. "Very well. Go and tell Jarl Sigurd that we will be pleased to receive King Harald, although I can't honestly say I'll be anything but appalled. And Gunnar—"

"Yes, Lady Rosamund?" He turned in the doorway.

"Mend your quarrel with Guthrun," she said tartly. "She let a whole tub of dye boil away this morning, mooning over you. Or thinking of a way to put a knife in you at night—I don't know which. But I won't have you quarreling like a pair of roosters under my feet with King Harald here."

"I am not your thrall!" Guthrun spat at him like a cat. Her gold hair was coming out of its knot. She had tried to hit him, and he had pushed her away and sat her down hard on the stream bank. "I am Norse. And I will never be a thrall again, not to you, Gunnar Thorsten, not to anyone."

Gunnar snorted. Guthrun had been a thrall in England until Jarl Haakon had come and stolen Lady Rosamund out of her castle, and Guthrun, born in England of Norse parents, had gathered her courage and gone, too. "Do you know how the Arabs keep their women? They wrap them up in veils—so no one but their husbands can see their pretty, bad-tempered faces, mind you—and they keep them in *hareems* with eunuchs to watch them. They have nothing to do all day but comb their hair and paint their toenails gold or other silliness. And at night, if they are lucky, their husband will send for them. But each Arab can have four wives, and as many concubines as he has strength for, so I don't suppose he sends for any one of them very often. And with nothing to do all day, they get fat very soon"—he eyed Guthrun's slim figure appraisingly— "and then he doesn't send for them at all."

Guthrun quivered with fury. "What about that—that whore with the black hair who does no work that you brought home with you?"

"She is a thrall," Gunnar said, "and whatever you may think, Guthrun, I have not been bedding her. Although she is somewhat more even tempered than you," he added calculatedly.

"I don't care if she's a thrall or an elf out of Alfheim," Guthrun snapped. "She clings like a leech. And her backside wiggles. She looks pleased with herself. And except for waiting on you hand and foot in a manner that is disgusting— so that now you come all lordlywise and expect *me* to do the same—she does no work at all. The other thrall-women, and most of the free ones, would like to kill her."

"If you had wed me, Guthrun, you'd have a right to complain." He sat down suddenly on the bank beside her. "Wed me, and I'll sell her."

Guthrun looked him in the eye. "Sell her first. I do not trust you, Gunnar."

He turned away and stared out at the water running coldly over the rocks in the streambed. A fish leaped up, snapping at a fly, turning mirrored, gray-green scales to the sun. "Then we are even. I don't trust you. You have too much liking for silly compliments and for spending your time in the boathouse."

Guthrun stared at the river, too, and addressed her remarks to it. "And maybe with a man who is not trying to make a fool of me for the whole steading to laugh at."

"Marry Yazid and you'll look a fool," Gunnar said, "in a veil up over your nose. And if you don't marry him and find yourself with a child on the way, you'll look like a bigger one, and I won't have you then, Guthrun."

"Yazid has lived in Norse lands for the last ten years," Guthrun said between her teeth, "so there is no question of my wearing veils, and you are only trying to find a quarrel. And I am not bedding him, whatever *you* think, so if I find myself with child, Gunnar, it will be yours."

"Are you?"

"No."

They stared at the river a while longer, watching the current bubble around the waterweeds on the bank. After a while Gunnar reached out a hand and pulled the rest of the pins out of her hair.

"It would be almost a shame to marry you and cover that up," he said huskily, but she knew that he was only trying to save his pride because she *wouldn't* marry him.

I should give in, she thought. She had been going to before he had come home with that black-haired thrall. Now her pride wouldn't let her. *Lady Freya, send a troll out of the mountain for that thrall-woman.*

Gunnar drew the back of his hand across her face, his mood gone from anger to something else almost as forceful. Guthrun tipped her head a little, into his hand, and didn't say anything when his other hand reached out, under the loose folds of her overgown, and came to rest on her breast. "Damn you," Gunnar said distinctly. She twisted her arms up suddenly, around his neck, and they rolled in the grass, half-passionate, half-angry still. He pushed her gown and shift up around her hips, his long hands hard and cool against her skin and then, while she lay and laughed at him, pulled his belt and trousers off. She didn't say anything, just lay there with her gold hair fanning out around her like a pool, but when he entered her, she wrapped her legs around his hips and sank her teeth into his shoulder. Whether in passion or fury, he wasn't sure.

Nothing has changed, he thought. He sat back and pushed her gown up farther, to cup her bare breasts. She gasped and twisted under him, and he let himself go, lost in wanting her, knowing that the sudden ache and desire that had come on him was on her, too. And nothing had changed. They had quarreled and made love alternately all year. Her arms were wrapped around his ribs, almost painfully, and his hands tightened on her breasts. They were quarreling still—like a jagged edge of glass laid along the top of a green desire. Likely they would be quarreling until Ragnarok if one of them wouldn't swallow pride.

King Harald Fairhair's outriders kicked up a choking cloud of dust on the roadway, and Rosamund stood in the gate with Gunnar and watched apprehensively. The king had a great many men with him. It had been her experience that that usually meant a king was going to ask for something, and she didn't know what this one was going to take it into his head to want.

Her women were gathered behind her and most of the seventy-five men that Haakon had left at the steading.

Enough to look imposing and make a proper welcome and
maybe give the king second thoughts.

The outriders stopped with a flourish, and someone
blew on a horn. Harald Fairhair drew rein in the gateway.
Rosamund curtsied, just enough for politeness. Harald
Fairhair was no king in the Trondelag, but it was as well to
be polite. Especially when Haakon was Mother Mary
knew where, chasing Harud Olafsson, who was less of a
danger now than this smiling blond man on a horse.

"Dear lady!" Harald beamed genially and swung himself
down from his horse. "You are most kind to welcome
us"—he kissed her hand and eyed the men behind her—
"with so courteous a display."

"Your Grace is welcome in Haakonstead," Rosamund
murmured politely. He wore a flowing shirt of red silk that
rippled in the light breeze, and she thought she could see
the pattern of mail under it. His gold hair curled around
his ears, freshly washed and gleaming, and his men were
all scrubbed clean, as well. They must have washed in the
river that morning. It was a long, gritty ride up from
Vestfold. The king rocked back on his heels and continued
to smile at her. He was an undeniably fine man to look at.

The king's men were beginning to swarm through the
gateway, a little more lordlywise but otherwise much as
Jarl Sigurd's had done. Rosamund made a stab at taking
charge of matters. "You will be tired and wish to rest. This
is my husband's steward, Gunnar Thorsten." King Harald
would know that already, she would be willing to bet. "He
will show Your Grace to the guesthouse"—so lately vacat-
ed by Jarl Sigurd. She would like to burn it down, she
thought, and then maybe be left in peace. She smiled at
King Harald. "Your Grace honors us."

With the *Eyrathing*, the June law courts, two weeks away,
most of Haakon's folk had by now come to the steading to
make the sea journey together. Was King Harald going to
stay that long, Rosamund wondered frantically. And if he
was, how were they going to transport him, because the
king and his entourage had come by the land road, and
there wasn't room enough in Haakon's ships for them. At
least the king had seemed pleased with his gift. A gift had to

be something important—valuable. Haakon had given the wali of Cadiz an entire longship. Rosamund shook her head. She had lived in the wali's *hareem* for a month, but in spite of that, Haakon appeared to find him a fine and reasonable fellow. Admittedly, he was a better man than Harud Olafsson, but she wondered if she was ever going to understand the way Haakon looked at things. It was not the way that most men did, to be sure.

She pushed the wali out of her mind and set herself to being pleasant to King Harald, who was sitting in Haakon's place at the high table and applying himself to a roast duck. Rosamund's ladies were seated according to their rank, either with herself and Gunnar and the king's court at the high table, or at a smaller table below it. The king seemed to find their presence a splendid addition to the feast. He smiled and complimented and patted hands, even Sigrid's, whose black hair was going gray and who had Erik the Bald scowling at her side. Rosamund had invited Sigrid and Erik in the hope that they might lend the force of their personalities to her position that evening, and, if need be, the force of Erik's men later. If Sigrid seemed inclined tonight to be charmed by the king, Rosamund knew that she wouldn't allow herself to be so charmed as to do anything politically unwise. Not if she realized that she was doing it, anyway. Rosamund found herself wishing fervently that King Harald would vanish in a cloud of sulfur like the devil.

At least Gunnar's thrall-girl was not in evidence, she noted thankfully, and Gunnar and Guthrun appeared to be in reasonable charity with each other. Gunnar was deep in talk with the king's poet, a squat, lank-haired man with a startlingly clear, true voice that should have come from the king instead, who had the looks to go with it. The king was too good looking, Rosamund thought. Dangerous. A man like that could talk people into things.

The only person who appeared unlikely to succumb to King Harald's charm was Fann, who sat pressed flat against the back of her chair and watched him like a robin that has met a snake. Her hair glowed as red as a fox's brush in the lamplight, and she had on a blue green gown that set off her fair skin and made her nearly pretty. King Harald beamed at her, apparently taking her stark terror for awe, and leaned across the table to kiss her hand. The king had a reputation for liking the ladies, Rosamund remembered despairingly, and none of the ladies at her table was unattached. The evening seemed to career inevitably toward nightmare.

Rosamund signaled behind her back to a thrall for more beer, and King Harald, distracted, drank it genially, wiped his mouth on the back of his hand, and told Rosamund how much he valued her husband's friendship in the Trondelag.

Rosamund had lived in Norway long enough to know that "friendship" spoken that way meant more than it sounded like. It meant an agreement of goodwill or mutual support, sometimes even a written treaty. "I am sure that my husband values equally any . . . *agreement* he has made with Your Grace," she said carefully. If she admitted to anything definitive on her own part, it might prove impossible for Haakon to repudiate it later with any honor.

King Harald chuckled and took another tack. He patted her hand. "I have heard it said that Jarl Haakon married a very wise woman, and I see that is so. Sometimes it is necessary that a wife be wise for her husband."

"In what way is that Your Grace?" Rosamund wiped her silver plate with a piece of bread and watched Harald's men-at-arms spilling beer on her table linens.

"Why, sometimes a wife will recognize what a husband will not. The Tronds can be a stubborn folk."

"Independent," Rosamund said. She smiled. "But then I am so new to Norway, and do not always understand these matters. That is why I always leave such things to Jarl Haakon, Your Grace."

King Harald fed a piece of duck to the half-grown wolfhound at his feet. The king's guest-gift had lost no time in transferring his loyalty, coerced by duck. "And in Jarl Haakon's absence, to Gunnar Thorsten?" Harald said. He eyed Gunnar speculatively.

"Of course," Rosamund said. "Gunnar is Jarl Haakon's most loyal man. He would never do anything the jarl wouldn't like."

"The jarl is fortunate," Harald said. Rosamund thought he looked irritated.

She nodded at the thralls for more beer. If he got drunk,

she thought, maybe it would help. A thrall-woman came with two pitchers and filled the king's horn with beer while he patted her backside. She giggled and sidled out of reach to pour water into Rosamund's. Rosamund took a deep gulp. Nursing Asa made her thirsty, and if she drank beer all night, she would be drunk herself, and King Harald was hard enough to deal with when she was sober.

There was a dogfight in the lower hall, and with the thrall out of reach, Harald tranferred his attention to that, pounding the table with laughter as one of his men-at-arms and one of Haakon's fell in the straw trying to wrestle the dogs apart. They pulled them apart finally, Haakon's man nursing a bitten hand and swearing. The contention proved to be a bone, disputed by Gerd and one of the hunting hounds that had come in King Harald's train. Someone tossed the other hound a second bone, and Gerd retired with hers in queenly dignity under a table.

"She's no beauty," Harald said appreciatively, "but by Frey, she can fight! Good blood, that." He fed his own pup a piece of meat and looked around him happily for other entertainment.

Rosamund settled back in her chair with a sigh of relief. The king seemed to have forgotten his mission for the moment. Maybe by the time he cornered her again, she and Gunnar would have thought of something. If they could arrange to leave for the *Eyrathing* early, it might help. There would be a full schedule of land disputes and blood-feuds to be decided, and if King Harald wished to wait through all that, then he could present his invitation to the Tronds personally with her blessing. He wouldn't get far—which, of course, was why he wanted Haakon's name to put to it. . . .

A sudden lurch of the table and a stifled scream broke her reverie, and she jerked upright in her chair to see Fann with her chair turned over behind her staring in patent horror at the king. King Harald still had hold of her hand, but his expression was fading from geniality to puzzlement, and there was every indication that pure fury would be next. Rosamund watched dumbstruck as Fann jerked her hand back as if a troll had grabbed it, screamed again, and ran from the room.

"Dear God." Rosamund stood up. "Your Grace—Your Grace must excuse her," she said ruthlessly, "Fann is not quite right in her mind. Most unfortunate. An accident when she was young." She gathered her skirts around her. "I must make sure that she doesn't do herself an injury—" She bent her head to Guthrun's ear. "Find him a woman," she whispered fiercely. "Any woman who isn't married who's willing—a thrall—I don't care!" She hurried out of the hall, abandoning Gunnar and Guthrun. A king who has just been made a fool of is not easy to soothe, but she expected they would manage.

She found Fann in her own chamber, curled into a hysterical ball on the bed. Rosamund stood a moment in the doorway to retrieve her temper.

"Have you lost your mind?" she inquired, when she thought she could refrain from tearing the girl limb from limb.

Fann raised a wet, red face from the tangle of furs on the bed. "He—he wanted me to—he said—" She stopped, hiccuping miserably, and Rosamund saw that she was shaking from head to toe.

"I can imagine what he wanted," Rosamund said more gently. "It was a compliment, you know."

"I couldn't!" Fann wailed.

"Nobody asked you to, you silly girl. But you don't refuse a king by squalling as if he'd tried to kill you. You have insulted him."

"I—I was afraid," Fann sniffled. She really did look dreadful. There was more to this than a moment's panic, Rosamund thought.

"Why on earth should you be? He wasn't going to rape you there in the roast duck, on all my good table linen." She smiled and looked to see if Fann would smile back. Fann wrapped her arms around her chest and rocked back and forth, shaking.

"Now see here," Rosamund said, "you didn't have to bed him if you didn't want to, but except for Donal, of course, it would be no bad thing to have a king's favor. It isn't worth howling over. And I am not angry anymore. At least not much."

"I prayed for forgetfulness," Fann said unexpectedly. "For that—that man in Birka—the one who b-bought me.

But it's no good. And now Donal wants to get married here, and then I'll—I'll have to—"

"Wait a minute. Haven't you been bedding Donal?" Rosamund looked at her with a little surprise. After all, they were betrothed, and there were no Christian priests handy; she had just assumed—

"Oh, no. That would be a sin," Fann said.

"There are times when a little sin is necessary," Rosamund said practically. She thought about telling Fann that she had first bedded Haakon just so she wouldn't be a virgin and Harud Olafsson wouldn't have her, which had seemed a small price to pay. But she thought that it was not the sin that Fann was so afraid of, not really. "Look you, child, what happened in Birka was unfortunate, and a sad way to lose your maidenhood. But a man and a woman together— that is the way of the world. This man in Birka didn't do it very well, I daresay," she added, half grinning. "Give Donal a chance, and you might find it different."

"Noooo." Fann shuddered.

Rosamund stood up. "Well, unless you are going to go in a nunnery, you will have to change your mind sometime. And Donal's patience may wear out, you know. And then you might find yourself with a man you won't like as well." Fann just curled into the furs and shook, and Rosamund sighed. "Get some sleep, child. The world won't look so black in the morning, I expect." She closed the door and hoped she was right. She didn't have *time* for Fann, she thought desperately.

Fann stayed in her mind, stuck like a burr, anyway. When everyone had been prodded off to sleep, and King Harald had gone away, mollified with the thrall-woman who had poured his beer, Rosamund curled up alone in her own bed and dreamed all night of her first time with Haakon. Or maybe it was only that she grew lecherous, she thought ruefully, with Haakon gone and nothing to do all night but lie there and think of King Harald and the thrall-woman. When she had come back to the hall, the woman had been sitting in his lap, feeding him honeycake. King Harald had inquired after Fann in a voice that said that he didn't care greatly if goblins had taken her, and gone back to letting the

thrall-woman stroke his hair. A woman who had screamed
and run at the sight of him was not one the king would have
a further interest in, and the thrall-woman's admiration of
his fine self was writ large on her face. Rosamund thought
that the thrall-woman would have slept with a giant out of
Jotunheim for a gold bracelet, which she learned later was
what Guthrun had promised her, but there was no denying
that the king was a fair man to look at.

Rosamund pulled the covers up over her ears and tried to
stop thinking about King Harald making love to the thrall-
woman, which would only give her more dreams. But at
least the king wasn't angry—yet. Guthrun was the one who
deserved a gold bracelet for that, Rosamund thought sleepily. She would see that she got it if there was anything left to
pay for it with when the king had gone home.

In the morning she dismally decided that Harald wasn't
going home, not until he had what he wanted. Or something attractive enough to stall him with, and there wasn't
that much gold in the whole steading. She left the king
and his lords making a leisurely breakfast of meat and beer
and good bread, and fled to sit on a flat rock behind the
dairy, where she wouldn't have to think about how much
they were eating. Barley bread and buttermilk was the
usual steading fare for the morning, but one couldn't feed
that to a king.

Danegeld, she thought with a snort of amusement. King
Alfred of England had paid the Danes the danegeld to stay
out of his land, and he hadn't been rid of them since. The
fjord below was blue, bright as a bird's egg. If only by
some miracle, Haakon's ships should come sailing up it . . .

No. Nothing there but the brown roofs of the boathouses,
unnaturally bright and silent against the green and blue,
frozen into stillness in the sun like the paintings that the
monks made. Gunnar had slipped away with a handful of
men when the feast had grown drunken enough that they
wouldn't be missed, and he and Yazid had floated Yazid's
half-built ship and towed it behind *Red Hawk* upfjord to
Erik's steading, where King Harald would be less likely to
notice it and take an interest. Even in its unfinished state, it
was clearly a great ship—and too great a ship for King

Harald to feel comfortable leaving an unallied jarl to own. Gunnar and Yazid had struck a truce in the face of a greater need and had both come home again at dawn in one piece, so there was one good to come out of the king's presence.

There should be, Rosamund thought. It was too fine a summer for her world to stay black all day, even with King Harald looming to blacken it. She took a deep breath of the air, crisp and sun washed. A beautiful country, Norway, wilder than England: by summer, a green and soaring loveliness; by winter, haunted, frozen, black on white; both with a beauty to catch the heart. And with a power in it, something out of the earth, a sense of change, of something coming. If only she were a witch who could sit on her rock and use it to magic King Harald away.

She looked up in surprise as a shadow dropped across her lap and saw Gunnar grinning down at her.

"Have you slept?" she asked.

"No." Gunnar's blue eyes were bright, with flecks of gold in them, and very slightly dangerous. "I have been thinking, and I have thought a great thought."

"Indeed?" Rosamund loomed at him suspiciously, wondering by the look of him if the great thought had come out of a beer vat.

Gunnar grinned, and the gold flecks in his eyes danced like a cat's. "I have thought of what to give the king, to make him go home again."

"You have agreed to this?" Rosamund looked at Yazid carefully, searching for some sign that Gunnar had beaten him black and blue to extract a promise.

"Yes." Yazid was his usual graceful self. "It is Allah's wish that I should serve Jarl Haakon. Also"—his dark eyes were a little rueful under the shadow of his head scarf—"the golden one will not have me, not to husband, not ever, I think, so maybe it is better that I go away for a little and let her have her poet with no more fighting."

So said Gunnar, no doubt. There would certainly be a fight when Guthrun found out, but it was still a good idea, no matter what devil had put it in Gunnar's head. "You are a wise man, Yazid. We are grateful, the jarl and I. Also, it will not be forever," she added gently.

"No." Yazid smiled, a little wistful. Only long enough for Guthrun to marry her poet. And for the jarl to come home. Such things were Allah's will. If a man believed that, they were somewhat easier to bear.

"My husband has spoken often of Harald Fairhair's war against the pirates," Rosamund said. She gave King Harald a blinding smile. The rebellious sea lords who had met Harald's fleet at Hafrsfjord had been "pirate" only because they preyed on Norse ships; raids against England didn't count. But that was a thought probably lost on a Norseman.

"Indeed," Harald said, "we sent a great fleet home to Ran that day." Ran was the sea goddess, robber by name and nature, a fitting spirit to welcome a pirate home.

"My husband says," Rosamund said primly, "that Harald Fairhair is a sea king of great power and a blessing to the folk of Vestfold."

Harald leaned back in his chair to bask in the compliment, but his eyes were watchful. He was learning to be wary of Jarl Haakon's Englishwoman, who slipped away like an eel from topics she didn't like and showed no signs of wishing to let him bless the folk of the Trondelag.

"And I have thought," Rosamund said, "that the folk of Haakonstead are owing Harald Fairhair something, for a battle that has brought good to all the Norse and cleared the sea-roads for us."

Harald's eyes narrowed. A point that he had been planning to mention. Somehow, the jarl's lady had forestalled him. "Indeed, lady, a grave responsibility, and one of much expense."

"Of course," Rosamund said smoothly, "I can do nothing without my husband's knowledge—" She fluttered her hands, helpless. "But I have thought that I *can* pay this debt with a service."

That's pricked his ears up, Gunnar thought. He was sitting well back, only a scowl in the background, letting the jarl's lady make the king comfortable with a fire and a cup of hot fruit wine and a chair draped in fox skins to set off his gold hair. Gunnar scowled again, letting the king think the jarl's lady made a mistake, and Rosamund gave him a haughty look.

Harald watched them carefully. The poet thought the jarl wouldn't like this "payment." So. That might mean it was useful. "With the jarl gone, we understand, of course." He patted Rosamund's hand. "But an arrangement, purely unofficial, between *friends*. Why, that is why we fought at Hafrsfjord—in friendship, for *all* Norse."

"Of course," Rosamund breathed, letting her hand lie in Harald's. She shot Gunnar a look that said to keep his tongue between his teeth. Plainly the jarl's lady did not like having the jarl's steward give her orders. "You must have suffered great losses, and my husband says that nothing is so important as a strong fleet. So I have thought and thought, and now I see a way to help." She retrieved her hand from his grasp and clapped it against the other one. A thrall stuck his head around the door. "Bring Yazid, please."

Gunnar sat forward. "Lady—"

"Gunnar Thorsten, this is not a concern of yours! Yazid is sworn to Jarl Haakon and me. Not to you."

King Harald watched with interest as the door swung open again for the Arab. He had seen him about the steading before and thought little of it, but now he saw that the man wore no thrall collar. He had a thin sheet of bark in his hand, with a drawing that caught Harald's attention with a snap. A ship. A ship with a difference: bigger, maybe faster, with a new sort of sail.

"This is Yazid of Alexandria," Rosamund said proudly, while Gunnar folded his arms and seethed. Yazid bowed. "He is a master shipwright, greater than any in Norway. If Your Grace accepts, I will give him to Your Grace's service for a year."

"How dare you!" Guthrun advanced on Gunnar like a spitting cat. The onions she had been carrying in her apron spilled from the corner of the bundle. Gunnar thought that she would probably pelt him with them in a moment.

He braced himself and smiled, his long face amused. "Don't hit me, Guthrun, or I'll hit you back."

Guthrun lashed out at him, onions rolling across the yard.

"Spiteful bitch!" Gunnar flung up a hand in defense. "I told Lady Rosamund not to do it, but she is willful."

"You are lying, Gunnar! *You* thought of it, to spite *me*!"

Gunnar caught her by the wrist. "No," he said seriously. "We have traded the king something that we could spare, to avoid giving him something that we couldn't—such as an alliance that would cost the jarl's honor to break."

"And you coiled yourself up like a snake and lied that you didn't like the idea, so the king would take the bait," Guthrun hissed. She looked over her shoulder to see that none of the king's men were idling in the yard. "But it was your idea—I know you! And when the king has gone away and you can admit it, you will preen yourself like a rooster, and the whole steading will laugh at me! I hate you!"

"No, you don't." He grabbed both her wrists and held them while she tried to bite him. "It is time we stopped this nonsense. We need Yazid to go to keep Harald Fairhair happy until Haakon gets home. But you are right, and I won't weep to see his back. There now, I have admitted it. But I will *not* let people laugh at you, so kiss me and make things right between us."

Guthrun jerked her hands away and rubbed her wrists. "When you have sold that black-haired whore, then you may ask me that. Maybe." She untied her apron and spread it on the ground, piling onions in it. "If Yazid goes," she said between gritted teeth, "then she goes." She stood up clutching the sack of onions. "In the meantime you may go and kiss a cow in the byre for all I care. And if that woman is still here in a week, I never want to see your snake's face again."

"There, like that. So." Rosamund, Guthrun, and Fann adjusted the last of the heavy clay loom weights and sat back on their heels. Whatever else might happen in Haakonstead, the weaving went on or they would all go naked. But today was a fine day, bright with sun, and she could see King Harald's men loading their horses in the yard. They would be gone this morning, and there were still two days before the steading would need to leave for the *Eyrathing*. Without King Harald hung like one of her loom weights from her belt, Rosamund felt that she could face anything, even helping to mediate a winter's store of quarrels. Guthrun was still tight-lipped and brittle as glass, and Fann sniffled and was doleful, but no doubt they would shake off their ill tempers when Harald and Yazid shook Haakonstead dust off their feet. The noises of the steading about its lawful business buzzed around her, and Rosamund considered the loom and decided that she would make a new shirt and trousers for Haakon to come home to.

A wail of despair rose from beyond the next chamber, and then Gunnar's placating voice over it. *Holy Mother, what next?* Rosamund looked at Guthrun. "You stay here." She marched to the door, weaving batten still in hand, and closed it behind her when she left.

Gunnar stood in the middle of his own chamber with the thrall-girl Riziya wrapped around his ankles like a vine. The look he gave Rosamund as she entered almost sent her out again, but she gathered up her skirts and marched through the tangle of overturned tables and strewn clothes. "Stop that howling."

Riziya gulped and looked up at her and burst into fresh tears.

"I told her I was going to sell her," Gunnar said helplessly.

"Noooo! I stay with Gunnar lord!"

"Well, you can't," Rosamund said, "so be quiet." She looked at Gunnar. "I'm glad to see you have developed some sense, but it doesn't appear to be very much. You've scared her to death."

"I have not!" Gunnar said indignantly. "I wasn't going to sell her into a slave market. I'll find her a good master. Thor take it, I told her I'd free her if I can find a man to marry her!"

"Noooo!" Riziya clutched his boots. "He will beat me!"

Rosamund sighed. "Very probably, if you do that." She leaned down and detached the girl. "Be quiet, or *I'll* beat you." She hefted the weaving batten. There were noises outside the door, and she walked over and dropped the bolt loudly. "You'll have the whole steading in here in a minute."

Gunnar's mouth twisted, grimly amused. "No doubt. They haven't had so much excitement since Hagar fell through the ship house roof. I thought you *wanted* me to sell her."

"For peace in the steading, yes," Rosamund said. "But I don't want it said that Jarl Haakon's steward ill treats his thralls. And she may be right. Even a good master may

sell her again. And if you marry her off—Gunnar, she's not
Norse. A husband mightn't give her the respect he'd give
a Norse wife. Damn the wali. May all his wives be a
trouble to *him*!"

Gunnar sat down and put his head in his hands, and
Riziya sidled up next to him hopefully. Her black hair was
tangled around her face, and she peered out at Rosamund
from under it.

"You should have been a monk, Gunnar," Rosamund
said, her mouth twitching. "You attract too many women
at a time."

Gunnar looked at her gloomily. "I can't drag her out of
the steading fighting like a she-cat, with King Harald's
men all over the place." He thought. "Not even with ours.
Earn me an ill name for the rest of my life. Riziya, stop
crying and listen to me."

Riziya gazed up at him. "Love you," she said firmly.

"You don't," Gunnar said.

"Do."

Gunnar looked at Rosamund. "She doesn't. She's just
scared."

"So should you be," Rosamund said. "That's Guthrun
outside the door."

"Oh, fine," Gunnar said. "Very fine. Probably with King
Harald and a herald and three lords of state and a poet,
just in case anyone should miss the goings-on."

Riziya put her head against Gunnar's knee and smiled. "I
stay with Gunnar lord," she said happily, "and be concubine."

"Father Odin," Gunnar said, "no!"

"Riziya, be quiet," Rosamund said absently, thinking.
"Lady Guthrun will break the door down if she hears that."

"Concubine," Riziya said. "Then Gunnar lord will not
need wife."

"Gunnar lord will not need anything but six feet of dirt
for a howe," Rosamund chuckled. She knelt down beside
the girl, remembering Gunnar yesterday morning, with his
great thought, and the cat light dancing in his eyes. "Look
you, child, how would you like to be a *king's* concubine?"

Rosamund held the baby on her hip, and Asa watched
interestedly as the king's cavalcade trotted out through the

open gates. Yazid rode behind the king, beside the poet and his herald, and Riziya was behind him, clutching the reins tightly in both hands, but with her black eyes bright and excited. "Gunnar lord" was very small cheese compared to the glowing picture that Rosamund had painted of a king's court. Rosamund had drawn her descriptions largely from fairy tales and her father's priest's description of heaven, but she expected the reality would be fine enough to suit Riziya. King Harald had a wife, Haakon Grjotgardsson's daughter, but remembering Harald's reputation, Rosamund doubted that one more mistress would make much difference to the poor woman.

Yazid turned back once to see Guthrun, with the morning sun shining gold in her hair, walking with Gunnar away from the gate. He drew rein and dropped back beside Gunnar's black-haired slave girl, who was now, like himself, the king's. "They have given him all their encumbrances," he said.

She creased her pretty forehead, not really understanding, and he smiled kindly. "Never mind. You will like it in Vestfold, I should think."

"I have a new gown," Riziya said. "And the king has given me a bracelet."

King Harald whistled as he rode. The black-haired girl would make a warmer bedmate than his wife, who was plain and didn't like him anyway. The hound puppy was a dog such as no other lord in Vestfold had. But the heart of the bargain was Yazid, who was better than gold. That was where the jarl's lady, who thought she was so clever, had made her mistake. With a ship such as Yazid could build, it would be easy enough to convince Jarl Haakon of most things—he would be persuaded or find his own ships gone down to dine with Ran, the sea goddess.

Yazid, riding behind Harald, thought he could read the king's thoughts like a scroll stretched across his helmet. There was an amused look under the shadow of Yazid's head scarf. In the Mediterranean he had once seen a ship with a false mast. It collapsed like cut string when an arrow hit it in the right spot. Yazid grinned and thought of Hagar the Simple shooting birds on the wing for the pot. Always through the eye. It spoiled the meat otherwise, Hagar said.

VI The River

"Ragnar is right: Oleg is a thief," Knut said disgustedly, watching the crew loading the ship's boat tied alongside *Gray Goose*. *Gray Goose* tugged at her anchor stone, drifting with the current near the shore, part of the great fleet of boats halted beside the prince's taxing house at Vitichev. Everywhere, small boats ran in on the shore or zigzagged like water bugs between the larger ships and the taxing house. Oleg's taxing agents nosed through the cargoes like ferrets, and there was a constant muffled roar of argument. Standing well out in the river, Oleg's own captains played dice and watched the fights. A merchant from Holmgard paid double for throwing the tax man in the water.

"Ah, well, a man with a town like that at his back can be naming his price," Donal said, heaving a half bale of skins into the boat, "there being only one road to Mikligard and that under his nose."

Knut looked at Oleg's boats, loaded down with the winter's tribute, or *dan*, and spat. "He thieves enough from the Slavs to let us pass free. Greed's an ill trait in a jarl."

Donal hooted. "That from a Norseman!"

"Nay, then," Knut said reasonably. "Raiding's one thing. Taxes are another entirely."

"Ah, but he's only refining the system, d'you see?" Donal looked with less amusement at the tax agent, a round little man in a fur hat. "Now then, push off. And see you mark Jarl Haakon's ships as paid. If anyone comes ferreting out here again with his hand out, the way I've seen you do, he'll find it floating." He nodded to the Norsemen in the boat. "Shove off, then, and unload for him. And see he doesn't get his little feet wet."

The tax agent glared at Donal and Knut and at the jarl

sitting with his dog on the deck and grinning at him. Prying the prince's *dan* out of the merchants was a trying service. It was easier to get it out of the Slavs, who were too cowed to protest and easier to add a mite onto the top for his trouble. The merchants screamed over every penny and went to the prince in delegations when they thought the agents were lining their own pockets.

Haakon's men set the agent on the shore and off-loaded the prince's *dan*, and then Hagar the Simple went into the tax house and stood over him until he marked the jarl's ships as paid and gave Hagar a wooden ticket to prove it.

Haakon pulled up anchor, and they drifted a while down the river and anchored again to wait with the rest of the ships that had paid already. The spring trip to Mikligard was a convoy, and they wouldn't raise sail until the last ship had joined on. The whole convoy made a joint sacrifice of a man and three bulls on the shore, and most of Haakon's crews went. Haakon, though, sat on the deck of *Gray Goose*, with Wulf and the tarnished ax at his feet and Donal fiddling with his harp, and no one saw fit to ask the jarl why he stayed away. After the swans at Gnezdovo and the black light that had blazed in his face when they had crossed him, it seemed to them that Haakon the Dark was not a good man to question about such things.

"It is the Scot," Hjalmar Sitricsson said, looking over his shoulder at Donal, head bent to his harp on the deck beside Haakon. Hjalmar spat into the dead leaves under the tree where they had raised the hanged man and the bodies of the bulls. "A Christian! We are Norse, not mice to follow a tame god."

"Nay," Knut said comfortably. "He was only born in that worship; he's no priest to be prodding other men to it."

Thorfinn Solvisson, who was their own priest for this sacrifice, took some of the bulls' blood and poured it in the water, and then each captain took some to paint on the prow of his ship.

Hjalmar Sitricsson shook his head as Thorfinn put blood in the little clay pot in Knut's hand. "I do not like it. That is for the jarl to do," he said stubbornly. "There will be others that think that, Knut."

Knut's free hand shot out and grabbed Hjalmar around

the forearm, fingers biting into the muscle. "Jarl Haakon is
Thor's man and will be until Valhalla, Hjalmar. And if *you*
don't know that, *I'm* not such a fool! So keep your tongue
quiet, or you'll lose it!"

Thorfinn looked thoughtful, hefting a second pot of
blood for *Curlew.* "Knut's right," he said finally. "That is
the jarl's business, and he doesn't think the way most do
and never has. And I reckon that be what makes him a jarl
and me a helmsman. And you, Hjalmar, being neither,
you'll keep quiet around me, also." He nodded briskly,
that point being settled, and went off to find Kalki Estridsson,
who was *Gull Wing's* new helmsman.

Knut raised the eyebrow over his good eye. "And if you
poke at Donal MacRae over this, Hjalmar, I'll put you off
Gray Goose onto another ship. He's a brisk man with a
knife, and I don't have time to settle a feud."

The Dnieper rolled wide and stately like a stout queen for
a few miles below Koenugard. Then it contracted suddenly,
caught in the iron vise of the southern heights, and turned
eastward, running sharp and dangerous under the cliffs.
There were over forty miles of this channel to negotiate,
with the river roaring like dragon's breath and the air wet
with spray, through seven cataracts and steep gorges where
the stone cliffs bent inward, jutting under the current, and
where the riverbed was fanged with rocks. The water boiled
in the rapids at nearly twelve knots, and Knut was right:
There was only enough time for the effort to pass through
safely and the pure terror that they wouldn't make it.

The cataracts had names. So great a power were they in
the lives of the men who rode them that they became
living things, watery beasts with a ship-hunger and a dark
intelligence of their own. The first was called *Essupi,* the
Gulper, narrow as a sword blade, hurling itself with a
hideous noise over rocks large as islands, jutting like teeth
from the water. At Ragnar's signal they halted in the
shallows above it, and Haakon made the men strip and
leave clothes and armor in the hold before they dropped
over the side into the water. Behind them the rest of the
convoy anchored and waited their turn, because there was
only one way to go through *Essupi* and that was babe-

naked on foot, with the empty ship guided by hand. The ones who didn't guide the ship carried swords and kept their eyes on the bank.

He had no mind to fight Pechenegs unarmored, Haakon thought, and the vulnerable feeling made the small of his back twitch, but a man who fell in that water with mail or even a leather cuirass to encumber him would have no need to worry over Pechenegs.

Even in the shallows the water roared swift and hungry, and the men felt their way carefully with bare feet, pushing the lightened boat along with oar handles, some at the prow to keep it from slipping ahead into fast water and breaking on the rocks in the middle.

"Slow, in Thor's name!" Haakon shouted. "Slow, or she'll ride over you!" He stumbled and righted himself quickly, while the current sucked at his waist.

Nearer the shore, Donal splashed along, sword in hand, and gave the cliff face a careful inspection. "Something up there, jarl," he shouted over the roar of water after a moment. "Just a shadow like, but I'm thinking they've their eye on us."

"If they've a mind to come down and fight in this, they are fools then!" Haakon shouted back. "But watch them anyway!"

"Oh, aye." Donal watched the flicker of movement on the cliff top. They would wait for a better stretch of the river most likely—if there was one. *Jesu, but this is the road into Hell, or the earthly twin of it.* Still . . . it was here that the Pechenegs could catch the boats separate from each other if they'd a mind to. He swiveled his eyes up along the bank again, quickly. They weren't coming down, seemingly. But whatever he was watching watched him.

The water boiled in *Essupi,* and Wulf, who had great sense for a dog, sat in the hold and let them tow him like a lord on a barge, but when the current finally slackened a little, he came out on the deck to make sure that Haakon was still there.

"Go away, you fool." Haakon pushed Wulf's muzzle away and leaned against *Gray Goose.* Ahead he could see Ragnar's crews drawn up to the shore and getting their clothes on with the haste of a maiden caught naked in her bath. Too naked. The cliffs were less precipitous here, and whatever was on top of them might come down.

"Beach her and dress!" Haakon shouted. "Fast!" There would be a pass from cliffs to river somewhere, and he wanted to be on the water and gone before the watchers on the cliffs could use it.

He breathed freer when they were out on the water again. Haakon could see Ragnar's short, bowlegged silhouette on the deck of his own ship, combing the water out of his beard, feet braced against the pitch of the ship. Behind them were more ships coming through *Essupi*. The feeling of being watched was still like a hand on the back of his neck, and it stayed with him. Haakon weighed the threat of the current against that of the Pechenegs and put his men back in their mail.

They camped that night above the second cataract, bone weary and shivering from the wet. Haakon made them put a ditch around the camp and set stakes in it, and there was nearly open mutiny at that. Haakon got a spade and climbed down in the ditch and said that he would dig it himself if they were wishful to rest. After that everyone had too much pride not to dig while the jarl was digging.

Ragnar hauled himself out of the ditch when his crew had finished their part of it and sat by the fire with his share of the salt fish and beer. "*Oof!* I ache like an old horse. This is a camp, Haakon, not a castle. Trolls take you and your ditch."

"Something worse will take you and your cargo if we don't ditch the camp," Haakon said. He bit into a fish, ravenous. "How many men did you lose, Ragnar, last trip?"

Ragnar sighed. "Too many. You are right. You will be king over something one day, Haakon, if no one kills you first."

"Nah, I've no mind for that," Haakon said. And Thor had said it was not to be. Everything Haakon might want in this life, the god had said, but never a crown. If that mattered now. "I've always thought my luck might go if I put a crown on it."

"They wear heavy," Donal said. "The better the king, the heavier the crown." He squatted down and undid the red strings on his harp bag. "The shipguard is posted, but

I'm thinking there'll be no trouble this night. They'll wait a better chance, likely."

"The fourth cataract," Ragnar said. "That is where they usually come, unless some fool puts his head out on a plate for them first. You are right about the ditch, Haakon," he added, loudly enough for the men huddled around the other fires to hear. "We should have ditched the camps last time. That is the way the old Romans did it, they say, and they conquered the world."

"And where are the Romans now?" Hjalmar said. "Bones in the earth or merchants in Mikligard."

"They are not Romans in Mikligard," Ragnar said. "Not really, not like the ancient folk. But it is a point of pride with them to say so."

"That for your Romans, then," Hjalmar said. He stuck his blistered hand in his mouth where the salt fish had stung his fingers. The calluses he'd earned pulling an oar hadn't kept the spade handle from rubbing raw spots in new places. "It is not for Norsemen to learn to fight from a people who are dead now."

Haakon thought that Hjalmar would dig in his feet against the learning of anything, new or old. Hjalmar's world was ordered by the things that had been so on the day he was born, and he viewed each change in that order with the suspicion of a pig being loaded for market.

"Everything ends," Donal said, fiddling with his harp. "New things are born before the old are dead." He glanced at Haakon. "That is what gives a crown its weight, I'm thinking—the trying to balance old and new. England had a king like that, one of our blood, not the Saxons."

Haakon settled in by the fire. His clothes were beginning to dry out. "What happened to him?" he asked, interested.

"Ah, he burned like a comet," Donal said. "But then he lost the balance somewhere. . . ." Donal ran his hand over the strings, a high, bright music that faded suddenly into something sad and wild. The men at the other fires quieted at the sound, and Donal began to sing.

It was a story that some of them had heard before, old enough so that by now the Saxons and the English had taken it for their own. But he hadn't been Saxon, this

Arthur, he had been of Donal's kind, or maybe the last of the ancient Romans who had ruled them once. It was little matter. He had been a king for Britain, a warrior lord who rose when the land had need of him, and burned brightly into memory, and then burned out. His fate had been of his own making: a dark sin made at the start, and a darker child born of it, to be the ending. But in between there had been glory and peace and a last great battle, and he had never died, so they said, but only gone away into Avalon to sleep.

> "Come again, so he will,
> Out of the hollow hill,
> Down through the summer field,
> Under the dragon shield,
> When our need be greatest."

Donal drew a last note from the harp and let it hang there, brightly, in the silence. When it had faded, they pounded their fists on their shields and shouted for another song, but he shook his head.

"Nay, I am going to sleep," he shouted over their noise. "Go you and do the same. If you are tired when our heathen friends out there decide to fight, you'll sleep longer than Arthur has." He put his harp away in the bag. "A fine tale, that, but I am thinking I would not be a king. Sleep you sound, jarl."

There was enough aggravation in being a jarl, Haakon decided in the morning, that Thor couldn't *pay* him to be a king. They towed the ships with ropes through the rapids, with the men complaining that there weren't enough thralls to do it for them, and they nearly lost Hjalmar, who was too busy complaining to watch where he was going. This cataract was called *Ulvorsi* for the island at the center, which split the current so that it boiled around it on both sides, masking the island in a cloud of foam and spray and pulling dangerously at the ships, even in the shallows.

They passed the next, *Gelandi*, the Yeller, in the same fashion, and when they were through, Haakon ordered them to halt and make camp. Then he sat down with Wulf on a rock and looked very thoughtfully downstream.

The presence that had dogged their heels was still there, but it didn't like the ditched camp or the number of other boats on the river that were close enough together to come and help fight. A few of the other merchants had had their camps raided at night, and some of them had started to ditch theirs like Haakon's, but mostly the tribesmen were hanging back in their mountains—waiting for the fourth cataract, everyone said. *Aifor,* the narrow rapids, and nothing got over it but birds. They would have to unload and carry the boats around the rapids, through nearly six miles of Pecheneg country. Haakon had yet to see a Pecheneg, but if they lived up to all the merchants' tales, they would have fangs and horns and tails like the Christians' devil, and eat men. Likely they were bad enough.

He got up off his rock and went to lay down the law to his crews concerning the ship watch and tomorrow's portage. They grew surlier with every bend in the river, from being wet and not having anything to fight but the water. Haakon was willing to put up with a certain amount of this because Norsemen were not thralls, but they were going to have to follow his orders in the morning. They could work off their ill humor on the Pechenegs.

The roar of *Aifor* began to swell, distantly at first, then louder, a far sound, like wakened giants. The water grew faster, pulled toward the dreadful torrent, and as they came around the last bend, they found the boats that had gone ahead of them beached in an armed camp on the shore, waiting. No one would move across the six-mile portage until every ship in the convoy had joined them. Haakon and Ragnar made camp with the rest and found Haakon's extra men welcomed in like sheep dogs when the wolves are about.

"Bastards have been sniffing around the camp all day," one of Oleg's captains said. "They'll wait until we're loaded down with the boats, but they've been trying us on for size in the meantime. We gave 'em something to think on not an hour since." He nodded to a huddle of sprawled forms a hundred yards from the camp, with a slow black dance of birds above them, beginning to settle.

Haakon whistled up Donal, Knut, and Wulf and went to look. They were not large men—dark haired with windbeaten skin, dressed in hides and rough cloth. They had a look of their home hills about them, accented in death—harsh, weathered, and fierce, men who lived knife in hand, to pull a living out of a harsh country.

"Naked as babes we'll be, carrying those boats," Donal said. He looked where *Aifor* howled, foam white, over the rocks. There were pelicans on the highest ones. As they watched, one came swooping down to land, just above the foam. She ruffled the water from her feathers and opened her beak like a cook pot for the fledglings in the nest. "Better to chance the water maybe."

"Only on wings," Ragnar said, coming up behind them. "There are stones all along the river raised to men who thought they could get over *Aifor.*"

"Has it been done?"

"One in twenty maybe. I'd rather fight."

Donal rubbed the scar on his cheek and looked at the Pechenegs.

"I expect we will," Haakon said. "Why haven't these been buried?"

"They are animals," Oleg's captain said. "We left these for a warning for their litter mates."

Haakon looked at the ragged bodies. "Men like this don't take death for a warning. They live too close to it." He shrugged. If they weren't buried, they might walk, and then Oleg's jarls might wish they had taken the time to dig a pit. But the hatred of the Rus and the Slav for the Pecheneg was bone deep and old as the land.

Oleg's captain spat into the dirt. "Then they'll get a worse warning. Someone will send an army one of these days to wipe the hills clean of these devils. In the meantime, we'll send detachments out to flank the caravan." He glanced at Haakon. "One man in three. One in two if you have more than you need to carry your ships."

Haakon thought. "I will give you two men in five, Captain. We will do our share, but these men answer to me. We did not come entirely to play watchdog to other men's ships."

Oleg's captain opened his mouth to argue, and Knut growled, "If there is more trouble than is worth our while, we are well enough armed to go alone."

The captain weighed the use of Haakon's fighting men against his dislike of Norse upstarts, and usefulness was the winner. He nodded and went away disgruntled, and Donal shouted after him, "Let the great prince be sending this army you talk of and earning his ship-tax, which he thieves from honest men for the right to come and fight Pechenegs for him!"

When he had gone, the three of them squatted down to look at the Pechenegs, and Wulf sniffed carefully at the dark blood congealing in the cloth. "They are fighters," Haakon said finally. "If I were the captain, I would not leave these unburied. They will walk in his sleep one night." He looked at the tall back of the Rus captain, who was sorting out the order of the march with the other merchants. "When he sends for the detachments, I want the men who will go with them to come to me first, for my orders. Donal, go and get Kalki and Thorfinn and tell them. And Hagar stays with the ships."

They waited two days for the rest of the boats to catch up. The Pechenegs tried no more raids, but there were shadows at night beyond the firelight, which made Wulf bristle and growl. Haakon thought that they wanted the bodies; Oleg's captain had had them dragged inside the perimeter of the camp.

"Damn the fool," Donal said. "He is only giving them something to take vengeance for. You don't warn off men like that by leaving their dead for the crows. These traders should let Haakon lead them."

"Well, they won't," Ragnar said. "The Rus are clannish. We're here on sufferance."

Donal drew his fingers across his harp strings in a little exasperated tune. "There are more fools made every day than God can count, but I am thinking that that one got his neighbor's share, also. Haakon, that is not a man I would let lead me in a fight."

"Yes, I have thought of that," Haakon said. "I am not a blind puppy born this morning. Donal, go to sleep." But when Donal had subsided, Haakon sat and looked thoughtfully at the camp and the ships and the dark pile of bodies, which was beginning to stink, and counted over in his head the ratio of men in the shipguard to men on the flank, and then counted with a stick in the dirt to be sure. In the morning he went and got Hagar and talked to him again.

Haakon grunted and gave another shove, and *Gray Goose* slid up onto the rollers. Everywhere in the camp other merchants were doing the same. The dugouts could be carried, but there were six miles across rough land till they could put out on the river again, and anything larger would go more easily on rollers. Every slave in the caravan had been put to carrying cargo or ships to leave free as many armed men as possible. One of the Rus captains had already taken out the scouts and flanking detachments to make sure the way was clear, and thirty of Haakon's men had gone with him, under Thorfinn Solvisson. Haakon had debated a long time over that. He didn't like putting his men under someone else's command, and if the Rus captain got in trouble, Haakon couldn't afford to lose Thorfinn, who was a helmsman. But he also needed someone who could stand up to the Rus if need be, which eliminated the rank and file, and not pick a quarrel if he could help it, which eliminated Donal. Also, Donal was a Scot, and there were some like Hjalmar Sitricsson who didn't bother to hide their distrust of that. Thorfinn was solid, Norse to his toes, and unbending. If Haakon gave an order, he would follow it and knock heads together to see that everyone else did, too.

It was hot, and the ground was dusty and full of rocks. The men were sweating in their mail even before they moved out. Haakon tied a cloth around his head to keep the sweat out of his eyes and adjusted the leather padding in his helmet. The metal was hot to his hand. A few feet away Ragnar was jamming a helmet on his own head and bellowing at his crew to move. A dust cloud was already rising from the head of the caravan, and someone started a rowing chant. The rest picked it up as they heaved the ships along. The Lapp slaves trudged behind with bales of skins and the amber and jet in wooden crates.

"Rich pickings," Knut said, hauling on his rope. "Father Odin'll take someone home today, mark me."

"As long as it's not us, Granddad," Donal said cheerfully. He had his harp bag packed safely inside a bale of skins, and his eyes were bright and watchful under his helmet. "I've too many sins to work through yet before I let them come and shrive me. And no priest handy for the ones I've already got to."

"Then talk less and pull more," Haakon said. "Maybe I should have just turned you loose to talk the poor savages to death. Where's Hagar?"

"Here, jarl." Hagar hauled on the towrope tied into the oar ports at *Gray Goose*'s midsection. His quiver and bow were slung across his back, and a handful of long signaling arrows stood up above the rest.

"Well, keep your bow strung," Haakon said.

Thorfinn Solvisson listened with one ear to the Rus captain giving out his orders to the scouts, and tried to scratch with his dagger hilt under his mail. It was perishingly hot, he thought. He was lucky to have mail, and this was a fine piece of English work, which stopped an arrow far better than the ring mail sewn to leather or the plain, boiled leather coats, which were all that most of the men had. But under the thick padding that cushioned it, his skin felt like there were ants crawling. He scratched again and looked south across the rocks and stunted trees to where the dust rose from the caravan.

"Yaaaah!"

Thorfinn snapped his head around. Mounted men on ponies, their black hair flying, seemed to have come up out of the rocks. Thorfinn slammed his shield up against Hjalmar's, his spear leveled at the oncoming riders. A few men went down, and Thorfinn staggered back as a pony, unable to stop, ran straight onto his spear. He twisted out of the way as it crashed down, and then rolled to his feet, hurling the broken-off haft of his spear into a brown face.

There were gaps in the shield line now, and with the weight of the charge broken, the scouts opened them a little further to draw the riders in where the Norse and the Rus, on foot, could pull the Pechenegs from their ponies or get under the animals with daggers. The attackers were not very many, Thorfinn realized. There was another cloud of dust in the sky, westward, and he thought that the other detachment at the rear of the caravan was fighting, too. He drew his sword and slashed at a dark warrior who dived off his hamstrung mount at him. The man hacked back. Thorfinn jerked his shield up, and the Pecheneg's sword glanced along Thorfinn's mail and bit through the links over the hip. Thorfinn pushed his shield farther out, into the Pecheneg's, making just enough time for a clean blow at the neck, and staggered back panting. The charge was broken, but it was much too easy. The tribesmen fought furiously, savagely, howling curses at the Norsemen in some unknown language. Thorfinn realized that now they were trying only to fight their way out. Something was wrong about that, and he tried frantically to pull his men back.

"*Odiiiiiiiin!* We have them!" the Rus leader shouted.

Something screamed overhead, a long-drawn whistle that rose and then fell away in the sky to the south.

"Get your shields up!" Haakon shouted furiously. "Around the ships!" The Lapps cowered behind the bales in the shadow of the dragon prows. Haakon's Norsemen and Ragnar's crew made a half-circle ring about the ships, with their backs to the cliffs and the river. A gap between the gray stone mountains opened onto the rocky plain where the caravan trudged along, and it was black with horsemen.

"Fools we were," Donal said, sliding into the shield wall beside Haakon. With the ships to defend and nearly half their strength gone, there was no hope of marching to meet them. All they could do was try to beat them off. "Fools we were to let him take thirty men, and where are they now?"

Haakon didn't answer. There wasn't much point. They could all see the dust of the forward and rear detachments. They were fighting—that was where they were, kept busy by a light force while the rest of the tribesmen came in on the caravan. He had told Oleg's captain that the land here was too tricky to let the flankers get so far from the caravan, and he had not been listened to, and he had been right. There was very little satisfaction in that, but he spared a hope that if anyone lost his ship, it would be Oleg's captain. Someone owed the Norns a debt for being stupider than the gods were willing to allow. Maybe it was himself, for not taking his ships and Ragnar's and going alone. Or for annoying Thor, who plainly had no intention of helping him in this fight. He wrapped the thong of his ax around his wrist and yelled, "Signal again!" at Hagar as the first of the horsemen came down on the caravan.

"Aye, jarl." Hagar was already nocking the third of his signaling arrows, long-shafted with bulbous, bone heads pierced to whistle as they flew. He drew the bow back and aimed high. Even in a fight Hagar was a placid bear of a man, the antithesis of Donal, who was crouched behind his shield, fighting and swearing steadily. Hagar never said anything or even looked angry. He merely shot his arrows or laid about him with his ax until there was no one left to hit. He let fly, and the arrow shrieked overhead, cutting through the howls of the Pechenegs and the Norsemen screaming back at them. He had one left, and he looked at it thoughtfully, then drew out his fighting arrows instead and began sending them over the shield wall into the Pechenegs. If Thorfinn didn't hear that one, he likely wouldn't hear another, and that meant they were on their own.

The Pechenegs howled around the caravan like a wind out of Hel-Gate. Haakon swung his ax and a man went down, and three more came up in his place, clambering over the bodies of their dead. They fought like berserkers, with an unyielding ferocity, clawing at the shield wall, hammering it back. They had archers in their own ranks, and their arrows rained down on the Norsemen pinned against their ships. Donal yelped as an arrow slammed into his mail and fell away, and beside him another man went down with a barb in his throat. Haakon jerked his shield up high, and his head rang as a sword blow glanced off his helmet. For an instant he saw the man's eyes—dark, furious, desperate. Then he swung the ax, and the Pecheneg went down with blood pouring from his nearly severed knee. Another, with a gold collar around his throat that was probably a chieftain's mark, howled and hurled himself at Haakon over the body of the first. And where in Odin's name was Thorfinn?

The caravan closed in on itself, driven relentlessly back against the ships and the roar of the river behind them. They were better armed and better armored than the tribesmen, but they were outnumbered and they had the ships to protect. Without the ships they were stranded. If the Pechenegs could get close enough, they would scuttle them; then it wouldn't matter whether Thorfinn ever came at all.

Haakon whirled his ax around his head and cleared a little space to breathe. Wulf's muzzle was dripping blood, and beside him Donal was still cursing in Gaelic and hacking with his sword at anything that came in reach. A pony hurtled toward them. Wulf snapped at its legs, and Hagar, who had shot the last of his arrows, pulled the rider off the stumbling beast with one hand and ran his sword into the man's stomach before he could get his shield up. He dropped, eyes wide in surprise, choking on blood. And still they came on.

The sun was boiling now, and the shield wall was growing ragged, hacked and splintered and hampered by embedded arrows. They were spread too thin along the line of the ships. Around the Rus boats, where the line was thinnest, the Pechenegs had begun to break through. Two of Oleg's men fell, and before the others could close the gap, the tribesmen poured through, swarming over the ship like wolves, hacking at the hull. The smell of blood was nearly as thick in the air as the dust, thick enough to choke on. Above them the carrion birds had begun to ride the air currents, black against the sun.

Thorfinn stumbled over the crest of the hill and caught his breath in a ragged gasp. Below was chaos—the beached ships straggled in an unwieldy line along the plain, overturned or tilted on their rollers where the tribesmen had caught the crews by surprise. A wavering wall of shields, dangerously thin, rocked and staggered between the attackers and the ships.

"Run," Thorfinn gasped, and Hjalmar and the others caught their breath and stumbled down the hill behind him.

"*Odiiiin!*" They swept straight into the rear of the

milling tribesmen, and the embattled men in the shield wall felt their presence almost before they heard Thorfinn's war cry. The onslaught of the Pechenegs wavered, and they began to turn, confused, pressed from the rear now.

"By Thor, we've got them!" Haakon shouted, and the ax felt light in his hand. Later he would be weary, almost too weary to move, but now he was tireless, and the ax seemed to swing itself, although he knew that was only battle fury and no doing of Thor's. Wulf raised a red muzzle and ran snarling beside him. Now they could fight and not huddle behind shields like things in traps. The warrior with the gold collar had been lost somewhere in the chaos, but now he leapt out again almost under Haakon's nose. Another black-haired warrior thrust a bridle rein into the chieftain's hand, and the chieftain flung himself onto the horse and pulled it onto its haunches as Haakon lashed out with his ax at him. The pony screamed and reared, and the chieftain raised a hand with a red sword and waved it. The Pechenegs dropped back as swiftly as they had come. Behind them the rocky plain was dark with bodies.

"You were right, jarl," Thorfinn said. He sat cross-legged by the fire with a riveter, and hammered new links into his mail where a sword had cut through. His voice was thin, with an angry edge to it, and he was bone weary like the rest of them. "We pulled back when we heard the signal, but the Rus didn't like it, and we nearly had to fight *them* first." He sounded disgusted. "They had orders to stay on the flank, and we couldn't make the thick fools see different until we waved our swords in their noses."

"They paid for it," Knut said quietly. The Rus captain and forty of the Rus from the caravan were dead because of that order.

"So did we," Haakon said. He and Ragnar had lost six, and it had so very nearly been more. He looked at Ragnar. "The Rus can go their own way if they've a mind to. No one orders my men but me from now on."

"The Rus may follow you now," Ragnar said. "Or they may not. They're prideful."

"Pride's cold company in a howe," Haakon said. He

made a fist at the pile of weapons and the hacked and
bloodied shirt of mail that lay on the ground beside him.
Dead men's armor, too precious to be buried with them.
"Go away and let me sleep." He rolled himself into his
sleeping bag beside the fire with his back to them.

Knut started to speak, and Donal shook his head at him.
"He blames himself," he said softly. "They were his men.
Though I am not seeing what he could have done. The
Rus would not listen to him, not before this happened."
He took his harp out of the bag and began to tune it, to
make a music for the jarl to sleep by.

The caravan had camped for the night where they had
fought, to lick their wounds and see their dead howe-laid
with the proper prayers. Here in alien land they could not
spare the weapons to bury with them, so they buried a
dead Pecheneg at the feet of each instead, for a thrall in
the next world, and to show to Father Odin that they had
done sword work, even if their swords had not gone with
them.

In the morning they moved on again, into the water
beneath *Aifor*, and the Pechenegs trailed them. They
didn't attack again, but they hung on the caravan's flanks
like hungry wolves. If there was a mistake, they would be
waiting.

They had three more rapids to pass: *Baruforos*, the
Wave-Force; *Leanti*, the Laugher; and *Strukun*, the Cours-
er; and they pushed their way doggedly through them,
with Haakon in what amounted to command. The Rus
merchants were less than willing to have a Norse jarl over
them, but they were traders first and fighting men second,
in defense of their trade. With forty-seven men dead for a
mistake and with widows to face, Haakon's restless quest
for order, for organization, for prodding the convoy into
some semblance of an army, was a wind they couldn't
stand against.

They lost one man of Ragnar's crew to the mocking
waters of *Leanti*, which bubbled as they fell across the
rocks, *Come you home to me*. And a boatload of the Rus
went under while crossing *Strukun*. But by the third week
in June, they limped into the waters off Berezany Island,
where the Dnieper mouth flowed into the Black Sea.

VII The Great City

At Berezany they fitted out the ships for open sea, made sacrifice, and set up rune-stones to the men who had been howe-laid above *Aifor*. Like Gnezdovo, Berezany had a colony of Norse and Rus dead that was larger than the city of the living. Berezany was only a waypost on the dangerous trek from Koenugard to Mikligard, a safe harbor to refit ships and bury dead, but its name meant Birka, Birch Island. The Rus had given to an alien outpost a name to tie them to home waters.

Then the men moved south from Berezany, behind the dragon prows and striped sails, full in the wind: black on red, red on green, green on black. Haakon picked up the lifeless ax and went to stand in the bow in the shadow of *Gray Goose*'s sail. To the south was Mikligard, and in Mikligard, Harud Olafsson. The ships would hug the coast past the mouths of the Danube to the Bosporus, and Ragnar had laughed and said the Pechenegs would trail them on land as far as the Danube, on the chance that a storm would wreck them ashore.

"A hopeful people," Donal said. "Look you." He pointed, and Haakon could see the horsemen strung out along the plain. "Desperate and land poor, they are. It's no wonder they want a share of Oleg's shipping."

Haakon watched the riders, the next wave in the great drift of steppe peoples who had pushed each other farther westward over the centuries. They had little choice, he thought. If they didn't fight Oleg, then Oleg would fight them, and then they would be thralls like the Slavs. He remembered the black-haired chief with the gold collar and a reddened sword raised blackly against the sun. Not a man to underestimate.

But it was not the Pecheneg chief, riding a scrubby pony along the shore, that occupied Haakon's mind now. He

thought about Harud Olafsson, Rosamund, and maybe even
Prince Oleg's dead Ana—all the reasons for this voyage of
hate and the justification for the dead men buried above
Aifor and for having made a quarrel with a god.

The narrow channel of the Bosporus cut sharply between rocky, shrub-covered hills from the Black Sea to
Mikligard on the Sea of Marmara. The merchant fleet
sailed down it, weary, triumphant, thinner in numbers
than when it had left Koenugard. As the sun-baked walls
of the channel slid past, Haakon thought of Harud, somewhere at the other end, and his hands itched.

At the mouth of the Bosporus, on the seven hills of a
triangular peninsula, sat Constantinople, capital city of
New Rome. Mikligard, it was also called—golden domes
and towers rising over white walls, above blue water.

"Mother of God," Donal said. He stood in the bow,
mouth open, the salt breeze ruffling his black hair. He
watched the golden city rise under the baking sun. "A city
of the angels, Haakon. Look you. Have you ever seen a
thing to match it?"

"It is fine enough," Haakon said, trying to keep himself
from gaping like a peasant, which did not accord with his
dignity.

The channel was thronged with ships, of every kind and
country: longships not unlike Haakon's own, lateen-rigged
ships of the Arabs, and the huge, oared war dromonds of
the Mikligarders, with long spouts projecting from their
bows. There was a heavy guard now because of the war
with the Bulgars, and smaller patrol craft skated like water
bugs among the traffic. Haakon's convoy idled, with peace
shields hung on the masts, outside the harbor chain that
was stretched across the entrance to the great natural
harbor of the Golden Horn. His crew, pointing and specu-
lating, impressed in spite of themselves, leaned over the
fighting shields hung along the oar ports. Knut and Hjalmar
Sitricsson admired the harbor chain and other defenses
with a professional eye.

"If the Rus ever came raiding here, they had Asgard's
own host to help 'em," Knut pronounced finally. "Still, it
could be done."

Donal dragged his eyes away from the splendor of trees and marble above the white walls, to laugh at Knut. "There's enough loot in yon city to circle Norway twice, you one-eyed thief, but you'll not get a smell of it. They'll be wary of the likes of us, friend."

"This is not a trip for raiding," Haakon said firmly, loudly enough for his voice to carry. "We are traders and peaceful folk, and I will break the head of the man who forgets it."

"Aye, as you're so peaceful," Donal said. He turned back, grinning, to drink in the sight of the city.

When their whole fleet had collected outside the chain, a trio of patrol boats came around from the walled harbors on the southern side of the city. They pulled up first alongside the Rus boats, and then worked their way through the fleet, stopping at each. A junior officer in a helmet with a plume on it came aboard *Gray Goose* and looked relieved when he found that Haakon could get by in Greek. He studied the crew list with Oleg's stamp on it, which Haakon handed him, and the wooden ticket from the taxing house, which proved that *Gray Goose* was part of Oleg's official fleet, while the officer's crew kept a watchful eye on the men in the dragon ship.

"You have a great many men for a trading voyage, Captain."

"It is wild country south from Koenugard," Haakon said. "As you will see from the list, we lost some anyway, to Pechenegs. Is there a limit to a ship's crew?"

"Not so long as they keep peace," the officer said. He looked them over. "Very well, match the men with the names on the list for me, and I'll stamp you cleared. When we drop the chain, follow the boat with the yellow sail and tie up where the pilot shows you. Stay in the channel, mind, going through, or you'll foul on the chain."

Beyond the harbor chain, the natural bay of the Golden Horn ran along the north wall of the city for nearly five miles. Within it were two smaller walled harbors and other docking facilities along the city wall, and across it on the northern shore, the suburb of Galata and its great tower. Guarded by the hills of the city, the Golden Horn lay flat and calm as glass, and under the protection of its harbor chain, the wealth unloaded on its docks could rest secure.

And there were rules, they found, for everything. Foreign merchants must stay in a certain quarter, and each country had its own. They could enter the city by one gate only with their wares, no more than fifty at a time. They were to go unarmed, and an imperial trade official was to accompany them whenever business was transacted.

"Thor's hammer!" Haakon roared, having heard all this. "Is there a special time to go and piss?"

The minister of the Docks smiled blandly. "It is only for your protection, Captain. And to see that all trade is conducted fairly."

Haakon growled and stuck Rosamund's knife in his boot when the minister wasn't looking.

"They are like that here," Ragnar said, when Haakon sent half his crew to help Ragnar's unload. The docks, like the harbor walls, were stone, with iron rings set in to tie the ships alongside. Farther down the outer harbor there was space assigned to beach unloaded ships. A massive stone gate, with sentries on either side of it, opened from the docks into the city. "Everything has a regulation here," Ragnar said, huffing along the boarding plank, with one end of a bale. "Even their own merchants . . . linen drapers can't sell silks, leatherworkers can't tan hides. There is a guild for everything. Even the fishermen have to report their catch to a government official. There is a great deal of government in Mikligard," he added dryly. "They spend most of their time thinking up new rules."

"If there are that many rules, it should be easy to find Harud Olafsson," Haakon said. "I only need to see the emperor and ask."

"I'm not sure you can see him," Ragnar said. "There are rules for that, too. The emperor may be approached at certain times, in certain throne rooms, by men who have made the proper appointments and requests, have the proper papers, and for all I know, are wearing the proper boots. There are twenty thousand people employed in the imperial palace alone, and most of them are there to keep you from seeing the emperor."

Haakon looked ready to explode, and Ragnar said soothingly, "Bide your time, and I may be able to see him for you. I told you I would. I have talked with him before;

that will make it easier. They always feel that if something has been done once, it may be done again. It is innovation they don't care for."

"And the Mikligarders consent to be ruled like this?" Haakon said wonderingly. "Are they sheep?"

"No, it is just their way. They are used to it. Also it has made them the richest city in the world. The emperor rules nearly as much land as the caliph at Baghdad."

Haakon craned his neck to look at the city wall towering over him. It came right down to the water here, and there were slaves on scaffolding, polishing the sea stains off the stone. Above the wall, like the tip of the sun against blue sky, he could see a polished copper dome and the tops of cypress trees.

When they had finished unloading, yet another official bustled out through the gate. He wore a blue tunic with gold medallions on it, close-fitting blue hose, and black shoes with straps that fastened with buttons at the ankles. He was very fine, and he wrinkled his nose at the weary Norsemen and informed Haakon in languid Greek that he would guide them to the warehouses and their quarters. All weapons were to be left with the ships. And no doubt they would wish to bathe?

Beyond the wall a wild maze of streets twisted and turned: past four-story tenements jutting dangerously over narrow alleys; by rich men's houses blank-faced to the street, achieving privacy from the lower classes by building inward to gilded courtyards hidden behind their walls; around multichambered churches of domed stone, topped by golden crosses; under the soaring arches of the city aqueduct; and past public cisterns and fountains that splashed on every street corner. All but the main thoroughfares were too narrow or too crowded for wheeled traffic, and the official in the buttoned shoes produced a camel boy and camels for transport to the customhouse and the warehouses where the foreign merchants kept their goods.

The streets were full of the singsong of peddlers. Fortune-tellers offered to predict a fine fate for anyone with a penny in his hand. The brightly decorated mule carriages of a fashionable lady trundled by, its occupant reclining comfortably on her way to the baths. There were tonsured priests in vestments, singing as they went, and men who seemed to come from every corner of the world: Bulgars and turbaned Persians, Syrians from Damascus, Jews from Palestine, Illyrians, Armenians, Goths. The criteria for citizenship in Constantinople were merely the use of Greek in everyday speech and membership in the Church.

Haakon was craning his neck around, watching all this go by, and nearly walked into a court official on horseback, brocaded and cloaked in scarlet, riding through one of the great open squares into which the narrow roads emptied at intervals. Through this square passed the Mesê, the main thoroughfare of the city, which ran, bordered by columned porticoes, from the landward walls on the west almost to the foot of the imperial palace.

Their guide looked amused, and Haakon ceased to gawk, not wanting to look a fool to this drawling fop with buttons on his shoes. But the sights were beautiful. The city soared, from marble houses and open squares constantly swept clean by thralls, to gilded churches and olive trees lining the roadway, and green gardens ablaze with red and orange flowers. Haakon had fought in the Frankish lands, in England and Ireland, and he had seen Moorish Cadiz and thought it fine. But Constantinople shone; it shimmered with white, gold, and a bright watery fire like colored stones. The riches of the world came here, and the inhabitants took them and built with them.

Ragnar and Donal walked beside Haakon and behind their guide, with the rest of their men keeping a suspicious eye on the camel boys. Wulf trotted at Haakon's heel, ears pricked. They crossed the Mesê between the best shops of the city, piled with Constantinople's luxury goods under bright awnings: silks and brocades, copper and goldwork, leather and glass, jewels and ivory reliquaries to hold the bones of saints. Where the Mesê ended, close to the imperial palace, the perfumers had their stalls, by imperial command, so that their scent would sweeten the palace air.

"There is nothing like this city short of paradise," Donal said, soaking in the warm water that lapped the edges of a green marble pool. "I am telling you, Haakon, I will marry a merchant's daughter and stay here."

"A merchant's daughter in Mikligard wouldn't have you," Ragnar said, scrubbing his beard with his fingers. He eyed Donal's scarred, wiry form. "Although you look some better clean."

They all looked better clean. Contrary to what the Mikligarders might think, a Norseman bathed whenever he could, but the chances on a sea voyage were not so many. Haakon's men splashed in the pool and shouted like children, ducking each other under the water and fighting, while the bath slaves stood by with towels and cleaned up the mess.

They were quartered with the crews of the Rus ships in a multistoried house in the section of the city suburbs reserved for foreign merchants. They were to conduct no business without an imperial official, but they were free to enjoy the city's amusements so long as they went unarmed.

"And be remembering you are traders." Haakon looked at each of his crew in turn. "Make trouble and we'll be barred from the city before we can do what we came for. And I'll leave you to rot wherever they put you until Ragnarok."

"It's *wasteful*, so much gold," Knut said.

The same official appeared the next morning, still looking slightly bored, to escort Haakon and his men to the merchants' trading quarters of the city. Most of Haakon's crew had some goods of their own in the three ships' cargo, so their guide had brought two more of his kind with him from the city prefect's offices.

The merchants' quarters in Mikligard seemed to cover most of the city, and nearly all the trading with Rus and Norsemen was done by barter, since they had come for the goods that Mikligard could offer. The amber, jet, and beads from Birka went for a cargo of wine in thin, long-necked jars; the walrus ivory was exchanged for wooden casks of cinnamon, ginger, and pepper, which were worth almost more than gold.

The Lapps he sold to a slave dealer at one of the main city slave markets, a huge vaulted stone hall and open

court through which the unfortunate of every race and
color passed daily, grouped by nationality, sex and age:
slaves for mines and field labor, for spinning and weaving;
eunuchs for Arabs' *hareems*, and the prettiest of the
women for concubines; horsemen, stable grooms, and
attendants in matched pairs for the fashionable.

With the Lapps trailing behind him, prodded along by
Hjalmar, Haakon prowled the slave market, while the
prefect's official fumed because it was all taking too much
time and he was bored.

"*What*," he inquired acidly on the third round, "are you
looking for, Captain?"

"For the man whose slaves are cleanest," Haakon said.
"And that don't flinch when I look at them."

"They are slaves," the prefect's official said wearily.
"*Does* it matter?" He twitched his nose delicately. The
slave market was not a perfumer's stall.

"It matters to me," Haakon said. "The man who values
his slaves will give me a better price. Also, it is not right
to sell anything to be ill treated. I would not sell a horse to
some of these dealers. If you are bored, go away."

"I am not allowed to," the prefect's official sighed.

Finally Haakon made his choice and then dickered over
the price for an hour more with a tall, beak-nosed man
with sandy hair who inspected the Lapps' teeth and limbs
for deformities. In exchange he offered a good cargo of
dried fruit and olive oil from his brother-in-law's warehouse, and Haakon settled in to argue over the size of it,
while the Lapps watched him, resigned, their dark eyes
wondering, fascinated by the city that their fate had
brought them to. They were not happy, but they were still
alive after the river and the battle and the sacrifice that
the dark-bearded man had kept the others from using
them for. They had seen the hanged man at Koenugard,
and a slave market was better than that. Any man might be
a slave, according to the will of Jumala and the way his
Haltia led him. That was life.

Relieved, Haakon parted from the slave dealer. The
Lapps could not be stored like a bale of furs, and they had
been a nuisance. Also they were a reminder of his quarrel
with Thor and the empty space that that had left in him.

He had got used to the god taking a hand in his life, it seemed. Too used, maybe, for a free man. Haakon growled at Hjalmar, who was looking at the women, to move, and headed away from the slave market, with the prefect's official trotting at his heels. Ragnar might have come back to their quarters by now, and he might have news. If nothing else, Haakon still had Thor's ax. It was scarred and tarnished, but it had held its edge, and it was still a fighting weapon. He could use it on Harud Olafsson.

"You have the patience of a house on fire," Ragnar said, dropping onto a bench and putting out a hand to Thorfinn, who was dipping beer out of a cask. "I have been selling my own cargo all day, and, as I have told you, you do not just walk into the palace and speak to the emperor as if you were ordering a load of fish. It is going to take time."

"How much time?"

"As little as I can manage with you pacing like a penned wolf and asking me every hour. But I don't know of another way to find Harud, unless you are wishful to start knocking on doors. In twenty years you might knock on all of them."

"I asked at the merchants' houses," Haakon growled. "And the slave market. There was one who remembered him, or thought he did, but he thought also that he had gone to ground in the palace somehow. Find him for me, Ragnar, or I will start knocking on doors there."

"They will lock you up," Ragnar said. "Or worse. I will try tomorrow, but you had best keep quiet about it. If that weasel gets wind of you, he'll find another burrow."

In the morning Haakon took his furs, sold them for silks at the imperial factory, and fumed because he was so close to the palace itself, and still so far, blocked by an array of trade officials, ministers of export, government silk dealers, undersecretaries, and the whole sprawling complex of the silk house and dye works itself.

The best silks came from the imperial factory, and certain dyes were reserved for its use alone. The salesroom shimmered with bolts stacked high on shelves and spread open on tables where a buyer could browse and choose. Traders from the western world had bought Mikligard

silks since the emperor Justinian had managed to steal the
secret of their weaving from the people of far Cathay, and
the silk house thronged with dealers of every nationality as
well as Mikligarders themselves. Traders bound for Italy
and the Frankish lands paid for shiploads of purple and
saffron and scarlet, heavy damasks, and veiling fine enough
to draw through a finger ring. Mikligard ladies in stiff
brocaded tunics, trailed by their slaves with cushions and
parasols, with more slaves to carry their purchases, chose
bolts for their own use. The silk house was colored like a
jewel box and was loud with unceasing chatter. Haakon
and his men went nearly unnoticed in the throng, with
their guide pushing a way for them through the confusion.
Mikligarders were a cosmopolitan crowd, and one foreigner more or less held very little interest. Unlike the
Christians of the West, they had no qualms over dealing
with the heathen. Mikligarders were passionately interested in their religion, but, so Ragnar said, they spent
most of their time in arguing incomprehensible matters
and seldom let it interfere with trade.

Haakon bought as much silk as the imperial monopoly
allowed to one trader, and the prefect's official put his seal
on it. Most of the silk he would sell at Hedeby on the road
home, but there was a bolt of deep blue-purple, like the
Valkyries' eyes, which was for Rosamund. It was damask,
woven along the edges with white in a border of vine
leaves. He thought guiltily of his mother and picked
another bolt, in green, for Sigrid, and a bolt of deep
purple satin to sweeten Harald Fairhair's temper with.

When he was done and it had all been counted and
sealed and the duty paid, he waited and watched the
crowd go by, while Donal paid for three lengths of red
damask for Fann. Haakon wondered if Donal were color
blind. It would clash horribly with her hair, but Haakon
didn't think that anything could improve Fann's looks
much anyway, so he kept quiet. Donal's infatuation with
that dull woman was one thing that Haakon hadn't been
able to figure out.

Ragnar was waiting for them when they got back.
"Well, have you seen the emperor yet?"

"Thor's hammer, no. Haakon, I told you—" He grimaced. "But I have found out some things, and you won't be liking them."

"He has left Mikligard."

"Nah, he is here, all right. He is in the palace under the emperor's wing, and he is the emperor's pet, and I don't know *how* you're going to get at him."

Haakon reached for the place where his ax would be if he hadn't had to leave it in *Gray Goose* and then thought about Rosamund's knife, secure in his boot. "I will think of something," he said grimly.

"Haakon, if you kill a man who's under imperial protection, the guards will cut your head off. Also, you have to get to him first."

"Aaaaah!" Haakon was disgusted and looked about him, apparently for something to hit.

"Sit down and keep your peace, or I won't talk to you anymore," Ragnar said. "You are not a man, you are an explosion, like the Greek Fire the Mikligarders use."

"What is that?" Haakon looked interested.

"A state secret," Ragnar said. "You have a better chance of getting Harud than of finding that out. Although you could name your price from any king in the world for it if you did. It is something that they shoot through those tubes on their warships, and it even burns on water."

"Why don't they use it against the Bulgars then?" Haakon asked, momentarily distracted from his quest.

"Because the Bulgars are fighting them on land," Ragnar said with a grin, "and Greek Fire is a problem on land. It explodes when you jostle it."

Donal had come in and sat down in a chair to tune his harp, and he whistled. "I have heard of that. Portable hellfire. This is an amazing country." He tested a harp string and looked at Ragnar. "What is it that makes the emperor keep Harud Olafsson—who seems to me a man of very small vision—so greatly guarded here?"

"I'm still not sure," Ragnar said, "but I think it has something to do with the war. I have been talking to a man I used to know, who is in the emperor's army here now, with a post at court. He says Harud is getting very powerful, and he didn't talk as though he liked that. He

also says that Harud has Stylian Zautzes, who is the
emperor's chief minister, supporting him. Didn't Oleg say
in Koenugard that Harud went with a Swedish jarl to trade
in the Magyar villages before he came here?"

"Yes," Haakon said. "What do Magyars have to do with
it?"

"Because the emperor's fleet has taken most of the
fighting men of the Magyars and ferried them across the
Danube," Ragnar said, "and turned them loose like so
many wolfhounds on the Bulgarian towns. The king of the
Bulgarians, who can't fight Magyars and Mikligarders both,
has sued for a truce. I smell a connection."

"Are you thinking this Harud brought the Magyars into
it for the emperor?" Donal asked.

"It's possible. You've never seen Magyars," Ragnar said.
"They are nearly as bad as Pechenegs. When they don't
like ambassadors, they cut them into pieces and send
them back. But Oleg said that old jarl Thjodulf has been
trading with them for a while. It might be that they would
listen to Harud because he had come there once with
Thjodulf. And like the rest, they want loot and land. They
might do it if he promised them the Bulgars'. To try it, he
must have been in a fine fear for his skin from you." He
glanced at Haakon.

"If he persuaded them, then, it is no wonder the
emperor is grateful," Donal said.

"Especially because they may need someone to make
them go home again," Ragnar said dryly. "When the
emperor has taken Bulgaria, he won't be planning to leave
it for the Magyars."

Haakon had been silent, thinking, tapping his fingers on
the carved arm of his chair. "This is all 'if.' *If* the Magyars,
and *if* Harud—I need something more than *if*. I am losing
time. I can't keep my men here with nothing to do, or
they will make trouble sooner or later. And I want Harud.
If the emperor is going to let him hide under his silk
skirts, then I will get him some other way, but *that* may
make trouble, and the other merchants won't like it.
Ragnar, are you going to see the emperor for me, or am I
going to push all your teeth out the back of your head?"

Ragnar sighed. "Yes, you pigheaded man, I am going to

see the emperor. But I am not thinking much will come out of it. I wasn't expecting wars and Magyars. It may be too big a complication."

Haakon just shook his head and strode out to pace somewhere else. Ragnar sighed again and got up too. Donal sat playing softly to himself and looking at the pattern in the brickwork walls. Haakon wasn't going to give up, but it might be that someone was going to have to be there afterward to pick up the pieces when he had finished finding Harud. Donal hoped the pieces wouldn't be Haakon's. A fine fighter and a brave man, but not invincible. Not against the emperor of New Rome, who had more soldiers than there were fighting men in all of Norway.

VIII The House in Galata

The sharp scent of the rosemary on the floor forced Harud to stifle a sneeze as he bowed before the emperor Leo's golden throne. It was only a minor throne in a minor throne room in the bejeweled rabbit warren that was the imperial palace, but it was studded with pearls and what looked like uncut rubies. Leo lifted a hand, and Harud got to his feet. Stylian Zautzes stood behind the throne, arms crossed on his chest and his dark face thoughtful.

"You should have told us what you were running from," Leo said. His pleasant face had an irritated expression that made Harud want to twitch. Harud was now dressed as befitted a servant of the emperor, in a blue silk gown in the Greek style, with the double-headed eagle of the imperial house woven into it.

"But I did, Basileus," Harud said cautiously. "My father slain and my lands in Ireland stolen by this man Haakon Olesson—" His stomach lurched. "Is he here?"

"We have had a petition," Leo said. He looked shrewdly at Harud. "For your head, Harud. Also a letter from the prince of the Rus in Koenugard, to assure us he would have no objections. We gave audience to a merchant of the

Norse who spoke for this Haakon Olesson, and he told us a
somewhat different story from yours. According to him,
your father attacked this Haakon's father by treachery
some fifteen years ago, and the man has only taken back
what is his. Also he says that you stole the man's wife and
sold her for a slave. There were other charges also, but
that would appear to be the one that provoked him to
chase you here. A most determined man."

"Those are lies," Harud said. He looked at Stylian
Zautzes, but the minister's face was impassive. If he was
going to help, he wouldn't do it now by interrupting the
emperor. "Haakon Olesson and this merchant are lying,"
Harud said, thinking desperately. "The woman was betrothed to me, and the whore was with child by Haakon
Olesson. But it is well that you told me of this, Basileus.
The man is dangerous. He had no claim to my father's
land and attacked him unprovoked. He carried the woman
off and looted her father's hold unprovoked also. He has
committed so many crimes in his homeland that the Thing
has named him outlaw. If he has gone to ground now with
the jarls of the Rus, he is close enough to your borders to
be a danger, Basileus."

Leo smiled. "Our borders are proof against one barbarian, we think."

But Harud thought that maybe he had struck home.
The jarls of the Rus were a force to be dealt with cautiously.
"The Rus have attacked here before, have they not, Basileus?"

"Yes. We chose to grant them trade rights," Leo said.
An emperor did not admit to having been forced. "But
they are scattered, petty chiefs, who squabble with each
other and have no unity. They are a nuisance on our
border, no more."

"But if they had a man to lead them? Unite them?
Haakon Olesson is a conqueror. He is an evil man, but he
has war-luck and men follow him. In Norway, he attacked
a—"

"We have heard enough stories," Leo said. "We do not
know which of you is lying, and we do not care. But in the
matter of our borders . . ." He raised a ringed hand and
beckoned Stylian Zautzes forward. "What is your counsel
in this, my friend?"

Zautzes looked Harud over. "Harud Olafsson has been useful, Basileus. And has been rewarded for it," he added. "But this Haakon, on the other hand, does not seem useful, and may very possibly be dangerous. Also, it appears that one or the other must go." He looked at Harud again and seemed to be amused. "If you do not give our friend here to this Haakon, he may come after him, which would be tiresome, and an affront to your dignity."

"So will it be if we do hand him over," Leo said. "We are not dictated to by barbarian merchants."

"Unthinkable." Zautzes spread his hands silently, but Leo understood him well enough. They needed Harud and had certainly no use for Haakon.

Leo raised his hand again and looked at Harud. "You have our leave to go."

Harud bowed, uncertain.

"You are under our protection," the emperor said. "But it might be wise if you did not leave the palace for a few days yet." When Harud had departed, the hunted look beginning to fade from his face, Leo turned back to Zautzes. "We cannot afford a quarrel with the Rus merchants."

Zautzes smiled broadly to cover a certain amount of relief. It had been his appointees, after all, who had provoked the Bulgars into war. If the war went badly, even his daughter might not be able to sweeten the emperor's temper. And they needed Harud to deal with the Magyars. "I see no need for an execution, Basileus. As you say, we do not wish a quarrel with the Rus. But there are other ways at our disposal, and the man is, as you said, a barbarian. It shouldn't prove difficult."

"He has seventy men with him, Zautzes," the emperor said.

"Ah, but there is one thing he wants," Zautzes said. "And if he wants it badly enough, he might leave them behind. Seventy men are conspicuous."

"They won't do it," Ragnar said. He raised his hand before Haakon could explode. "I spoke to the emperor himself. It meant starting with the third assistant to the fourth junior secretary for petitions and fighting my way through enough clerks to row a longship, but I saw Leo himself."

"And he said no?" Haakon was pacing the sleeping chamber he shared with Ragnar and Donal and a half dozen other of his men. The room seemed much too small for him.

"He said he would consider the matter and advise us," Ragnar said, "but he meant no. He is much as I remembered him. A little older, but no different. I could see by his face that he was annoyed, but he had no mind to give us Harud."

"Leo will regret that," Haakon said. "Everything Harud touches turns black. This emperor will find that out."

"Maybe. But not in time to help us. I can't winter here, even if they'd let us."

"Are we such pariahs, then?" Donal asked. He had been lounging on one of the beds, listening to Ragnar's description of Leo's court.

"You, maybe not," Ragnar said. "You are Christian, and not Norse. But for us and the Rus—they don't like us in their city too long. We might get to looking at their treasure and thinking how a raid could be done."

"Like Knut," Donal laughed. "If we stay here too long, he will burst from sheer greed. Still, I am Norse enough. I go where the jarl goes." He stood up, slung his harp bag over his back, and glanced at Haakon. "You look like a penned wolf. Come outside before you begin to walk into the walls."

Haakon scowled, but he went with him. Of all his men, only Donal could prod him along like that. Donal was ten years younger than Haakon, and in most ways much his opposite, but a friendship had grown between them that was more than just the shoulder-to-shoulder comradeship of fighting men. Donal was interested in anything new or different, and like Haakon he had an eye for beautiful things, which went beyond mere gold. Constantinople held endless fascination for both of them. Haakon was in a fury over Harud, but that didn't wipe away his curiosity. While he tried to think of a way to pry Harud out of the emperor's palace, they prowled the bazaars and side streets of the city.

They stopped to peer at the pale and intricate beauty in an ivory worker's shop. There were rugs on the floor, and their rainbow colors set off the soft glow of ivory carved to myriad uses. Haakon ran a finger along a jewel casket ornamented with flowers and three-dimensional scenes of the old pagan gods of the Greeks. Another casket had a face of the Christ and three more men with circles around their heads, and Donal said it was made to hold a saint's bones.

"Or a piece of the True Cross," he added cheerfully, "of which there are enough to build a house."

"Why do Christians keep such things?"

"They work miracles, so it's said. Besides, wouldn't you keep something that had been touched by a god?"

Haakon thought of the ax, stored with the other weapons in *Gray Goose*'s hold, and didn't answer. He turned to inspect another piece, a triptych carved with the Christ and the Virgin, and side panels that swung open to reveal the figures of warrior saints in ancient armor.

"That is very fine work," the shopkeeper said. "A bargain at that price."

"I can see that, but my gods would not care for it, I think," Haakon said.

The shopkeeper looked only mildly shocked. His customers' souls were their own affairs, and this was, after all, a business. He hopefully pushed a few nonreligious pieces forward, but Haakon shook his head.

"I have all the cargo I have room for." They prowled away on to the next shop, trailed by the gaggle of street urchins who invariably attached themselves to passersby, offering wilting bunches of flowers or baked goods, or begging outright. Haakon threw them a handful of copper coins to get them out of the way, and they scrambled after them.

Constantinople was baking hot in the summer, and the heat shimmered visibly above the pavement. It was worse than Cadiz. Haakon could feel his shirt beginning to stick to his back. They inspected sandals and gaudy horse-trappings in a leatherworker's shop, and a case of enameled jewelry displayed on silk. The street they were on came out on the Mesê, where the best shops were, and Haakon and Donal pushed their way into the traffic along it. The light was beginning to fail, and the shopkeepers were setting tapers out to light the dusk. In summer Constantinople was as busy by night as by day. It would be too hot to sleep yet for some hours, and the people still thronged the streets to shop and gossip and catch any faint breath of air that stirred. The scent of the perfumers' shops at the palace end of the Mesê was overpowering. Haakon turned into one and bought a flask of attar of roses for Rosamund.

Donal looked wistfully at a wineshop that also sold fat pies with spiced meat inside them. The aroma was nearly as strong as the perfume. Haakon grinned, and they shouldered their way inside and found an empty place. Haakon had found his mood improving with their expedition through the city. Someday, he thought, he would bring Rosamund to this golden place and show it to her, and they would stay in one of the white villas with the flat roofs that capped the hills.

A burly man in an apron put two cups of wine and a plate of pies in front of them, and stuck Haakon's coin in the pouch at his belt. A few of the street urchins had followed them in, and he shooed them out again on the toe of his boot. Haakon recognized one thin, dark-haired child to whom he had tossed a penny earlier. Determined little bastard, he thought, amused. Mostly they stuck to their own stretch of street. The children who worked this part of the Mesê gave the boy a shove too, and he slipped away into a shadow, but he didn't disappear entirely.

Haakon wolfed down two of the pies, took a deep drink of the wine, and looked around him. The noise was deafening. There was a constant babble of talk, and in a small dot of cleared space on the floor a girl was dancing, with a drummer sitting cross-legged beside her. A second girl with a flute was perched on a counter, her skirt spread out around her, and the customers were tossing coins into it. Donal wiped his mouth and cocked his head to the flute song. After a minute or two he took his harp out of its bag and began to play an accompaniment. The drummer laughed and stepped up the beat, and the flute girl looked over at him and waggled her head in a friendly fashion as she played. The dancing girl was wearing several layers of veiling and not a lot more. She looked at Donal over her shoulder and wriggled, a little shiver that went from the bracelets on her ankles clear up to her fingertips. Donal looked back, appreciative. Haakon was wondering what Fann would think of that, when he felt a hand on his arm.

It was the street child, and he crouched on the tiled floor to be out of the proprietor's sight. "You are the Norse lord who is called Haakon?" he whispered.

There was something furtive about the child, and Haakon didn't answer.

"The one who has been seeking the other Norseman who lives in the emperor's palace?"

Haakon's hand shot out, and he grabbed the boy just below the shoulder. "What do you know about Harud?" he hissed.

The child wriggled, and Haakon held on. "Nothing, lord. I have a message, that is all."

"From who?"

The child shrugged. "Just a message. I am to say that there is one in the palace who wishes this Harud an evil, and she will help you if you will meet with her."

"Where?"

"The third house from the east wall in the Street of the Birds, across the harbor in Galata. Tonight."

"What kind of house is that?"

"I don't know, lord. I was only told to tell you. And that you must go alone because it will be dangerous if you are seen."

"*Who* told you?"

"A lady."

"What kind of a lady?"

The child wiggled free. "I don't know," he said, backing away. Haakon thought he looked frightened.

Still, it sounded possible enough. Harud made enemies as easily as breathing. That he had made one among the emperor's women was not a matter for surprise. And if she had paid this child to help her sell the emperor's pet to a man who wanted to kill him, then the child had a right to be scared.

"I will come," he said.

The child nodded and darted from the shop.

"You have gone mad," Donal said flatly. He put his harp carefully down on the bed. "There is a full moon. We should lock you up until it passes."

Thorfinn Solvisson and Knut and ten more of his crew stood leaning against the wall, waiting while Donal argued with him. They knew the jarl well enough to know when he wasn't going to be swayed, but they thought Donal was right.

"Look, then," Haakon said reasonably. "It is in Galata, which is across the harbor and not part of the city proper, so first I will get my weapons from *Gray Goose*. Also I will take you with me while we look at this house. But if this is a woman from the palace, she is going to be frightened of what she is doing, and if you come lumbering in behind me, making a noise like a bull seal in the mating season, she is going to run and I won't learn what I want to from her. So if this house looks safe, you are going to go away again when I tell you to. Is that clear?"

Donal looked at Ragnar. "What do you think?"

"I think it is dangerous," Ragnar said. "But I also think Haakon is right. The woman will run if she thinks Haakon will make her conspicuous."

Donal looked thoughtful. Something about this invitation made the skin prick on his neck. "I've never met Harud Olafsson face to face, so I can't be knowing. Haakon, does this sound like Harud to you?"

"Truthfully, it doesn't," Haakon said. "Harud would send a thug to wait in an alley for me. He wouldn't do something elaborate that might get the emperor's attention and make trouble for him."

"Well, I'm coming," Donal said. "When we get to this house, then I'll be deciding if I'll go away again."

They took *Gray Goose* across the harbor and beached her outside the town wall. There were sentries at the gates, but they passed Haakon and his men through with no trouble. Anyone who crossed the Golden Horn beyond the harbor chain had already been cleared by officials from

the city, and there was no prohibition against weapons in
Galata as long as a man didn't look as if he meant trouble.
Haakon had Donal, Thorfinn, Hjalmar Sitricsson, and nine
others with him, and he had made them all swear terrible
oaths to go back to the ship if he told them to and keep
their noses out of his business. He hoped they were going
to do it. Donal looked rebellious, and Hjalmar swiveled
his head around like an owl every few steps and looked so
surly that passersby gave him a wide berth. If he wanted
to be inconspicuous, Haakon thought irritably, he should
have come alone, but that would have been too foolhardy.

Knut had stayed behind in the city to keep the rest of
the men under his thumb and to see that Wulf didn't get
out of the room where Haakon had locked him. Ragnar
had said that if this mysterious woman had wanted Haakon
to come alone, she obviously didn't think he needed an
interpreter, and so he had stayed too. As Haakon had set
out, Ragnar had gone to check on their stored cargo. It
was always possible that this was neither an ambush nor an
assignation but merely an attempt at thievery.

Galata was a maze of streets even more crowded than
the city across the harbor. Many of the foreign merchants
who lived here permanently had their homes in Galata,
and it also seemed to be the prowling district for young
men from the city looking for a night's amusement. Haakon
saw none of the golden-domed churches that crowned
Constantinople proper, but there were whole streets lined
with taverns and houses where women sat in lighted
windows and called to passersby.

The third house from the east wall in the Street of the
Birds appeared to be one of the latter. It was a two-story
wooden building, with a balcony that leaned over the
street. The balcony was empty now, but Haakon could see
the flutter of draperies as figures moved behind the balcony windows. The lamplight from a tavern across the
narrow, cobbled street showed a wooden door with an iron
grill across it. The ground floor windows were curtained,
but light and the murmur of feminine voices filtered from
behind them.

Haakon rattled the iron grill across the door, and a

white hand swung the inner door open. "We are closed tonight," the woman said.

"Wait!" Haakon put a hand through the grillwork. "I was to meet someone—"

The woman's dark eyes widened at the men behind him, and she looked frightened. "You were to come alone, lord," she whispered.

Haakon looked past her into the room. There were more women in loose trailing gowns, seven or eight of them maybe, and a few children, who looked like slaves. He didn't see any men. The woman tried to close the door.

"No, wait!" he said again. "They will not come in with me." He knew his Greek was faltering, but she seemed to understand him. She shook her head.

"They cannot stay in the street. Someone will ask questions. It is dangerous." She tried to shut the door again.

Haakon looked at Donal. "Go back to the ship."

"Jarl—"

"I can defend myself against a houseful of whores and children!" he snapped. "Now do it!"

Donal peered through the door behind him, caught Haakon's expression, and jerked his head at Thorfinn and Hjalmar. "Let's go." Haakon watched them until they turned the corner.

The woman unlatched the iron grillwork and beckoned him in. "Quickly!" She was tall and beautiful, with pearls in the dark hair that was knotted on her head and rings on her long, slim fingers. "This way!" She tugged him past the outer room through a doorway beyond, and most of the women followed them and clustered in the doorway. Keeping guard maybe, Haakon thought. They were all as tall as he, but with a delicate grace in their slim waists and fine features. Haakon wondered what nationality they were. There was something exotic about their graceful carriage and their low, mellifluous voices as they murmured in the doorway.

The room inside was a bedchamber, with a curtained bed, silk draperies, and heavy cushions on the floor. The dark-haired woman curled herself onto a cushion, with her

feet tucked under her, and motioned to Haakon to sit.
One of the children darted in with a tray of wine and
sweets and put it on the floor.

"Eat, lord."

Haakon shook his head. He didn't trust anything that
might have poison in it.

The woman laughed gently and picked one up and
began to eat it herself, but Haakon just smiled and shook
his head again. He didn't like the sweets they made here.
They were heavy and cloying and left a bad taste in his
mouth.

"Are you the one who sent a message to me?" As he
spoke, the other women moved closer. There was something odd about them, about their movements, but he
wasn't sure what.

The dark-haired woman nodded. "You wish to make an
end to your quarrel with Harud Olafsson. It may be that
we can help you."

"Oh, yes, we can help you."

"Indeed, lord."

"Yes, we know Harud."

The women murmured and laughed in the doorway
behind him. Haakon shifted uncomfortably on his cushion
and looked at them. The sensation grew stronger of something not right in those lovely faces.

"Yes, we can help you," the first woman said. Haakon
barely had time to fling himself to his feet as her hand
twisted into the folds of her gown. The knife blade flashed
in the lamplight, and he snatched up the tray of wine and
threw it at her. The other women crowded through the
doorway, and he realized with a crawling of his skin that
there were no windows in the room.

He lashed out with his fist as they came at him, and
knocked one woman back into the rest. The first woman's
knife scraped down his chest, and she shrieked in fury
when it caught on the mail under his shirt. He twisted the
knife out of her hand and sent her sprawling, then jumped
up on the bed and pulled the hangings down to throw at
them, blessing whatever god had put it into his head to
wear mail tonight.

The women stumbled among the cushions as he flung

the hangings at them, but they kept on coming. And what in Thor's name was he going to do, he thought frantically. He jerked the ax out of its sheath on his back in the seconds that the tangle of hangings kept them at bay and held it in front of him warningly. It was no part of a man's honor to kill a roomful of women. But if he didn't, they would kill him. There were eight of them, and they all had knives.

They flung themselves at him, and he lashed out with the flat of the ax, and then they were on him, their hair tangled wildly about their faces, shrieking and clawing at him with knives, fingernails, and teeth. The mail turned the knives from his chest and back, but he was bleeding from cuts on both hands, and one blade came within an inch of his throat before he kicked the woman off him. If it hadn't been for sheer good luck, he would have been dead before he had even got his ax out. Now there was nothing else he could do. He could kill them or he could die here in this room, clawed to death by these furies. Haakon swung the ax, blade out, and one of the women dropped, blood pouring from her throat. The others backed away, and Haakon jumped down onto the better footing of the floor. He lashed out with the ax as they tried to circle him. Then they were on him with a rush, all at once, and he wrestled with them, panting, using the ax like a club, until he had them backed away enough to swing. The tarnished blade bit deep into a blond woman just above the hip, and she fell. Haakon swung the ax again and caught the woman who had opened the door to him, as she lunged for him with her knife. The blade sank into her ribs, and she twisted to the floor with a shriek. They tried once more, and another woman died, and then the rest backed out of the doorway and ran.

Haakon stood, gasping for breath, blood running from the ax blade and his gashed hands. Three of the women were dead, but one lay watching him, her blond hair spread in a tangle on the bloody cushions. Her gown was red with blood over her hips, but Haakon thought she might live if the wound was seen to. Something in him balked at just walking away to let her die. Warily he knelt down beside her and pulled the blood-soaked gown away.

The wound was worse than he had thought, and the blood ran in a crimson river down over a penis and an old scar where the testicles had been. Haakon jerked his eyes up to the painted face framed in its fall of blond hair. The eunuch gave him a look he wasn't ever going to forget, and died.

Haakon dropped the bloody gown and backed away, gagging. He looked closely at the other bodies. They were the same: not women. Eunuchs. Painted and jeweled. They had clawed at him like cats with their knives.

He stepped over the bodies and looked at the outer room. The child slaves had gone. There were more wall hangings, cushions, and silver trays for wine. The smell of incense was thick in the air. He choked and looked back at the dead things in the bedchamber. This *was* a whorehouse, and these were whores, but—Haakon shuddered in spite of himself and pushed the front door open without looking further. Outside he took a deep breath of clean air, but there seemed to be a sweet, sickly smell to it that hadn't been there before. Or maybe it had only been unnoticed, the dark, twisted side to the beautiful city of gold.

"This is not at all proper." The third assistant to the undersecretary of the deputy in charge of foreign petitions wrung his hands. "You cannot stay here."

"Why not?" Haakon planted his feet on the red and blue marble and showed no inclination to move. He was not so tall, really, not if one measured him, but he somehow seemed to loom menacingly above the assistant to the undersecretary. Nor was he armed, of course, not in an antechamber of the imperial palace. He simply stood, like one of the marble pillars that supported the painted roof, and so far none of the assistant's efforts to shift him had met with any success. The assistant could call the guards, but that would make a row, and rows were not encouraged.

"You will be sent for," the assistant said desperately. "When an audience is arranged, you will be sent for."

"That will no doubt be when the next snow falls," Haakon said pleasantly. "I will wait here."

The assistant nearly stamped his foot. "No, I assure you.

But it will take some time, and for now, you will have to
go!"

There were three carved chairs against the frescoed wall
of the antechamber. Two were occupied by other petitioners
seeking audience with Leo VI and looking interested. The
third was empty, and Haakon went and sat in it. "I will
wait," he said. He stretched his legs out in front of him
and appeared to turn to stone.

"A most persistent man. Perhaps you should see him."
The emperor Leo looked irritated, but Stylian Zautzes's
dark face was nearly amused. "It won't look good if it gets
out that a foreign merchant was nearly murdered and the
emperor refused even to grant him a hearing."

Haakon nearly lost his determination before he reached
the audience chamber. Another official of some sort, in
green hose and tunic and shoes with buttons, came to lead
him through the vast, sprawling grounds of the imperial
palace. Haakon thought afterward that they had done it to
impress him, because they walked for miles, and he
thought at the end that they had come in a circle. But it
was awesome all the same. There were gardens, endless
gardens, dotted with pavilions, ponds, and a fountain
where a golden pinecone spouted wine into the air. Broad
stairs led down to what the official said was the emperor's
private harbor, where the imperial barges lay moored to a
marble quay. Pheasants, ibis, and peacocks paced in stately grandeur along the walkways, under colonnades of
green marble and red onyx. The roofs of the palace
complex sprawled unendingly, above living quarters, reception rooms, swimming baths, stables, and an indoor
riding hall, and beyond them, offices, palace workshops,
and the silk house.

The high golden domes of churches loomed over all,
and Haakon's guide said that the greatest of these was the
Church of the Holy Wisdom, the *Hagia Sophia*, where the
emperors were crowned. It stood beside the square of the
Augustaeum, and even Haakon, who was no Christian,
caught his breath. The cascading domes dwarfed even the
bronze figure of the emperor Justinian, in a plumed

helmet and bearing the world in his palm, which dominated the Augustaeum. At the other end of the black-paved square was the Hippodrome, which could seat sixty thousand spectators for races and public entertainment.

Having passed all these wonders, they came at last to the *Chalkê*, the Brazen Entrance to the emperor's palace. The outer roof and doors were gilded bronze; inside, the ceilings were set with mosaics of Justinian's great general Belisarius riding home in triumph—so the official in the green tunic said. The walls and floor were dressed with marble: emerald, red, and white, patterned with undulating lines of blue.

The official gave Haakon a look that said plainly that he felt Haakon sullied the splendor of the palace with his mere presence, and then the official moved off to speak to another official who spoke to a man-at-arms, who spoke to another, and eventually a page with a double-headed eagle on his tunic trotted out and beckoned to Haakon.

The emperor Leo received Haakon in what was no doubt merely an everyday throne room. It was set about with porphyry and gilding, but it was small. There was room for no more than the handful of men-at-arms and a dark-faced man with a black beard, who, from Ragnar's description, was undoubtedly the chief minister, Stylian Zautzes. A pair of eunuchs, plump and easily recognizable in men's clothing, waved a peacock-feather fan above the emperor's jeweled head. The emperor looked as if he didn't wish to see Haakon, either. There was no sign of Harud Olafsson.

As instructed by Ragnar, Haakon prostrated himself the requisite three times before the porphyry dais on which the emperor's throne was set.

"You may rise," Leo said tiredly. "What is your petition? We have heard a great many petitions today and we are weary, so we wish that you will make the matter brief."

A man-at-arms, who himself appeared to be Norse, or maybe Rus, began to translate.

"I understand, if the emperor speaks slowly," Haakon said in Greek. "No petition, Basileus. Justice. Ragnar has asked this already, and the emperor has refused. Now a houseful of—things, such as these"—he eyed the eunuchs with distaste—"has been sent to kill me. Is this the emperor's justice?"

Leo's face took on a look of mild surprise. "We know nothing of this."

Haakon folded his arms on his chest and looked first at Stylian Zautzes and then at Leo. "I do not believe that, Basileus. These were eunuchs, dressed as women, and one said she—he—came from the palace."

Leo shrugged. "That is a very easy lie to make. And there are many eunuchs in the city—some slaves, some civil servants, some very high in our government. We do not know them all." He smiled gently at the foreigner's ignorance. "That is like wishing to know all the red-haired men in the city, or all the lame ones."

"There is only *one* man with any reason to wish me dead, and that is Harud Olafsson," Haakon said flatly. "And Harud is hiding here."

Leo stiffened. That was close to an accusation. And the emperor was holy, sacred. Even the things he touched were sacred. No man spoke unwisely to the emperor and lived. Still, there were a great many Rus in the city, and there was no knowing what this annoying dark-bearded man had said to them concerning the aborted attack. Leo could not afford a riot just now. "We know nothing," he said again. "You may leave us."

"I will remember the emperor's justice," Haakon said politely, with a look that belied his mild tone. "Also the Rus and the Norse in the city will remember, so that if there should be any . . . accident befalling me, they will know who to look to." He bowed again and then deliberately turned his back to push open the painted doors. The men-at-arms started forward, hands to their sword hilts, but there was no command from the emperor, and they dropped back again as the doors swung shut.

A curtain rustled behind the throne, and Harud Olafsson slipped out and bowed before the emperor. "Is it not as I have said, Basileus? The man is a danger. He thinks himself able to threaten even the emperor's sacred person."

"But we do not wish trouble with the Rus, not while we are at war." Leo looked at Harud and Stylian Zautzes. "What is your counsel?"

"Kill him, Basileus," Harud said. "It would be safest."

Zautzes looked at Harud wryly. "Safer for *you*, certainly," he said. He turned to the emperor. "But in this case, I must agree. This man is unpredictable. There is no knowing what he will do next."

"No," Leo said.

"Basileus—"

"We will not be publicly branded a murderer. Not now. It would not be good. But we agree he is dangerous. Therefore, we will set a time—one week from tomorrow—when all Rus now trading here must leave the city. For reasons of our war with the Bulgars we do not wish to have so many of them here at once. That will take care of the Rus and this Haakon both. We do not wish to be bothered with them further. We have the truce with the Bulgars to occupy us." He looked at Harud. "And the Magyars to be resettled when the khan of the Bulgars has capitulated to us."

Harud opened his mouth to speak, but Zautzes shook his head at him slightly. One did not argue with the emperor. But if one were careful, it would be possible to circumvent him, quietly.

"You will have to give it up." Ragnar heaved himself up onto a bed and kicked off his boots. "I have just come from the Rus captains, and it's a good thing they want your men with them on the home road, or you wouldn't be able to turn your back on them, either. As it is, I wouldn't stay overly long in Koenugard if I were you."

Haakon looked up from the cargo sheets he had been tallying and gave Ragnar a questioning eye.

"We have been given a week to leave the city." Ragnar spat. "I have pointed out to the captains that we will have to fight Pechenegs on the way home too, and that Jarl Haakon has seventy men who will not be a help to the Rus if the Rus have put a knife in Jarl Haakon." He glared at Haakon. "What did you say to the emperor?"

"That I do not like it when someone sets his male whores to kill me," Haakon said. "Also that I want Harud Olafsson. Nothing so very new."

"Well, you have made him angry," Ragnar said. He looked to be in no very good temper himself. He would have gotten a better price for the rest of his goods if the Mikligard merchants hadn't known he had only a week left in which to strike a bargain. "And you have made the Rus angry, which means Prince Oleg. He is not a good man to anger. Harud Olafsson isn't worth it."

"Not to you, Ragnar," Haakon said quietly. "He is greatly worth it to me. And maybe also to Prince Oleg."

"Not," said Ragnar flatly, "if you don't kill Harud, but only interrupt Oleg's trade."

Haakon stood up. He was beginning to be angrier than Ragnar, and he had no wish to fight with him. "I am going to check the warehouses."

He stalked down the staircase and out into the street, glaring around him at the shifting bustle of the city. It was beginning to make him feel hemmed in, as if he were fighting his way through a net—against the Rus, the emperor, and a web of protocol, regulations, and as many officials as there were mice in a grain house, always separating him from Harud Olafsson. Somehow there was a way to get at Harud. There must be, or the emperor and his dark-faced minister wouldn't be taking so many pains to see that Haakon didn't find it. He thought about the whorehouse in Galata and glowered around him at the passersby. He took no notice of the shadow slipping along behind him.

At the warehouse Haakon gave his name and showed his ship clearance to a sleepy guard at the door. The guard yawned and motioned him through with only a half glance at it. The day was baking hot, and when another man came up and offered him a drink from a wineskin, the guard raised it and took a deep swallow.

In the shadows of the warehouse, Haakon checked the goods in the section allotted to him and Ragnar, examined the seals to see that they hadn't been tampered with, and sat down to think on a bale of silk bolts. The warehouse was stone, cooler than in the street outside, and there was no one to tell him things he didn't wish to hear, such as "Go home."

Haakon pulled Rosamund's knife out of the scabbard he had fitted for it in his boot and looked at it to remind himself why it was that he couldn't go home. It was long and thin, with a faint blue sheen to the blade. Valkyrie blue in the shadows, like her eyes. He rested it on his knees and put his head in his hands. Without Thor Odinsson, maybe he wasn't *going* to get Harud, but there was no going home otherwise. For maybe the first time in his life, Haakon didn't know what to do, and he sat there and let the dark misery of that realization wash over him like a tide. A shadow crept through the dimness, among the piled bales.

It was the faint flicker of reflected light, like the light from the knife blade on his knees, that caught his eyes. Haakon spun, knife in hand, to see the man leaping at him. The attacker had a knife too, long and thin as Rosamund's, thin enough to slide between links of mail. Haakon dodged frantically and slashed out with Rosamund's knife to knock it aside. The man moved like an eel. Haakon lunged at him and backed him a little way up against the bales. The man struck out again, looking a little frightened now; the Norseman wasn't supposed to have a knife. Haakon's rage boiled over, and he caught the man's knife hand in his left, and snapped it at the wrist. He jerked the man upright and drove Rosamund's dagger into the chest to the hilt. The man sagged and slid backward off the blade, with blood in his mouth. Haakon stood over him with a black wolf-look in his eyes that boded no good for someone.

"By Thor's hammer, I have had *enough!*" he bellowed, and rolled the body with one foot toward the warehouse guard as he came running in, peering through the dimness. Talking to the emperor of Mikligard was like talking to his city walls. Talk got nothing but a knife in the dark. That had been his mistake from the first: to try to do the thing with *talk*.

IX Sarak Khan

"They demand to know *why* you wish an audience with King Symeon." The monk's lined face was apologetic, and

he spoke in careful Greek to Haakon. A troop of heavily
armored cavalry reined their mounts into a ring around
them, gazing impassively at the Norsemen, lances at the
ready, while the Norsemen scowled back.

"It is enough that I wish it," Haakon said. "I am no
enemy of Symeon."

"But you see, you have come from Constantinople," the
monk said gently. "They are at war here and wary of a
trap."

Haakon thought it over. "We will give them our weapons," he said finally. "For good faith."

The monk breathed a sigh of relief. He had been in
Haakon's company since Haakon had bought him out of
the slave market in Constantinople, and he had developed
a great respect for the Norseman's temper in that time.

The cavalry commander nodded and shouted an unintelligible order in Slavonic, and half the troopers dismounted.
Haakon gave Knut and Donal his own orders, and they
passed them on down the line. The Norse grumbled
greatly, and Knut thumped one or two in the ribs and
reminded them that they had sworn. They settled eventually to a watchful, surly silence. The jarl hadn't led them
astray yet, but this giving up of weapons—this was not
good, and they must have them back. They would tell the
jarl so when they stopped. The troopers remounted, con-
fiscated weapons in hand, and the cavalcade moved on.

Behind them the ships lay beached on the Black Sea
coast, with twenty-five men to guard them and orders to
raise sail and make for Berezany Island if there was
trouble.

Ragnar the Noseless was in Mikligard with the Rus
captains, loading his own ships and fuming because he
didn't want to go through Pecheneg country alone and
because Haakon was sticking his own nose in a wolf's
mouth and would be lucky not to have it bitten off to the
neck. When Haakon had told him where he was going,
Ragnar had looked honestly horrified and said that he
would raise a rune-stone to him in Norway. Haakon had
shrugged and told Ragnar to camp two weeks on Berezany
Island before heading north up the Dnieper, and it might
be he would have less trouble with Pechenegs. Ragnar had

narrowed his eyes suspiciously but asked no questions. Haakon thought that Ragnar would take his advice about Berezany, but that Ragnar would also not wish to know anything more until he was well out of the emperor Leo's reach.

Haakon looked around him as they made their way through the coastal hills of the Bulgars to the king's capital at Preslav. It was plainly a country at war, and the king's men were right to be wary. The ravages of the Magyars and the emperor's troops showed in abandoned villages, ruined fields, and the blackened timbers of burned buildings. The land had the look of an old battlefield, and the air seemed to have the smell of blood in it still.

Brother Gregory trudged along beside Haakon, sadly taking in the wreckage. The peasant folk would be in Preslav now for refuge, he supposed. Gregory sighed; so much laid waste since he had left for Constantinople. Gregory had been the abbot's clerk in his monastery, and his only sin had been to be in Constantinople on church business when his king had decided to make war. He had huddled miserably for months, first in the emperor's prisons and then in the slave market, and he wanted only to go home again. He was not a fighting man like the Norseman who paced along beside him, with his hound at his heel. Gregory was unsure what proposal the Norseman was going to put to King Symeon, but Haakon had promised Gregory home and freedom for getting them to Preslav. The old monk eyed Haakon thoughtfully and decided that if Symeon were willing to listen to him, the emperor Leo would very likely regret the day he had angered this dark-bearded man. There was a great deal of satisfaction to be had in that, and Gregory said a prayer to be forgiven the sin of vengefulness.

The Bulgars were yet another of the predatory people of the steppe who had settled in Slavic lands and then assimilated Slavic custom and Slavic language. They counted themselves the descendants of the Huns, but their king spoke Slavonic and styled himself "tsar of all the Bulgars and the Greeks." They were a Christian kingdom, having been converted in the old khan Boris-Michael's day, with only a short lapse into the religion of their ancestors when the venerable Boris had retired to a monastery and left the rule to his eldest son, Vladimir. Vladimir had attempted to reintroduce the old gods, and Boris had emerged angrily from his monastery to depose Vladimir, reinstate Christianity, and set his orthodox second son, Symeon, on the throne. Thereupon Boris had returned to his cloister, and Symeon had set about making his capital city, Preslav, a residence to rival the glories of Constantinople. If Haakon were expecting a warrior king who lived in the saddle and had no thought but to his arms, he would be greatly surprised.

Preslav, even jammed with the refugees of the Bulgarian countryside, was impressive, not so fine as Constantinople perhaps, but equal to any other great city Haakon had seen. The buildings were decorated with stone and wainscoted with wood of various colors. The palace buildings soared loftily over all, and the churches were adorned with marble and frescoes without, and with gold and silver within. Symeon had been carefully educated at Constantinople, and while it had not encouraged him to look with favor upon that empire, he had brought home with him a love of literature, art, and industry. When he received the Norsemen, Symeon was wearing a robe covered in pearls, with chains of coin about his neck, bracelets on his wrists, and a girdle of royal purple. A golden sword of state lay at his side.

Haakon had dressed in his finest shirt and trousers to do justice to the occasion, and they sized each other up thoughtfully while Brother Gregory made the necessary presentation and stood aside to interpret if it became necessary.

Symeon was much of an age with Haakon and was said to have the look of his father about him: dark hair and beard, wide eyes and a fine-boned face. His crown was in the Greek style, hung with dangling chains of pearls, but there was something about him, in spite of the delicate features, that made Haakon think of the wild Pecheneg warriors rather than the emperor Leo.

"If you have come from Leo in Constantinople," Symeon said in Greek, "we will tell you again what we have already told him once: We have agreed to a truce, and a truce does not mean a surrender. The last proposal of terms was unacceptable."

"I am from Leo in Constantinople only in the sense that I have come from his city," Haakon said, picking his words carefully. It was too easy to insult a king unwittingly in an unfamiliar tongue. "I am Norse, from Norway, and a free chieftain in no one's service. This Leo owes me a debt that I wish to see paid. Getting nothing from him but thugs with knives to trail after me, I have come to the king of the Bulgars because I have heard he is at war with Leo. It seemed to me that together we might give Leo cause to wish he had dealt more honestly."

"Any man at odds with Leo is welcome in Preslav," Symeon said. "But fifty men—that is useful, of course, but not enough to turn the tide. Still, if you wish a commission in my army—"

Haakon shook his head. "No, I am not seeking service. But I have also heard that the Bulgars must ask for truce because Leo has sent the Magyars to harry their backs. What if another people should harry the Magyars while they are...occupied? A land-hungry people. Pechenegs, for example."

"We would thank God for the blessing," Symeon said frankly. "But the Pechenegs answer to no man, and most ambassadors who are sent to them come home in two pieces."

"The Pechenegs will not trust us," Brother Gregory added. "Like the Magyars, they are dangerous neighbors, and our kingdom has never done aught but quarrel with them."

"No. You need a...a...someone between you—" Haakon groped for the right word.

"An intermediary?" Brother Gregory said.

"Yes."

Symeon's eyes grew shrewd. He studied Haakon and the Norsemen crowding into the audience chamber behind him. "You? That is possible, but also very dangerous. Most likely they will make a wine flask from your skull, Norseman, and someone will mourn you in Norway."

Haakon laughed. "That is always possible. But if I do it? If the Pechenegs come and fight the Magyars for you?"

"That is a great *if*," Symeon said. "But yes, then, if you do it, you can ask any reward we find it in our power to give. And we would greatly like to see Leo's face and that of his thief of a minister."

"You are mad then," Donal said with conviction.

Haakon raised his eyebrows. "You knew what I was intending when we left Mikligard."

"Aye, but to go with no extra men—"

"The king can't spare them," Haakon said. "And they are unfriends with the Pechenegs anyway. The Pechenegs will see Bulgars and attack."

"They will see Norse and attack," Donal said. "Or are you thinking they have grown civilized since we sailed down yon river?"

"Norse don't raid where there is nothing to take," Haakon said. "Unless the Pechenegs are fools, and I doubt it, neither will they." The cargo was still stored on the ships, under guard with Kalki Estridsson in command, who was no doubt pacing the beach and wondering if the jarl would be back or no. Haakon grinned. "And we have Brother Gregory. No doubt he can call on your god for aid."

Donal made a rude noise and took his harp out of its bag to play as he rode. Donal sat a horse like a centaur, which was more than could be said for the Norse. They were seafarers and rode when they had to go to a place that was inland, but they would never make cavalry. They were one day out on the trail, the worst time for a man unused to the saddle, and even Haakon gritted his teeth with every lurch in stride from the dun beast that had been lent him out of Symeon's stables. The ground was rocky, which added nothing to their comfort. Wulf trotted along happily enough at the dun's heel, and Brother Gregory sat stoically on his mule, with a broad straw hat to shield his tonsured head from the sun. Among his other languages, Brother Gregory could speak the old tongue of the Bulgars', which was kin to that of the Pechenegs, and to his horror King Symeon had taken the Norseman's proposition seriously enough to order an interpreter to ride with him. Brother Gregory's abbot had seconded the command, and Gregory had bowed to the will of his churchly lord and his earthly one. He tried hard to believe that God would hold him in His hand on this journey and prayed repeatedly for faith, but the farther they rode north along the barren coast, the harder it became to find God in the dusty land and the tall, grim-faced pagans who rode behind him.

Donal watched him with sympathy and began to make a lighthearted music on his harp, to match the beat of the horses' hooves. They were all grass in the wind that blew from Jarl Haakon these days, the little monk among the rest. He prodded them along like cattle at herding time, driven by the fury that had finally erupted in him in Mikligard—to the king of the Bulgars, to the chieftain of the Pechenegs, straight to hell maybe. But Donal was Jarl Haakon's man, and, having said so once, he wouldn't argue again.

In the ordinary way, no one came through Pecheneg country on horseback because it was the river that gave the only refuge from attack. It was late in the season for the Rus to be on the river, and too early for their trip back up it, and so the Pechenegs kept to their huts along their summer grazing lands and tended the few fields that they planted for grain. The Norse nosed their way into the land like hounds on the scent, knowing only vaguely where they needed to go. They were very close to the Pechenegs' summer graze before they were seen.

They came over the lip of a hill that sloped shallowly to a wide valley through which a tributary of the Dnieper ran, and Haakon flung up his hand. Donal and Knut and Thorfinn Solvisson drew rein behind him. The plain was dotted with grazing animals and a scatter of round shapes like huts. They were still too far to make out more than that, but it wouldn't be long, Haakon thought, before someone spotted them, even at this distance. The Pechenegs would know who had business to be on this hill and who had not. He ran his eyes swiftly over the valley. Just at the base of the hill a smaller stream, deep and swift running, splashed its way down to join with the river. A tangle of wild vines and summer flowers grew beside it, and Haakon stiffened as he caught a flicker of movement along the bank. He beckoned up Brother Gregory, who came reluctantly and peered down into the undergrowth.

"I'm going down," Haakon whispered. "Tell them that we come in peace. Get the words clear in your mind now, so that you won't be forgetting them if there is trouble."

Brother Gregory liked his lips and prayed for fortitude, and kicked his mule down the slope behind Haakon. Wulf padded silently behind them.

A stone rolled under the dun horse's hoof, and rattled down the hillside. There was a swift flurry of movement and a scream, and Haakon saw a woman on the bank with her hands full of wildflowers. He started to laugh. All this preparation for one girl picking posies by the river. Then she screamed again and began to run, not away from the river but toward it, stumbling frantically along the bank with her hands stretched out.

"Dear God! There! In the river!" Brother Gregory said, and Haakon saw a small hand and face rise from the current and go under again. Haakon kicked the dun horse into a dead gallop down the hill, cursing himself as it stumbled and slid on its haunches. He had frightened a child into falling in the river, and it was plain that the mother, even if she could swim, was being left behind by the swiftness of the current as it carried the small form into deeper water. The dun hit the riverbank, and Haakon dug his heels into its flank and shouted in its ear to run as the ground leveled out. The woman was wailing behind them. He could see the child in the water some distance ahead of him . . . closer . . . then he was past the struggling form and throwing himself from the saddle. He stumbled as he hit the ground, righted himself, and dived. The water was cold—not so icy as the fjords at home, but it was quick and dangerous. He surfaced, spitting water, and flung out a hand as the child's body swept by. He pulled it to him and lifted its head from the water, letting the current take them both for a moment.

The child was limp in his arms, and he thought miserably that he had failed before he had even reached the Pechenegs' chief. Failed and caused a death. And if the

Pechenegs would forgive him that, which was unlikely, he himself could not. Since he had angered Thor, his life had been blighted with failure and ill luck, and it might be that this, too, was part of that. The water rushed over his head, and he choked.

Vaguely he could hear shouting from the shore and a drumming in his head that was probably the feel of drowning. Better maybe to go under the river and be done with it.

No. The voice came from somewhere, maybe only his own mind, fighting for life. The child made a faint sound and thrashed in his arms. It was alive! Barely maybe, but alive. Haakon tucked the little body into the crook of one arm and began to swim.

The current clutched at him like hands, buffeted him against floating debris, dragged at his ankles like Ran's reivers to pull him under. Slowly the shore grew nearer, and the drumming in his head became a softer sound that whispered, *Swim*. He held the child's head from the water and fought the river and the water in his own lungs until he felt mud under his feet.

The sun was a bright dazzle as he lurched into the shallows, and the child had gone limp again. He dragged it to the bank and held it up by the heels to let the water pour out. The child gagged and choked and began to wail, and the dazzle grew brighter until Haakon could see no more than the lights that burst in front of his eyes and blinded him. The child slid from his grasp, and Haakon fell, to lie with his face in the mud. A voice from somewhere said, *You redeem yourself, Haakon Olesson....*

There were gray shadows where the blinding lights had been, and a face of fearful beauty, red bearded and fire eyed, looked out at him from it.

"I thought to drown and be done with it," Haakon whispered.

The god shook his head and pointed somewhere Haakon couldn't see. *There is a plan for that one. Most men make little difference in the world, but this child is one who will matter. And when such a seed is sprouted, there are always the dark ones who would break it before it comes to fruit.*

"My horse and I, we frightened the child," Haakon said. "It was my fault."

No. It would have happened anyway, but now the battle has been fought and won, and you have served me by that. Also you have come to know yourself, and that is no bad thing for a man. The face lost some of its fierceness and looked even a little amused, although no less fearful. Always it had been fearful; no man talks to a god as he does to his spear brother. But there was the flicker of a smile along the mouth as he said, *It is a stubborn man, Haakon Olesson, who must be half drowned to learn the pattern of his life. You were not meant for drowning; you were meant for me.*

. . . He must have been unconscious. The god's face faded, and he was left with a pain in his chest and mud in his mouth. He retched up more water and looked around him painfully. Wulf stood over him, growling low in his throat, and the Norsemen were a ways up the bank, bunched together behind a shield wall, with Brother Gregory unhappily in their midst. They must have crossed at the ford where the child had fallen. Between them and Haakon were what looked like three hundred Pechenegs, the chieftain with the gold collar, whom Haakon remembered from the battle beside *Aifor*, at their head. The woman they had frightened by the bank was clutching her wet child and talking to the chieftain very fast in an unintelligible language. The chief reached out a hand and touched the child's cheek, so maybe the woman was someone important.

Haakon groaned and rolled over, and the ax, still in its sheath on his back, bit into his spine. The Pecheneg warriors all took a step toward him, and Haakon unslung the ax in a hurry. The sun flashed on the blade, and he saw that it was gold again, as bright as the emperor's imperial throne in Mikligard. He nearly dropped it. The Pecheneg chief headed for him, spear in hand, with the woman running beside him, and Haakon decided he had best worry about the ax later.

"Brother Gregory!"

Brother Gregory crossed himself and emerged from

behind the shield wall. He called something to the Pecheneg chief, and the chief stopped and nodded abruptly. Brother Gregory picked his way down the bank to Haakon, praying as he went. The Norse stared suspiciously over their shields.

"Tell them that we have not come to raid or to make war, but to talk," Haakon said. "Tell them we are not Rus."

Brother Gregory repeated this to the Pecheneg chief, and the man looked at Haakon thoughtfully. The chief was maybe forty-five, with a harsh, weather-beaten face and gold at this arms and throat. The woman spoke to him again, and he nodded and turned to Brother Gregory.

"I think God has had a care for us after all," Brother Gregory said in Greek. "The woman is the chieftain's sister, and she says that the chieftain owes you a life-price for saving the child, so he will listen to you. We are honored guests, it seems."

Haakon stood up slowly and put the ax back in its sheath, while the chieftain eyed it with interest. "Thank him, and tell him I will tell this to my men."

The Pechenegs lived in round huts of some sort of hide, which could be moved as their herds moved. The Norsemen eyed them with the look of a mouse invited to enter a trap, and Haakon left them camped in the open, with Knut and Thorfinn to keep order, and went into the chieftain's hut with Donal, Brother Gregory, and Wulf. A short round woman in plain clothes brought Haakon a tunic and loose trousers such as all the Pechenegs, men and women alike, seemed to wear, and took his own away to dry. The floor of the hut was covered with rugs and cushions, and when he had changed, Haakon sank into them gratefully. Donal looked around him with interest, and Brother Gregory appeared to be praying again.

After a while two more plainly dressed women, who were probably slaves, came in and put up a little brazier and set dishes of meat to cook on it. When they had gone, the chieftain and his sister appeared and sat solemnly across the brazier from Haakon. They also had changed their clothes and wore tunics and trousers bright with embroidery and alternating bands of color. The child was

with them, clutching at its mother's trouser leg. It stared
at Haakon with bright black eyes, and Haakon looked
interestedly for some sign of the god's hand about it, but
saw only a child, perhaps two years old, over its fright now
and curious about the foreigners. He wasn't even sure
what sex it was. It wore the same tunic and trousers as the
rest, and its black hair was cropped off square above the
ears, as if someone had set a bowl on its head for a guide.

Another slave brought in a tray of bronze cups and
handed them round, and the chieftain pointed at the
dishes of meat on the brazier.

Haakon dipped his fingers in the meat and chewed
interestedly. It was highly spiced and very good. The little
cups held a drink that tasted like fermented, sweetened
milk. It was very strong, and Haakon decided that it was
best treated with respect. He nudged Brother Gregory
and Donal to eat, also. He was unsure of custom here, but
he was certain that to refuse would give offense. The child
took a piece of meat and held it out on a flat palm to Wulf,
who picked it off carefully. The child laughed and edged
closer to the big dog, one eye on its mother and the other
on Haakon to be sure that that was not forbidden.

"Tell the woman that Wulf likes children," Haakon said
softly to Brother Gregory, and the old man complied.

A smile split the chief's face, and he nodded. He dipped
his fingers in a bowl and stuffed his mouth full of meat,
motioning to the others to do the same. The child scooted
over to sit with its head against Wulf's shoulder and fed
itself with one hand and the dog with the other.

When the meat and drink were gone, the chief sat back
and began to speak, slowly because there were some
differences between the Pechenegs' tongue and the old
language of the Bulgars that Brother Gregory knew.

"The chieftain of the Norse is welcome in the yurt of
Sarak, the khan of the Pechenegs," Brother Gregory translated. "This is the khan's sister Temulun, and the sister's
son Tulu, whose life is owed to the chieftain of the Norse.
They are grateful."

"The nephew of Sarak will be a great man when he is
grown," Haakon said. He bowed solemnly to the child.

"My spirits have told me so. I am glad to have served him."

Brother Gregory looked slightly startled at that, but he translated it, and the child's mother beamed proudly and ruffled the baby's hair. She was pretty, Haakon decided, when he got used to the brown skin and the slightly slanted eyes. Donal appeared to think so too, Haakon noticed, and decided he would have to keep a hand on Donal's collar while they were in the Pecheneg camp. Likely the woman had a husband somewhere, and Haakon didn't trust Donal's affection for Fann to keep him celibate. If Haakon had had Fann, he would have bedded other women at every opportunity. He frowned at Donal with a slight shake of his head, and Donal stopped staring at Temulun and stared around him at the inside of the chieftain's yurt instead. Donal spoke neither Greek nor the Turkic tongue of the Pechenegs, so there was little to do but stare while Haakon and Brother Gregory made their proposition.

The yurt was plainly a chieftain's dwelling, even in the harsh conditions in which the Pechenegs lived. The walls were draped with embroidered hangings, and the rugs on the floor were good ones. Bought in Constantinople and stolen from the Rus, Donal suspected. The iron brazier was intricately made, with scrollwork legs, and the bronze drinking cups were incised around the rim with hunting scenes. A great deal of stolen wealth passed through the Pechenegs' hands, Donal thought, but they were nomads with no settled economy, and mostly they used it for adornment. He looked around him interestedly for the silver-banded skull cups that Prince Oleg's men had talked about, but he didn't see any. At least it appeared that they wouldn't go that road themselves. As Haakon and Brother Gregory talked, Sarak, the Pechenegs' khan, grew more interested. He leaned forward, chin on hand, and once he shouted for a slave to bring a tray of damp sand, where Haakon drew a map with a pointed stick.

Finally the matter appeared to be concluded to everyone's satisfaction, and Donal watched, startled, as Sarak drew a red silk bag out of the front of his tunic, and presented it to Haakon with what was almost a bow.

Haakon opened it and drew out a necklace of pale turquoise medallions, blue as a bird's egg, linked with gold.
The khan spoke solemnly, and Brother Gregory translated.
"He says that it is magic and has great powers in the East."
The medallions were flat and carved in curved patterns,
like the jade Haakon had seen in Mikligard, which came
from Cathay. It was plainly a piece of great value. It was
also, among the Norse, an ornament such as women wore.
Haakon fastened it around his neck and gave Donal a look
that dared him to make remarks. In his Pecheneg clothes
and the turquoise necklace, the jarl had a decidedly
Eastern look. Donal salaamed gravely and hid a grin as
Haakon glared at him.

The necklace was not to seal the treaty, although a
treaty had been made, but was a personal gift from Sarak
to the man of the North who had pulled small Tulu from
the river. Sarak had no sons, it seemed, and Tulu would be
khan after him, Brother Gregory said.

"These people place great value on their children. They
lead a harsh life here, and death is easy. The children are
their continuance."

That Sarak also remembered Haakon from the fight
above *Aifor* made no difference. The Pechenegs had a
healthy respect for a man who could fight, and it was the
Rus, not the Norse, who were the enemies of their blood,
the Rus who had left Pecheneg dead unburied. Haakon
had seen through the Pechenegs' feint, where the Rus had
not, and that marked him as a war leader to be reckoned
with—a man to follow. It had been a good fight, by *Aifor*,
and the khan of the Pechenegs and the jarl of the Norsemen
refought it, laughing now, over a campfire, while Brother
Gregory translated and looked scandalized. And Haakon
continued to wear the necklace and the finely embroidered Pecheneg clothes, while Sarak called in his men and
armed them for war. The Norse knew better than to make
remarks about their jarl's clothes, but Haakon suspected
there would be fine stories later, around the hearth fire in
the winter, when there were no outsiders present to hear.
For now, greatly outnumbered, they eyed the Pechenegs

with a wary respect, and even Hjalmar Sitricsson grew impressed as he watched Sarak's tribe gather.

They came in from the outlying pastures, on shaggy, agile little ponies, with yurts and families loaded onto wagons behind them. They carried spears and knives, but their best weapon was the bow. Even boys of six could hit a moving target from a running pony. Where the men went, the women and children and the herds were not far behind, moving, always moving, in search of new graze, new arable fields, pressured always from behind by the Rus and the other nomads of the steppe. They were fierce, harsh as the things that drove them; when Haakon headed the dun horse southwest again three days later, he rode at the head of an army he would have been willing to bring against almost any enemy. The golden ax was slung across his back, lovingly polished, and he thought that there was a feel in the air now that hadn't been there before—the smell of victory in the wind. He had very little doubt of his war-luck now.

The Norse towered above the khan's people, but the plain behind them was black with their ponies. There are few worse ways to fight a battle than slogging it out hand-to-hand in the broiling sun until one side is dead. That was the way of many of the armies of Europe of that day, but it was not the way of the Norse, nor was it the way of the khan's people. Like the Norse, they were raiders, as fast-moving on their ponies as the Norse were in their dragon ships, able to strike and go and strike again. They lacked only organization, Haakon thought, and a small band could terrorize a whole countryside.

Haakon had sent three of his men for couriers, three hours apart and by different routes, to tell Symeon, king of the Bulgars, where the Norse and the Pechenegs would strike. He had left it to Symeon what to do about that—a commander of auxiliaries does not give orders to a king— but Haakon remembered the hawk-look under the jeweled crown and decided he had very little to worry about. Symeon of the Bulgars was a warlord like the ancient khans of his people before they began to call themselves kings and live in cities. Symeon would be waiting for him.

Wulf was in his usual place at the dun horse's heel, the two beasts having negotiated a compromise: The dun horse would not kick, and Wulf would not bite him. Donal rode beside them, whistling cheerfully, with his harp well wrapped in a blanket on a packhorse's saddle. Donal would risk his hide in battle, but never his harp. Brother Gregory lurched along on his mule on the other side, between Sarak Khan and the jarl, and hoped that his interpreter's skills would not be called for in the battle itself. That was cowardly, and he prayed fervently for fortitude, but it was slow in coming. He had said mass that morning for Donal and himself and heard the Scot's confession in Latin, which had been less shocking than he would have thought, for a man who had lived so long among the heathen.

Haakon, seeing how Brother Gregory's thoughts lay, leaned down and said gently, "When the fighting starts, old father, I want you back with the baggage. We have our signals, the khan and I, and a fight is no place for the White Christ's priests." Norse priests were warriors like the rest, but Haakon had raided a monastery once, in England, and learned that Christian priests were useless. He decided he had best not explain his knowledge to Brother Gregory.

"There have been some," Brother Gregory said. "Great men of God, warriors in their faith. Alas, I fear I am not one."

"No matter," Haakon said. "You've done what you came for. I expect your king will be grateful."

"We are not allowed to accept reward in this world," Brother Gregory said. "But for the monastery—a new bell, perhaps." He smiled, suddenly content. A new bell, to the glory of God, and his fortitude now as the price of it. A reason for courage.

Haakon shook his head, baffled. He had the Norseman's instinctive dislike of Christians, but he had learned a certain tolerance from Rosamund. Brother Gregory was a brave old soul, in his way. Haakon thought that Donal had gone to Brother Gregory's mass more out of kindness to the monk than anything else, although Donal had said cheerfully afterward that he had confessed all his sins and

could now take on more without overloading God's tolerance. Still, the things that Christians considered sins were
a constant source of wonder to Haakon.

The Pechenegs came down on the Magyar villages like
wolves hunting through a sheepfold when the shepherds
are gone. As the smoke rose from the first of the burning
villages, Haakon saw Sarak lift his bow in triumph with the
same shrill cry Haakon remembered howling in his ears
above *Aifor*. The baggage and the rear guard caught up,
and the survivors from the village, women and children
mostly, were sorted out. They would be slaves now, but
they still had to be cared for. There had not been many.
The Magyars fought back with a ferocity to match the
Pechenegs, and the flaming village was sickening with the
smell of burning flesh. The Pechenegs and the Norse
moved on.

They swept through the Magyar lands like a Hel-Wind,
behind the grim, fierce figure of Sarak Khan. The Magyars
had not been settled here long, but since they had come,
there had grown up a considerable debt to pay between
Pecheneg and Magyar for stolen women and slaughtered
herds. Behind the khan rode Haakon the Dark and his
fifty Norsemen, not overly happy on their horses, but with
ax and spear reddened from blade to haft. The golden ax
gleamed through the blood, and with every blow he
struck, Haakon said silently in his mind, *Harud Olafsson*.
The pattern of fate, so darkly shrouded by the Norns from
the eyes of men, blazed like the axhead in his mind now.
From the Pechenegs to the Magyars to the Bulgars to Leo.
And when Leo saw that Harud's Magyars had lost their
usefulness, he would throw Harud to the wolves that were
hunting him. Haakon thought he knew Leo well enough
to be sure of that.

"Yaaaaahhh!" The Pechenegs rode for the next Magyar
village. Haakon raised the golden ax and shouted a praise
to Thor Odinsson, which rang above the high, harsh cries
of the khan's horsemen.

With the knowledge that their own lands were burning
behind them, the Magyars demanded passage north across

the river by the emperor Leo's fleet. They asked it at
sword point, and in that fashion they got it. When the
admiral of the fleet saw the Pecheneg horsemen approaching
from one direction, and King Symeon's heavy cavalry and
the Bulgarian fleet from the other, the reason became
clear. The admiral threw his orders to the wind and rowed
for his life. With the milling confusion of the Magyars
between Symeon's fleet and the emperor's, the emperor's
ships got clear, shielded by the raging curtain of their
mysterious secret weapon. The Greek Fire was shot from
long iron tubes at stern and bow and burned hellishly on
the water. One of Symeon's ships went up like a torch, but
the rest hung back and let the emperor's galleys go.

It was the Magyars that they wanted. At truce with the
emperor Leo, Symeon had taken his entire army, infantry
and heavy cavalry, to hammer the Magyars back into the
Pechenegs' reach. Now he sat, in gilded armor, lance in
hand, astride a black war-horse and watched the Magyars
crumble and the retreat become a rout. The Norsemen
were riding with the Pechenegs, and they sat their horses
unhandily, but they fought as the Norse always did, in a
red, half-berserk rage, cutting like a scythe through anything that stood in their way. Symeon saw the dark-bearded
jarl swing his ax around his head and cut a man nearly in
half.

The god was alive in the axhead as he had been before.
Haakon's arm felt tireless, and he knew that the strength
was not his own. He had made his peace with Thor, and
he knew that something else had been settled between
them as well: Haakon Olesson would have no more doubts
of the god's hand on him, and Thor would give him his
vengeance. A Magyar warrior, lips drawn back in a grin of
fury, leapt at him, and the ax swung up and sliced downward through his helmet. There was blood everywhere.
The ax handle was slippery with it. But the Magyars were
moving, herded together against their will by the onslaught of the Bulgarian army and the bows of the Pechenegs.

In the end they broke and ran. As the battle rage died
down in him and the bone-deep weariness that comes
when there is no further need for strength took its place,
Haakon looked slowly around the battlefield.

The Magyars were no more. Their lands were swept clean, and their fighting men lay twisted among the far smaller numbers of the Pecheneg and Bulgarian dead. The ones who had run were scattered, leaderless. They might wander for months in the mountains before they began to regroup.

Haakon slid down from his horse and cut a piece from a dead Magyar's tunic to clean his ax. A shadow fell across the ground, and he looked up to see Symeon, king of Bulgaria, with blood on his gilded armor and blood on his lance, and the hawk-look bright in the dark eyes under his helmet. The emperor Leo had best look to his borders, Haakon thought.

X Symeon and Leo

They were burning the bodies; already Symeon's army was saddled and ready to move south. The carrion birds circled above them, floating silently. Haakon felt a tug at his trouser leg and found the child Tulu smiling up at him. The women, children, and the herds had caught up to the army, and the Pechenegs would stay here for a while, Sarak Khan had said—there was good graze and loot from the blackened Magyar villages. Tulu tugged at Haakon's trouser leg again and held out his arms insistently. Haakon scooped him up.

The child seemed less interested in the grisly leavings of the battlefield around him—war was the way of his people, after all—than in the fair-skinned, dark-bearded man who had pulled him from the river and who owned the wonderful dog. Tulu pulled something from his shirt front and held it out. It was a scrap of dirty silk, and inside was a bird's egg, as blue as the turquoise in the necklace Sarak Khan had given to Haakon. A hole had been carefully punched in either end and the egg blown out of it. A treasure, plainly. Haakon admired it solemnly and tried to hand it back. Tulu shook his head and pushed it again at Haakon. Then, suddenly shy, he buried his head in Haakon's

shoulder. It was Tulu's own gift, Haakon realized, as great a
treasure in its way as the turquoise necklace, which had come
from Cathay. Haakon nodded and put it carefully in the pouch
that hung from his belt. Tulu smiled and then wriggled down
from Haakon's arms. Wulf was nosing about the remains of a
cookfire, and Tulu trotted toward him purposefully. He wanted
to say good-bye to the wonderful dog, too.

Haakon watched him indulgently. Two bitches from the
motley pack of dogs that belonged to the khan had been in
heat, and Wulf had gallantly made love to them both, so
Haakon expected that he had probably left Tulu a present
as well.

"You have made a friend of the little khan," Brother
Gregory said, coming up to his elbow. His brown robe was
dusty, and his mild, lined face looked weary with the
passage of events too strong for his cloistered soul. But he
eyed the Norseman thoughtfully. A man who had it in him
to be kind to the little ones had a great capacity for good in
the world. "What did you mean when you told Sarak that
your spirits had said that this one would be a great man?"

Haakon shook his head. "I don't think I could explain it,
old father. My gods are too different from yours." But he
felt the golden ax almost like a live hand on his back.

Brother Gregory sighed. He would have liked to con-
vert this Norseman; surely a work to honor God, that
would be. But Gregory was as sure as he was of his own
faith that it wasn't worth trying. "The king wishes you to
come to him before we ride," he said. "He has a gift to
give you and, I think, also an offer to make."

For a moment Haakon watched Tulu tumbling in the
dust with Wulf and then turned to follow Gregory. He
wondered if King Symeon's gift could be a greater thing
than the bird's blue egg, and he doubted it.

The king's gilded armor was clean again and polished,
and there was a gold crown with pearls in it set around his
helmet. Haakon felt trail worn and scruffy in his rusted
mail under the gold and white stripes of the king's silk
tent. A slave poured two delicate silver goblets full of
wine, and Haakon drank his sparingly.

"Stay with my army, Haakon Olesson," Symeon said

suddenly. "I will give you a commission and anything you wish out of the loot of Constantinople." There were only the two of them. Symeon had shooed the slaves and Brother Gregory away, and he spoke carefully in Greek for Haakon's benefit.

Haakon raised his eyebrows. "You are so sure you can take the city?"

Symeon laughed. "To be honest, no. But we will give Leo great trouble, and it is going to cost him dearly. Dearly enough to pay any price you ask."

"With respect, no," Haakon said. "My quarrel is not so much with Leo as with the man who is hiding under his purple skirts. The debt I owed Leo has been paid, I think. I saw his fleet go yelping downriver for home. And I have a home to go to, too, when I am done here. If I don't sail soon, I won't make it by winter."

"*Mmmm.* I would have preferred to stay friends with Sarak Khan," Symeon said, "and I think you might have ensured that. Now he will raid my borders."

"Not if you keep good patrols," Haakon said. He looked at the heavy scale armor and plumed helmet of a cavalry officer going by. "Sarak is no fool. It will still be easier for them to raid the Rus on the Dnieper."

"Where will you go now, then?" Symeon said.

"Back to Leo," Haakon said. "I expect I will find him in a somewhat different frame of mind as regards Harud Olafsson. It was Harud who thought of the Magyars."

"I see," Symeon said. "No Magyars, no use for Harud. Very likely. Also, the Magyars have angered *me*, and he will lay that at Harud's door. Leo is a practical man. I knew him when we were boys—my father sent me to be educated at *his* father's court. He was like that then. The old emperor had very little use for him; he had a maggot in his head that Leo wasn't his son, and once he nearly had him killed. I think he would have if he had lived longer. That sort of life makes a man practical very fast." Symeon drained his goblet and looked thoughtful. Weighing the chances of persuading him, Haakon thought, and giving it up. "Very well, then. If I cannot change your mind, what will you take for reward? I promised anything in reason, and I pay my debts."

Symeon hadn't thought he would have to keep that

promise when he had made it, Haakon thought. The king
had thought the chances much better that Haakon would
end up as a cup for Sarak Khan to drink from. Haakon
decided it would be best to be conservative. "Enough
silver to reprovision my ships, and a mail shirt for any man
of my band who doesn't have one who fought for you. Also
the loan of your horses from here to the coast. If you will
send a man of yours with them, we will send them back
from there."

"That is little enough," Symeon said. "What for yourself?"

"Only that you break your truce with Leo."

"That is *my* war and will be done anyway. If I do not
reward you, it will be said that I am a miserly king, and
that is no good reputation to have when I wish to keep an
army content. You will not refuse gold if it is offered?"

"I have eaten and drunk with the king of the Bulgars,"
Haakon said solemnly. "I could not refuse."

"Very well then."

"As the king wishes." Haakon bowed low and went away
chuckling. A man who had made it a point of honor to be
generous often found himself more generous than he had
intended. There would be more gold pried from Symeon
by *not* asking, Haakon thought.

"Haakon Olesson!"

Haakon swung around.

"When you meet with our cousin Leo, give him our
best wishes!" Symeon shouted. He looked cheerful and
dangerous. Behind him, slaves were already beginning to
pull down the gold and white tent.

"There is fighting, Basileus. Bad fighting. The Bulgars
have broken their truce." The dusty courier pulled himself
up from the porphyry floor and knelt before Leo VI. The
messenger had not even taken time to put on clean
clothes, and no one had asked him to. "The general sends
to know your orders."

"Our orders?" Leo's normally mild face was furious, and
the pearl drops on his crown shook. "Our orders are to
push that son of a caravan whore back across his borders!"
Leo liked bad news no better than any other ruler, and
being made a fool of even less. He had just concluded an

explosive interview with the admiral of the Danube fleet, and the courier's message was not unexpected. That did not render it welcome. Leo gripped the golden arms of his throne and glared at the courier. "Our orders are to level Preslav. Our orders are to win this war or we will find another general!"

The courier shook in his boots, and Leo made an explosive noise and got a grip on his temper. "You have our leave to go!"

The courier fled, and Leo swung around to face Stylian Zautzes. The guardsmen behind him stared straight ahead, wisely appearing blind and deaf. "We have further orders. The fools who decided to tinker with the customhouse—yours, were they not, Zautzes?—get rid of them before we find them." He stared at Zautzes blackly. "If the lady Zoe talks us out of it, we will not get rid of *you* as well. But she had best be persuasive."

Zautzes gritted his teeth. "Yes, Basileus."

"And send us Harud Olafsson."

Stylian Zautzes's dark face was nearly as vengeful as the emperor's. "Gladly, Basileus."

The three ships lifted their wings to the breeze, southward to the Bosporus again. Wulf sniffed the sea air happily and barked at a gull as it swooped overhead. Wulf took to voyaging in a manner most unlike a dog. Knut was in the hold, happily rummaging in the chests King Symeon had sent aboard, while Haakon took the helm. There was enough gold and silver in coin and odd bits of plate and jewelry to double the profits of the voyage—not bad pay for a few saddle sores.

"Likely we won't be allowed back in the harbor," Knut announced gloomily, but his heart wasn't in it. The chests of coin had cheered him immensely, and if Jarl Haakon could turn the Bulgarians' war around, no doubt he could solve a problem like getting back into Mikligard. The longer he sailed with Haakon, the more Knut decided that the jarl was an extraordinary man. There were two wounded among the Norse, but no dead. Haakon's war-luck was still with him.

"Ah, then, they won't be knowing it was us that turned

the Pechenegs on their Magyars," Donal said. "The emperor will be keeping his temper for Harud Olafsson, I'm
thinking. The emperor let himself get restful, like, with
the truce and all, and Symeon took him by surprise. If he
hasn't fed Harud to the crocodiles in his zoo yet, he'll be
glad enough to feed him to the jarl instead."

Haakon didn't say anything. He leaned on the tiller and
watched the headland, which rose above the channel of
the Bosporus and grew slowly larger in the distance. He
could feel Harud Olafsson getting closer, vengeance getting closer. The thought crossed his mind that Harud
Olafsson was an evil thing, but a little one, insignificant in
the world and perhaps not worth the trouble of this
vengeance. A man who always hid behind another was not
a proper enemy. Haakon shrugged his shoulders. It didn't
matter. He wanted Harud anyway. Even Thor, it seemed,
had decided that if Haakon wanted Harud that badly, he
should have him. The ax, slung across his back as always,
was still, but Haakon was sure now that the god was there.
He was only waiting until Haakon finished with Harud.

"It is not my f-f-fault, Basileus!" Harud said desperately.
He could feel fear clawing at his throat, and he began to
stutter.

"You are not implying, are you, Norseman, that it is the
fault of the emperor of New Rome, the chosen of God?" A
chastened and vengeful Stylian Zautzes stood behind the
golden throne and bared his teeth a little as he spoke. His
own position was precarious, resting solely on his daughter's long legs, amber skin, and the things she could do to
keep Leo happy. Later, the emperor would realize that
except for this mistake Zautzes was an able minister; for
now, Leo had been humiliated by an upstart khan of the
Bulgars and was in no mood to take the long view.

"The Magyars did as I said they would!" Harud said. He
looked at Leo. The emperor's face was unreadable. "It is
not my fault that the Bulgars found other allies!"

"The Magyars were your idea," Leo said flatly. "Perhaps
in the sight of God a bad one, unworthy of us. We do not
find your counsel to be useful now."

Harud had a bad temper. When he was in command, he

had always given it free rein. Now, as a supplicant, he found it hard to control, and his nerves were lashed raw with fear. "You found it useful enough before," he snapped, "when you wished me to do your work for you! It was *I* who went to the Magyars and risked my skin in their camps, not you! Is this the way you repay me now?"

Leo's hands clenched, the guards behind him stiffened, and Harud knew that he had gone too far.

Gray Goose bobbed outside the harbor chain, with *Curlew* and *Gull Wing* in her wake. A patrol craft scuttled like a beetle, oars out, across the water to them. The officer on board was the same young man who had come out to them the first time that Haakon had sailed into Mikligard's waters. He recognized Haakon and saluted cheerfully as he came across the boarding plank onto *Gray Goose*.

"Pleasant to see you again, Captain. I rather think you're expected."

Haakon raised his eyebrows in surprise, but he didn't ask any questions. If the emperor knew who was the cause of his current military troubles, then the emperor's officers were peculiarly friendly. On the other hand, if Leo didn't know Haakon had been mixing in his war with the Bulgars, there was no reason for Leo to expect to see Haakon's face again in Mikligard. For all Leo knew, Haakon should be halfway up the Dnieper to Koenugard by now. Haakon decided that caution was in order. If he was expected, his welcome might be one he wasn't going to care for.

"We've had orders to find you a good lodging if you put into port again," the officer said. "But your men'll have to stay outside. The truce with Bulgaria's gone to hell, and we're touchy just now about security."

Stranger and stranger. Haakon waited to see if he could feel the pricking on the back of his neck that sometimes meant danger, but nothing came. Haakon was suspicious by nature. He narrowed his eyes at the officer while he puzzled it out. He had expected to have to argue his way back into Mikligard; now they were bowing him in through the gates. It wasn't for love of Haakon Olesson, and Haakon didn't *think* it was only to lure him to his death.

They could have done that just by burning his ships in the
harbor with the Greek Fire that Leo's vessels carried.
None of the Rus were still in Mikligard to object.

"I don't want lodging," Haakon said finally. "I want an
audience with your emperor."

"Certainly. That will have been arranged." The officer
seemed to notice Haakon's growing mistrust at that, and
smiled. "Your ships were sighted before you were into the
channel, you know." He coughed apologetically. "If you'll
pardon me, Captain, these are busy times. Will you come
aboard? We'll take you straight to the palace harbor." He
looked at Haakon's water-stained shirt and breeches. "I
should, uh, change my clothes first, though."

Haakon put on his best, blue wool with fine braiding
around the wrists and hem, and a quantity of gold jewelry.
Whatever was happening, it didn't seem threatening, and
the young officer looked more amused than anything else.
When Haakon crossed the boarding plank onto the patrol
craft, Wulf padded at his heel and the officer didn't object,
so Haakon let him come.

The patrol boat put out oars and shot across the blue
waters of the harbor. Fat gulls sat on the swells. Behind
him, Haakon could see Donal and Knut leaning over the
bow of *Gray Goose*, twin mirrors of suspicion. Haakon
tried to make himself receptive to any evil thoughts that
might be emanating from the patrol officer, but try as he
would, he couldn't achieve any impression other than that
a joke was in it somewhere—not at his expense, but not
for his benefit, either.

The patrol craft circled south along the sea wall of the
city and through the marble gates that guarded the Boucoleon
harbor, where the emperor's private yachts lay moored.
Haakon set himself not to be impressed, but it was hard.
On the wooded slope of the palace grounds above the
seawall, a lighthouse soared up, and beside it, marble
stairs ran down to the quay. The quay was marble, too,
decorated with sculpture, and everywhere were slaves
scrubbing the sea stains away. The emperor's imperial
yacht was moored at the quayside. It had a red and purple
canopy with gold fringe, and curtains that could be let
down against the weather. Tables and silk-covered couches

were bolted to the deck, and as the patrol boat drew near, Haakon could see more slaves scuttling along the quay with bowls of fresh fruit and tall silver ewers.

The sun was broiling hot, but there was a brisk little sea breeze, and the patrol officer turned his face toward it gratefully. Haakon looked with a certain sympathy at the man's iron helmet. He had left his own and his mail on *Gray Goose*. They wouldn't have been much real use here, and he had decided not to insult the emperor by putting on mail, under the patrol officer's eye.

A crowd of brightly colored figures appeared at the top of the steps, and the officer snapped to attention and nudged his passenger. "An informal audience, as I understand it," he said. "But don't forget you're speaking to the emperor."

The emperor of New Rome, Leo the Sixth, Basileus, languidly descended the stairs, his courtiers behind him like a flock of bright attendant birds. Haakon decided his own expression probably resembled a country lout at his first midsummer market fair. He closed his mouth and tried to stop gaping. He had seen the palace complex before and had even been warned by Ragnar about a mechanical throne, which was installed in the main reception room. It could, so Ragnar said, suddenly lift its occupant to the ceiling and leave the supplicant below, gazing at the emperor's boots and looking foolish. But now it was the immensity of this one man's power that was borne in on Haakon. Leo was slight and graceful, not a tall man, and the palace grounds seemed to spread unendingly around him, dwarfing him at the center of the guards and pages and fan bearers who attended him. And yet it was all his, and so was the gold and white city beyond it, and the lands beyond that. Now that he had actually beaten the emperor at his own game—maybe—Haakon fully realized what it was that he had challenged.

The patrol officer poked him in the ribs again and hissed at him to bow. Haakon obediently flattened himself. It made him grit his teeth, but some things were not possible to argue with.

"Ah, the Norseman," Leo said, inspecting him. "We were just going to take in the sea air. Do come with us."

He swept along the marble quay and across the boarding plank, which was laid with carpet and bordered with gold pots full of bright, unfamiliar blooms.

Haakon and the patrol officer followed. Haakon didn't believe in coincidence, and the patrol officer had as good as said that the emperor awaited him. More and more he thought that Leo was setting the stage for something. Leo arranged himself in a gilt and ivory chair, and a small black page settled the purple folds of the emperor's gown about him. Two more pages waved fans, which seemed to be made entirely of peacocks' tail feathers.

"You may sit."

Haakon sat gingerly on the edge of a couch upholstered in opalescent blue silk. The patrol officer stood at attention behind him. Whatever Leo was planning, Haakon decided that it wasn't murder. The emperor of New Rome didn't bloody his own hands. Or the upholstery of the imperial yacht. Wulf seemed unconcerned as well. He sank down at Haakon's feet and put his nose on his paws. Two seamen unmoored the barge from the quay, and there was a rattle below the deck as the oars were run out. The rowers must have been on board already. The barge moved in stately fashion past the marble harbor walls.

"You came to us once before," Leo said conversationally. "We confess that we did rather expect to see you back."

"Why was that, Basileus? We had your order to leave the city." Haakon decided he might as well be blunt. He thought it was the answer Leo was expecting.

Leo smiled, a man with a good joke. "Ah, but you struck us as a persistent man. Also, to be honest, our spies came back to say that the other Rus went home, but that your ships were beached on the coast."

Haakon stiffened. How good were Leo's spies? "I told you, I came for Harud Olafsson. We waited to see if we couldn't think of a way to change your mind, Basileus."

"And did you?"

"No. But when we heard from the fisherfolk that the Magyars were driven back, we thought you might have less use for Harud. And so we came back to see."

Leo looked even more amused. "Ah, you should have been more patient still, Norseman. When you came back here in so great a hurry, did you not pass any traffic in the channel?"

Haakon thought: Leo's patrol craft, fishing boats, a few of the little log boats that the Slavs built... "Some, Basileus," he said, the source of Leo's amusement beginning to dawn on him.

"Your quarry, Norseman. Rowing north with the devil behind him. You should have looked more carefully."

Haakon ground his teeth. "I had no reason to, Basileus." No reason to suspect that Leo would take his attentions from his war just to arrange an elaborate hunt, with Harud for the quarry and Haakon for the hound. He wondered what Harud had done to provoke Leo so far. Harud would be running in sheer terror now, Haakon thought.

Leo looked satisfied. He reached out a delicate hand for a peach from a gold bowl and began to eat it. "Ah, well, we daresay you can still catch him."

"They gave him a log boat and two slaves and turned him adrift!" Haakon said. He slammed his fist into the bow planks and then stuck it in his mouth because he had hit a nail. "And now they are using *me* for the hound to catch him, while they sit on their fat rears and amuse them-selves with the idea!"

"Well, you annoyed them, you know," Donal said prac-tically. "The emperor wouldn't have taken to that. I expect he thought you owed him some for it. It took some imagination to think it all out. Also a good spy," he added thoughtfully, "or he couldn't be sure you'd be back to hear about it."

"If his spy were all that good, he'd have told his emperor we'd been with Symeon," Haakon growled.

"How are you knowing he didn't?" Donal grinned. "Like I said, he seemed to be thinking you owed him something."

Haakon swung around and looked at the receding sky-line of Mikligard, gold on its promontory in the evening sun. "He said . . . he said when I'd caught Harud, to come back if I'd a mind for a post in his army."

Donal whistled. "A practical man, that. And would you?"

"I'd sooner serve Harald Fairhair," Haakon said. "Him at least I understand. We will catch Harud, and then we will go home. I want to see my wife."

"But all that gold, jarl," Donal said, prodding him out of his black mood. "Doesn't it call to you at all, then?"

Haakon's scowl faded, and he started to laugh. "It does, Donal, but it would take an army." Plainly, if he went back, it would be with no mind for serving the emperor. "If I should ever have one. . . ." He shrugged. "For now, we will catch Harud and go home. I am getting weary of this."

Weary enough so that it was only his vengeance oath that pushed him on? Donal wondered. Harud Olafsson seemed to grow smaller as they chased him. Now he was only a terrified man in a log boat.

XI Harud Olafsson

They passed through Pecheneg lands again with no trouble—Sarak Khan's folk were still in the Magyars' country and had a peace-oath with Haakon in any case—although it was a wearisome journey upriver, with more portage than the downward trip. The absence of the Pechenegs from their accustomed haunts would have made Harud's journey easier too, of course. Haakon's ships reached Koenugard without a smell of him, and with Haakon nearly frothing at the mouth for fear Harud had taken some other route.

Ragnar the Noseless was waiting for them in Koenugard, and he came stalking down the riverbank almost as soon as Haakon had beached his ships.

"I thought you'd be away home by now." Haakon dropped down over Gray Goose's side, with Wulf beside him. Wulf butted his head into Ragnar's hand to be scratched.

"Huh! I'd a mind to know what you've been doing," Ragnar said. "Also maybe to protect you from the Rus, who are still in a temper for being thrown out of Mikligard like thieves."

"And did you have to fight between Berezany and

here?" Haakon got behind *Gray Goose* with the rest of the crew and pushed her farther up on the sand.

"No, we didn't!" Ragnar shouted over the noise. "And I'd a mind to know the why of that, too." His expression softened some as Haakon came back, wiping wet hands on his trousers. "I'm glad to see your thick hide in one piece, and I'll buy you a pot of beer while you tell me what in Odin's name you've been doing. Then we will go and tell Prince Oleg, and likely that will get the Rus off your tail."

"For drawing the Pechenegs off... maybe," Haakon said. "But they'll be back next season. That river is too good a reiving place to let alone."

"No, it's Harud Olafsson's head that Oleg wants."

"Thor's fire take him!" Haakon realized that no one had seen Harud in Koenugard, then. "I don't have it! And if the Rus feel like fighting me over Mikligard, let them." He looked like a man who wanted to fight *someone*.

Donal came up and put a hand on Haakon's shoulder. "Come and drink beer, jarl, since Ragnar has been rash enough to offer. We'll find Harud, I'm thinking. Look you, where else can that weasel have *gone* but north?"

"As many roads as there are stars in the sky, no doubt," Haakon scowled, but he let them lead him up the river walk into the town and settle him in an alehouse, with a pot in his hand.

When Haakon had told his tale, Ragnar concurred with Donal. "There *are* no other roads that Harud could take. The Magyars wouldn't hide him, even if he could find what's left of them. He won't stay anywhere near Mikligard— it's a fair bet that Leo told him he was setting you on his trail, to amuse himself. Leo is like that. And Harud won't linger in Pecheneg country just to find out why the Pechenegs aren't there. He'll thank the gods and keep running. He'll skirt around Koenugard most likely, to hide his tracks and because Oleg doesn't love him, but he'll keep on north—to Jarl Thjodulf in Sweden, who brought him here last year, would be my guess."

Ragnar proved to be right, although Haakon fidgeted for three days while they were proving it. Oleg told his merchants and his *druzhina* to keep the peace with Haakon

and be thankful for their safe passage home. Then Oleg
sent his spies out, and they came back to say that Harud
Olafsson had skirted around Koenugard through the outlying Slavic villages, stolen food and what little silver he
could find, and gone on. Harud had only two men with
him, but they had been fighting men before some evil had
landed them in the Mikligard slave market. Harud was
still a jarl, and for all the villagers knew, he might have
been under Prince Oleg's protection, as he had claimed.
(Oleg swore nearly as loudly as Haakon at that.) Harud, in
fear for his life, had the ferocity of a rabid dog, and the
villagers had been too afraid of him to protest.

Haakon, Ragnar, and Prince Oleg sat down for a council
of war.

"I am nearly certain that he has gone to Thjodulf," Oleg
said. He rubbed his red-gold beard thoughtfully. He was
still not admitting to any personal quarrel with Harud
because it might annoy his wife. Her temper was touchy at
best, as befitted her station, and Oleg wished peace in his
house. But the matter of the Slav villages, where Harud
had been thieving—they were under the prince's protection, and that was reason enough for the prince to meddle.
"I will give you a letter of friendship that will set my hand
against any Rus who raid your ships," Oleg said finally.
"And a letter to Thjodulf, although I am not sure how
much good that will do. He has made his last trip through
my lands anyway, and he is a stubborn old soul."

"It will be worth having anyway," Haakon said. He
could always fight Thjodulf if he had to. He thought he
would rather deal with a Swedish jarl than with any more
princes and emperors, who switched their loyalties the
way most men changed their shirts and then thought of
elaborate reasons why they had done so. "I will send you
word when Harud is dead," he added politely.

Oleg's eyes hardened just for an instant, and Haakon
saw a hatred in them that went clear to the brain. Then
the prince arranged his expression carefully and nodded.
"Thank you. There were only Slavs in that village, but
they are my folk all the same. Harud Olafsson is a beast I
do not wish to have running loose in my lands any longer."

Haakon was suddenly grateful to be only a jarl and not a

prince with alliances to keep him tethered and make him tell lies to himself. Donal was right: To be a ruler was like walking on a rope, and it was far too easy to lose the balance and fall. And if the ruler held the balance, then the strain of it would kill him one day, Haakon suspected. He praised Thor Odinsson silently for forbidding him a crown and looked at Oleg with a certain amount of sympathy.

"My thanks for the safe-conduct. Ragnar, shall I leave a ship and some men with you, for the escort I promised, or do you come with us?"

Ragnar scratched the old scars of his nose and got to his feet. "Oh, I am coming, Haakon. I am wishing now I had gone with you to the Bulgars. Donal will make a fine song of that, and I will not be in it. So now I will stay to the end."

They left in the morning, heading north for Gnezdovo, sails spread and oars out against the current. It was harder going, but once they had passed Gnezdovo and the marshes between the Dnieper and the Dvina, they would have the current in their favor again. They wouldn't catch up to Harud until then, Haakon thought. Three men in a little boat would move faster. He spent most of the way to Gnezdovo pacing the deck and scowling northward, until even Knut was jumpy. The third night Donal sat the jarl down by the fire and sang to him, while Ragnar poured enough beer into him that he was too hung over to crawl out of his sleeping bag in the morning. That tactic had an unfortunate effect on the jarl's temper, however, and they didn't repeat it.

All the ships' crews knew that they were racing the coming winter, as well as Harud Olafsson. They wouldn't reach Gnezdovo until the first of October, when by rights they should have been home in Norway. Every day after that, that they spent in hunting Harud, was a day that risked their having to winter here in this alien country, leaving their wives and women to think they had died in Mikligard and to fight off the reivers who thought so too. Haakon knew it as well as any of them, and it was part of the reason he paced.

Harud had been through Gnezdovo and hadn't bothered to hide his presence. Haakon bought a sheep and killed it

on Orm Persson's howe, partly for Orm's spirit, partly for
good weather, and partly to ask Thor Odinsson that Orm
should not have died for nothing, chasing a will-o'-the-
wisp they were never going to catch. Wild grasses had
grown up on the bare mud now, and with the winter rains
there would be moss on the rune-stone that Thorfinn
Solvisson had carved. Haakon thought of the other howe
behind them in the Pecheneg country above *Aifor*, and
gritted his teeth. He would be bringing their widows a
share of the profits when he had sold the trade goods, but
that would be cold comfort to a woman who was expecting
her man to come home. Any man risked death in battle. If
Haakon could come home to say that Harud Olafsson was
dead, there would be justification. If not, the widows
would have fair reason to hate him. The men pushed on
through the marshes to the Dvina, and the jarl's temper
grew more surly each day, until finally only Donal would
come near him. The men were wet and miserable with
tramping through bogland, and their hands were blistered
raw from the towropes, but one look at Haakon was
enough to stop any complaints. They clung stubbornly to
the notion that somehow Jarl Haakon would see them
home by winter. No one wanted to poke a hand in the
dark cloud that hung around Haakon these days.

If Harud Olafsson knew he was pursued, he was too
frightened to hide his tracks. He fled headlong, leaving
traces in the cleared camps along the Dvina, where other
homebound merchants had passed earlier in the season.
At Dvina Mouth he left the log boat and stole a fishing
craft, which was somewhat better able to stand up to an
autumn storm in the Baltic. From there he ran for Sweden
and Jarl Thjodulf Ottarsson's Uppland steading, with Haakon
and foul weather both like Hel-Spirits on his heels.

Jarl Thjodulf was old, and the autumn cold made his
bones ache. He would go viking no more, he thought, on
the river-roads to Mikligard or the whale-roads to the
west. He had outlived and outfought most of the men who
had been born in his year, and if he died a straw death
now by the fire, it would probably be forgiven him. He

stretched his hands to the flames' warmth and let the
women cluck about him and put a rug over his knees.
There had been too many changes, he thought, since he
had first sailed south with the dragon ships. The Rus lands
had all been wild country then, and every man made his
own way through them. Now Oleg held the reins on all
the land around Koenugard, called himself "great prince,"
and honest sailors paid him ship-tax to pass through.
Thjodulf thumped on the floor with the staff with which he
walked now, and shouted for more ale. Even the Magyars,
the wild, untameable folk who had let only Thjodulf
Ottarsson come to trade with them, were no more; en-
ticed into a war they knew nothing about, they were
scattered and destroyed.

Thjodulf's mouth tightened. He had had that news from
a merchant heading home only a week since, as well as all
the season's gossip from Koenugard, and Thjodulf knew
well enough what evil had come down on the Magyars. He
had brought it himself, like a plague ship, in the form of
Harud Olafsson. Gossip said now that Harud had done
worse in Norway and been named outlaw in Birka, but
Norway and Birka could see to their own affairs—indeed,
were already seeing to them if the tale of a Norseman
hunting Harud in Koenugard was also true.

The steward of the house brought the old jarl his ale
himself, and with it the news of a stranger at the steading
gates, asking shelter of Thjodulf Ottarsson. Thjodulf found
that he was not surprised when the man was Harud
Olafsson.

"Why are you here?" The old jarl's voice was steady, but
his gnarled hand shook on his staff. It might have been
with the cold, but Harud Olafsson saw something in the
pale gray eyes that told him it was not.

"To take service, jarl." Harud forced a smile. Outside it
was raining, and his hair was plastered flat around his face.
"If you will let me. Mikligard was fine enough, but I'd a
mind to see the north lands again, and I found you a fair
man to serve."

"I was counted as such," Thjodulf said. "Before I brought
death in my ship to the Magyar folk."

Harud's eyes flicked around the room. He was swaying

on his feet, and he coughed. His two slaves had run away
as soon as the ship had touched Swedish ground. The jarl's
hall was full of thralls and women and half a dozen fighting
men. The steward stood by the jarl's chair, with his spear
in his hand. Harud licked his lips. "The Magyars were
savages," he said.

"They were *mine!*" Thjodulf said. "*Mine, to me!* Too
savage to know what sort of war you drew them into. Now
they are dead."

"I didn't plan on that."

"No." Thjodulf looked at him with grim eyes. The
firelight glowed in the old jarl's white hair and beard. He
looked like a judge come to make a ruling at a Thing that
was just between the two of them. "But it was a small
matter to you, wasn't it—so many lives? I have heard more
since I let you take ship with me. Everything you touch
withers and turns black in your hand. Find another hole to
hide in. You will get no shelter here."

Harud braced himself with one arm against a birch
trunk, panting. He could feel a tight knot in his chest,
which was only partly weariness. The rest was fear. Haakon
would go to Jarl Thjodulf, and Jarl Thjodulf, who was a
soft fool and mourned a tribe of savages, would tell him
where to hunt. Harud would have to find a place to lie low
until Haakon had given it up. Beyond the stand of birch
trees, the high meadow was bare, windswept and rocky, a
desolation for Hel to rule over. Farther north the bare
ground rose sharply into trees, wild mountains where no
man's hand had been. Harud turned and staggered that
way. The wind keened around him, and the sky was
leaden. Winter was coming, wolf-winter, sharp-fanged enough
to bite ships in two. Maybe if he ran far enough, Haakon
would turn back, sail home before he trapped himself in
Sweden for the winter. Haakonstead was a fat land, fat
enough to tempt other jarls who found it unguarded.
Harud pinned his last hope on that and ran on. He hadn't
eaten since the night before, but he was afraid to stop.

Sigurd Njalsson sat in his hall in the Trondelag and
thought much the same thing that Harud Olafsson had.

"Haakonstead's still half-empty, jarl." Thorleif, helmsman of Sigurd Njalsson's warship, grinned at his chief and stuck his wet boots to the fire. "Jarl Haakon won't be home this winter; maybe not at all."

Jarl Sigurd contemplated the possibilities of that. Haakonstead had looked very fine indeed when he had gone there for King Harald in the summer. And since Haakonstead had struck no bargain with Harald, they could expect no defense from him now. In fact, Harald himself was likely enough to be there in the spring, behind a spear.

"Hroald Weather-Eye gives us two weeks before the coastal lanes turn bad too," Thorleif said hopefully. "We could see to the matter now maybe, before King Harald takes a hand."

"And if Harald puts his nose in, it won't be to hand the steading to the widow," Sigurd said. "He'll put it in his own pocket, and then he won't need any friend in the Trondelag. He'll have a foot here himself, and I'll have wasted a whole season spent courting him in Vestfold. I'm thinking you're right." Sigurd nodded at this line of reasoning. "Haakonstead should have a Trondelag jarl."

"Most of the fighting men will have gone away to winter in their own steadings by now," Thorleif said. "But there's Haakon's stepfather upfjord. And what about the widow? Can she hold the men that are left and call the others back?"

Sigurd shook his head. "She's English. You saw her in Haakonstead. I doubt they'd come in to fight for an Englishwoman, with the jarl dead. I'm more worried about that poet he's left as steward, but he can't do much with a handful of men. And the mother and stepfather have lands of their own. The Tronds don't like one house holding too much." Jarl Sigurd picked up his sword and scabbard from the floor beside his chair and laid it comfortably across his knees. "By the time that poet and the Englishwoman can call them in, we'll be sitting in Haakonstead. That makes a strong position to argue the matter from."

"Aye." Thorleif let his fingers run over the blade of his

ax. "As easy as taking milk out of the dairy. Especially if they've decided Jarl Haakon's dead."

"If they haven't," Jarl Sigurd said cheerfully, "they will when I tell them so."

Haakon fidgeted, looking northwest in the moonlight at the white mountains that rose between Uppland and the Trondelag: menacing, impenetrable. Something came out of them and blew down the back of his neck. A voice in his ear seemed to say, *Go home*. He shook it away. It wasn't the god's voice, only his own nerves. He wriggled out of the sleeping bag and sat up, so that Donal woke up too and swore as the cold air came in. Harud Olafsson was only half a day ahead of them now, crawling higher into the wild country.

"What are you looking at?" Donal whispered sleepily.

"The mountains."

"Whatever for?"

Haakon shrugged his shoulders and sat silently, looking off at them.

"It will be the thin air, no doubt, that has got into your brain," Donal said. He was not a man who liked to be awakened.

"The same madness, no doubt, that made me take a Scotsman to go viking with," Haakon said sourly.

Donal looked affronted. "And have I not turned into as satisfactory a thief as a Norseman, then?"

Haakon chuckled suddenly. He never minded it when Donal called him a thief. Donal had a sea rover's instincts himself, for all his pious Christian upbringing. The piety had been all on his mother's side, Haakon had discovered. Donal's father had taken his Tay Valley keep in a war and furnished it finely by raiding the English. "It is only that it is late in the year, and Rosamund may be thinking me dead," he said, looking at the mountains again. "I thought her dead once. It is worse than dying yourself."

Donal's face sobered, awake now. "Fann, too. She'll—I don't know what she'll do if she thinks I'm not coming back."

At least Rosamund wouldn't shriek herself into hysterics, Haakon thought, or take to her bed, both of which seemed likely to be Fann's choice. He remembered Rosamund standing on the battlements of her father's hold, directing arrow fire down onto himself and his men, the first time he'd seen her. If she'd had a bow, she'd have shot him. He came close to asking Donal what strength there was in Fann that bound him so closely to her, but he closed his mouth again. There were some things that couldn't be asked if a man wanted to keep his friendships. "Rosamund will look after her. Don't be worrying." He put a hand on Donal's shoulder, awkwardly.

Donal pulled himself out of the sleeping bag and sat up. "She has a kind heart, your lady. Fann will be all right in her care." He looked contrite. "Ah, then, it is me who is supposed to keep *you* from worrying—what is a harper for?"

"I've often wondered," Haakon said sarcastically, and they both laughed.

"I've made a fine song of the road to Mikligard, so I have. It wants only the ending." Donal whistled softly, a tune that ran forward headlong and stopped. "Tomorrow, I think, we'll be finishing it."

"Finish and be done with it," Haakon said. Harud Olafsson dead, to avenge the trail of evil he'd left behind him; the last of Olaf Haraldsson's seed blotted out, to lay Ole Ketilsson's ghost and Ole's own dead children finally at rest. And then a fast voyage home to take the taste out of his mouth. He wanted to be done with Harud.

Haakon lay back down and tried to sleep, but it wouldn't come. In the end he and Donal sat side by side and watched the sun come up over the hills below them.

Harud ran, stumbling up from the ravine through rock and rough grass turning brown with the autumn cold. They weren't far behind him. He could feel them with his skin, the way a wild pig senses the hounds. He gasped, his breath shuddering in his chest. Jarl Thjodulf wouldn't hide him; the land wouldn't hide him. He looked around him wildly, trees and a cold sun spinning over his head, and sought something, anything, for a shield against Haakon Olesson.

"Harud Olafsson!"

The shout rang out below him, in the rock-strewn ravine.

"I have come for you, Harud! Come out and fight me!"

Harud looked around him frantically. A boulder balanced on the lip of the ravine. He pushed and sent it crashing down. Then he turned and ran into the shadow of the trees. The pine needles broke under his feet like birds' bones.

There was a yelp and a curse from the ravine, and then the deep baying of a hound. Harud dodged among the trees. They gave him no shelter, and the cold sun mocked him. He heard men's voices in the ravine and the scattering of rock as they climbed.

"I have come for you!" Haakon Olesson's voice bellowed up at him.

Harud stumbled and righted himself, half crouching, in the stand of pines, as the pursuers scrambled over the lip of the ravine. There were maybe twenty of them, harsh-faced men, weatherworn, with Haakon the Dark at their head and the great gray hound at his heel. One of the others was limping, Harud saw with satisfaction, and leaning on a comrade's shoulder. Harud got to his feet, his sword out, and pulled up the shield he had dragged with him. He had carried very little else, not even food, and he was still hungry. The sun, alternating with the darkness of the trees, made a pattern like a gameboard, which flashed in his eyes. At the center of the pattern was Haakon Olesson.

The forest hunched into stillness. Harud raised his shield. He had lost his helmet long ago, climbing into this wilderness. His pale eyes blazed at Haakon in a last fury. There was no arguing with death now, no more turns to take, and even Harud knew it. "You take a lot of trouble to avenge a whore," he spat.

Death didn't answer, only lifted his shield and his ax. The axhead shot out light like fire when the sun hit it. Haakon looked at it. "No," he said quietly, not to Harud but to the ax. He turned to another dark-haired man beside him and gave him the ax to hold. Then he looked at Knut One-Eye. "Give me yours."

Knut unslung his ax, and Harud wondered if Haakon

the Dark had a god on his side as it was said and the one-eyed man was Odin All-Father come to take his vengeance. A wind came up from nowhere, and the trees spoke to themselves above him.

Haakon lifted the ax and came at him, and the others ringed them around.

"You are brave, Haakon Olesson, to bring twenty against one," Harud said. His voice was thick with fear.

"No," Haakon said. "Just the two of us, Harud. And the ghosts who want your blood." The dappled light flickered on his mail, and Harud found it hard to see him clearly.

Haakon swung the ax, and it bit into Harud's shield as Harud flung it up to guard his neck. Harud's sword lashed out and grated along Haakon's shield. Harud felt a burning in his stomach from hunger and a rising fury that couldn't quite overpower fear. The ax came down again, and he heard the air sing as it went past his ear. He lashed at Haakon frantically, and Haakon slammed his shield into the blade in a little shower of wood chips. He pushed, and Harud staggered back, feeling the pine needles under his feet, brittle and slippery as glass. His shoes had holes in them, and the pine burrs bit through.

Harud swung again at Haakon's head, and this time it was Haakon who slipped, down on one knee, while the ring of watching men tightened around them, weapons half-out.

"*No!*" Haakon shouted, and even the big gray dog dropped back and crouched, snarling, as Haakon whirled the ax at Harud, rising, and then reversed the blow and struck again, backhanded. Harud reeled back and saw the eyes of the watching men grow hooded, waiting, like judges. The ax crashed into the shield again, and it splintered. For an instant Harud saw Haakon, outlined against the blackness of the trees and the blinding sun, and thought that Jarl Thjodulf looked over Haakon's shoulder. The ax came down into his skull.

Harud's body crumpled slowly, the terror and fury fading from the face as it fell. Haakon looked at Knut's ax. The blade dripped, the blood pooling in the pine needles at his feet. Harud Olafsson was gone. There was only a twisted thing under the trees, with its skull broken open.

Haakon dropped the ax and walked away, his hacked
shield hanging from his hand. The ring of men parted
silently to let him pass. Knut started to follow, but Donal
put a hand on his arm.

"Let him bide for a while."

Wulf sniffed at the blood and howled, a sound that
might have come up from the earth itself, from Hel-Gate
opening to let Harud in.

Ragnar the Noseless came forward stiffly, an odd expression on his face. "I said I would be here at the end, but I
am wondering now if I am glad of that. That was a fight I
will remember at night, in my dreams."

Knut picked up his ax and began to clean the blood
from it. He cocked his one good eye at Donal, who still
held the golden ax in his hand. "Why mine, and not that
one, which he has never fought without since he found
it?"

"This was the jarl's fight," Donal said. "Only his." He
held the golden ax gingerly. "This one has sometimes a
mind of its own."

Haakon had gone no one knew quite where, so they sat
down to wait for him, and Donal put a splint on Hjalmar
Sitricsson's leg. He had twisted it getting out of the way of
the falling boulder. They left Harud lying among the trees
until the jarl should come back and say what to do with
him.

When Haakon had been gone for an hour, Thorfinn
Solvisson slithered back down into the ravine to retrieve
the gear they had left there and doled out salt fish, while
Knut sniffed out a spring-fed stream and filled his helmet
with water.

Hjalmar looked at the golden ax stuck through Donal's
belt. "Why do *you* have that?"

"I'm afraid to put it down," Donal said frankly.

"Where is the jarl?"

"I'm not knowing that any better than you," Donal said.
He sat down, put a piece of fish in his mouth, and cupped
his hand into Knut's helmet for water to wash it down. He
was beginning to think he *did* know; the ax had an
unearthly feel to it through the wool of his shirt. If the jarl

talked to pagan gods and they answered him, it was not something to be discussing with Hjalmar Sitricsson. Donal had known only one man before who claimed to talk to God, and that had been a monk at Lindisfarne, as ancient as he was holy. This was something different altogether, and there was an almost terrifying power in it. An old power, closer to the earth than the monks.

Where is my ax?
This time there was no mistaking the voice. "With Donal MacRae," Haakon said. He was weary, bone tired, and somehow his fine red vengeance had brought him very little solace.
You felt no need for my help? Haakon couldn't tell if the voice was angry or not.
"He was such a . . . small man, at the end. It didn't seem like honor to bring a god's strength against him."
Too small, maybe, for Haakon Olesson to have fought?
"Maybe." Haakon was uncomfortably aware that he had felt so as he had brought Knut's ax down for the last stroke. "Why didn't you tell me, lord, that it would be like this?" he burst out.
That there would be no pleasure in it? Would you have listened?
"No." When had he listened to anyone over it, even Rosamund? Or thought of anything but to nurse his hatred for Harud?
There are some things a man must learn for himself, Thor's voice said, and Haakon thought that that was a great piece of truth telling. *Some men never learn. You were chosen, Haakon Olesson, because you can. And now that you have learned, what will you do with knowledge?*
"Go home," Haakon said. The wreck of his vengeance was still a foul taste in his mouth, but somehow he knew that was the right answer. "I will go home. And then I will go where you send me, lord."
Go home first, Thor said. *You have a matter to settle there.* The presence faded from the trees as suddenly as it had come.

"Jarl, where have you been?"
"Jarl, here, drink."

"There is salt fish, jarl."

They clustered around him, proffering fish and water. Haakon wondered how badly in need of it he looked. "I am all right." He pushed them away. "You are not nurse-maids. Pack your troll-taken fish away."

"What about that?" Knut jerked a thumb at Harud's body.

"Bury it," Haakon said shortly.

They scraped a grave out of the hard ground and tumbled Harud into it. Haakon looked at Hjalmar Sitricsson. "Can you walk?"

"Aye, jarl."

"Then we march. Now. And sail for Norway."

They cheered at that, blithe and glad of a homecoming, but Donal caught Haakon looking back, once at Harud Olafsson's grave and once at the peaks that broke the sky between Sweden and Norway. He handed him back the ax. "So much time taken to kill a snake—would that be it?" he asked softly.

"Mostly," Haakon said, knowing that Donal read his thoughts too well to deny it.

"It was a snake that needed killing," Donal said. "Even at a price. Do not you be fretting for it."

"No," Haakon said slowly, "not now. That is done. But I think there is trouble waiting."

Donal looked grim. "Then that is not a matter for faultfinding, but only for a sword in the right place." He didn't ask how Haakon knew.

The others had fanned out down the slope already, and they set out after them. The dappled sun and trees masked the unmarked grave. By spring the wilderness would have taken it altogether.

XII The Islands in the West

Fann stared despairingly out into the gray waters of the fjord. *He isn't coming,* she thought for the twentieth time.

He isn't coming. The litany of fear ran unendingly through her head. Donal wasn't coming back, and she would be left with these pagan people, who terrified her with their rough ways and their evil gods. Lady Rosamund wasn't evil, but she was one among so many, and in time she too might turn her back on God, as the jarl's mother had done.

Fann's hand crept to the silver image of the Virgin, which hung under the neck of her gown. Fann was shaking. *Holy Mother, send him back to take me away from here.* If Donal came back, she would have to marry him, but Fann wasn't as afraid of that as she was of being abandoned here forever among the Norse.

The autumn wind blew up fiercely and stung her eyes. It churned the fjord into foam. If they were coming back, they would have been here by now. Fann knew that Lady Rosamund thought so too, although Rosamund wouldn't say it. Fann could tell by looking at her taut face, by Guthrun's hovering around her, and by Erik the Bald's frequent messages, which were supposed to be cheering but only succeeded in convincing everyone that he and Sigrid also thought Haakon was dead. And if Haakon was dead, then Donal was dead, or captured and a slave in some Eastern city. . . . Fann's fingers clutched the silver image, and she choked on a sob, staring down at the whitecaps on the fjord, letting her misery engulf her.

Holy Mother— There were ships on the fjord. She peered through the wind and then screamed. Not Haakon's ships—warships, long and lean, with sails scarlet like blood. Fann had lived along the vulnerable coastal rivers of Scotland long enough to know a viking ship when she saw it. There were two of them, with black serpents coiled across the red sails and dragon snouts lifted above the water. She turned and ran shrieking toward the steading as a shout from the shore told her that the sentries had seen them, too.

"Warships! Warships on the fjord!" The steading exploded into life as the sentries came scrambling up the hill. There was no question that the ships might be friendly; friendly ships would have taken down the dragon heads before the Land Spirits saw them and took fright.

"Whose are they?" Rosamund stood in the hall doorway, with Asa under one arm.

"Sigurd Njalsson's," Gunnar said. "Those are his sails."

Rosamund pushed the baby into Bergthora's arms. "Take her—take *all* the children, and get into the hills—the sheepherders' shacks—and stay there!"

"You, too, lady," Gunnar said.

"No, the women stay. We don't have enough men, Gunnar. The women will have to fight."

Gunnar opened his mouth to argue with her and closed it again. She was right. Behind her in the hall, he could see the house thralls milling in a frightened herd, with Guthrun's gold head in their midst, shouting them into order. In the steading yard, the men were running for the armory.

Gunnar grabbed a thrall. "Get a pony and ride for Erik Allesson's!" If Erik the Bald could get men to them in time, they might have a chance. *"Run!"* There were sounds of fighting outside already. The thrall *might* get through. "If you don't get to Erik's, they'll catch you!" he shouted after him, in case the thrall should think of running the other way.

Three men spilled into the hall with a bundle of spears and axes. The rest were forming themselves into a shield wall between the outer buildings or clambering up onto the roofs with bows. There weren't very many men; of the seventy-five Jarl Haakon had left, a good half were home on their own steadings for the winter. No one had expected an attack. Gunnar shouted a curse on Sigurd Njalsson and grabbed Guthrun by the arm. There wasn't much to say, so he just kissed her. There were shields stacked by the door, and he snatched one up as he ran. Behind him, Guthrun grimly took her apron off and picked up a spear.

They had formed the shield wall between the outer buildings at the top of the slope above the fjord, where they could push Jarl Sigurd's men down as they tried to climb from the shore. It gave them a little advantage, Rosamund thought, steadying herself against the unaccustomed weight of a shield on her left arm. But not enough. There would be close to a hundred men in those two

ships, far more than were in Haakonstead, even counting
the women and the thralls. The fighting men had made
the shield wall, with the women and thralls behind them
to hold off anyone who broke through or could circle
around.

Rosamund gritted her teeth and let go of her spear long
enough to wipe her hand on her skirt. She had never
fought anyone before, not with a weapon. She had fought
Haakon with talk and seduction when he had taken her
father's hold, and she hadn't really wanted to kill him, not
even then. Now it was different—Rosamund thought about
Asa in the sheepherder's shack with only Bergthora to
defend her. She shot a glance around the steading yard, at
the hall, the dairy, and the cattle byres. This was *hers*, and
now she would gladly put a spear in the man who tried to
take it. *But I am no warrior.* Mere willingness to kill
would give no skill to her arm. *Christ give me the skill*,
she thought.

Jarl Sigurd's men were howling a war cry outside the
shield wall, and she saw one of her own men go down. A
warrior with a scarred face staggered toward her, and she
leveled the spear.

Fann crouched sobbing inside the storehouse door. In
the steading yard they were fighting, Jarl Haakon's warriors against the others. There weren't enough to hold the
steading; Fann had heard Lady Rosamund say so. The
men from the serpent-sailed ships would break through,
and then they would come for her. She cowered against a
grain sack, which spilled a thin trail of meal onto the floor,
as she tried to shut the memory out: Fierce, blond-bearded
men with bloody hands, pulling her into a boat, with her
father dead behind her on the riverbank. They had put
their hands under her gown to amuse themselves while
she had screamed for Donal, who was tied up and unconscious. They hadn't raped her. She would fetch a better
price as a virgin, so they had left that to the man who had
bought her. Now it would happen again. Cold, paralyzing
fear swept over her, but something made her peer around
the door to watch the fighting, as a rabbit watches, frozen,
while the wolf comes for it.

A handful of Jarl Sigurd's men were in the yard. There was too much confusion to see quickly what was happening. Fann saw Lady Rosamund, with her kerchief fallen off and her pale hair spilling down her back, put a spear through the belly of a man with a sword in his hand. He tumbled down, and Guthrun and two house thralls closed in on the man who followed him. Fann realized that some of Jarl Sigurd's men were coming around past Haakon's warriors on the flanks, to attack them from the rear. They hadn't expected to find the women waiting for them.

Two more came running, shields up, axes raised. An ax came down, and a thrall fell, spouting blood. The body rolled against the storehouse door, the fallen spear clattering on the step. Lady Rosamund turned on Sigurd's axman, and he backed against the door and raised his ax again. The door swung silently in. He was close enough for Fann to smell him, the sickening scent of sweat and blood. He would kill Lady Rosamund, and then he would find her. . . .

Fann's terror turned to panic. *Never again*. Never again those bloody hands under her gown and the horror of a body pushing itself into hers. She snatched the dead thrall's spear from the doorstep and with both hands drove it into the axman's back. The man had a leather cuirass over his shirt, but Fann put the whole weight of her body and the strength of her fear into the spear shaft. She felt the point go through the leather and grate along the spine.

He fell forward, taking the spear with him. Rosamund lowered her shield, gasping for breath, to see Fann shaking on the doorstep. Rosamund put her foot on the dead man's back and pulled the spear out. She handed it silently back to Fann.

The shield wall still held when Jarl Sigurd's men began to draw off, but everyone in Haakonstead knew they would be back again. The steading yard was littered with the dead, and the defenders, gasping and bloodied, swayed on their feet.

Rosamund let the shield and spear fall where she stood. *I have killed a man. Christ forgive me and give me the strength to do it again.* She looked around her. Guthrun had the same look of weary horror on her face that Rosamund thought she herself must wear. Fann was still holding her spear with both hands. It was red all the way up to her fingers. The child had fought like a demon, Rosamund thought. There was a kind of grit at the bottom of that timid soul after all.

There were far too many dead, women among them. Rosamund knelt and brushed a bloodied wisp of hair from the sightless eyes of one of her servingwomen. A hand touched her on the shoulder. She looked up.

If was Leif Hildisson, one of Haakon's sworn men, whose home steading was downfjord. "We saw the warships and came in to fight, lady," he said. "Me and the few others I could get to. There's not many of us, but we fouled the land trails behind us. Jarl Sigurd can clear them in half a day, but it'll hold him back some maybe."

"That was good, Leif." Rosamund stumbled over the words. Her tongue felt thick. "I expect he'll try that way next. There—there will be soup in the kitchen. Go and eat while you can." She got to her feet and looked around her for Gunnar.

He came limping, with a rag, dirty with blood and dust, tied around his shin.

"The devil take Sigurd Njalsson into hell with him," Rosamund said, looking at the wreckage of the steading yard and the dead on the ground. "What will he do now, Gunnar?"

"They've only stopped to think it out," Gunnar said. "They weren't expecting you and your women." She stood spear straight and bloodied, and Gunnar remembered that Rosamund was an earl's daughter. She had her mother's kindness, but her courage was her blackhearted father's. "They'll be back and probably send some men around by land, to strike from both sides. I've ordered the landward side shored up as much as we can."

Rosamund nodded. The men were overturning sleds and hay carts, anything that would make a barrier between the outer buildings. "Leif Hildisson says they fouled the downfjord trail coming in, but Jarl Sigurd can clear it. Do you think our man got through upfjord to Erik?"

"I don't know," Gunnar said. He thought he probably

hadn't. Sigurd's men had been halfway up the hill. They
would have seen him.

That thought was plain enough on Gunnar's face. "Then
we are trapped," Rosamund said. "Unless Haakon comes
home." And no one thought he was going to, now. She
wondered wearily if she cared what happened to her if
Haakon didn't come home. But there was baby Asa and
the steading folk, and they were hers to look after now.
She counted over the winter stores in her mind; at least
they couldn't be starved out. But there was no place to go,
and no way to get there if there had been. Sigurd's men
had holed the hulls in all three of Haakon's warships. Not
badly enough to wreck them—Sigurd wasn't wasteful—but
badly enough so they wouldn't float without repairs. And
even if they could get to the ships, which was doubtful,
Sigurd would be back before the hulls could be patched.
Sigurd Njalsson didn't want a ruined, empty steading; he
wanted to take over Haakonstead, the power that went
with it, and any of Haakon's sworn men who would swear
to Sigurd instead after he had beaten them. Rosamund
hoped they would see Jarl Sigurd at the bottom of the
Trondheimsfjord first, but she couldn't be sure. Loyalty
didn't fill empty bellies, and a man had to serve someone.

The spear and shield lay where she had dropped them,
and she couldn't make herself pick them up again, not
until she had to. *I have killed a man*, she thought sickly. *I
will kill again*. She turned her mind away from the blood
on the spear, back to the matters that counted now. "We
must hope our man got through to Erik, Gunnar. We can
do no more." She knew without even talking about it that
there was no point in trying to send for help from King
Harald. If Harald Fairhair had been willing to save Haakon's
steading for him, then Sigurd Njalsson wouldn't be here
now. "Put the men who are in the best shape on watch and
let the others sleep." The wind was still blowing, and
there was a fine mist in it. The sky was leaden with rain.
Rain to wash the blood away, she thought.

"What about the children? Those sheepherders' shacks
won't hold storm weather out."

Asa. Rosamund bit her lip. She wanted to weep. How
long since she had had the luxury of tears? "The children

must bide where they are. We can't chance leading Sigurd's men to them." If they lost, then she would bargain with Sigurd for the children. Anything he wanted, for the children. She couldn't say that now; the men wouldn't see it so. Rosamund was wearily aware that if they lost, she would maybe have to fight her own men and Sigurd both, to let him take the steading and the silver and let the children go free. She gathered up her skirts and brushed futilely at the blood on them. "I must see to the wounded, Gunnar. Find me Guthrun, will you?"

They carried the wounded through a driving rain into the hall and put the dead as far away from the building and the well as they could. There was no time to bury them and no place to do it. Sigurd's men were Odin-knew-where, prowling around the perimeter of the stead-ing, picking out the weak spots. Two hours later, at nightfall, Rosamund and Gunnar gathered the leaders from among those who could still fight and sat down by the fire to plan how dearly they could cost Jarl Sigurd for Haakonstead.

Jarl Sigurd sat in his tent on the shore and looked up the slope at the glow of lanterns in the steading. He grinned. So Haakon Olesson's widow thought she could hold him off, did she? She'd learn to bow to the inevitable in the morning and to wish that she had sat by her fire and spun. They'd caught the thrall who had been riding for Erik Allesson's and left the body where they had caught him.

Sigurd looked at Thorleif, his helmsman. "I want that English she-cat taken alive. We might get a fair price for her from Erik Allesson. It'll be *all* the old man can do by the time he gets the word."

"What if he doesn't want her? Erik's a close man with his money."

"He'll want the brat, if he doesn't want the mother," Sigurd said. "His wife's grandchild's up there somewhere, and it may not be weaned yet. I don't want the thing to die before we can sell it to Erik. If he doesn't want the Englishwoman, she'll make a fine enough dairymaid and learn that no woman kills one of *my* men and enjoys life afterward."

Sigurd looked up through the rain at the steading and thought it out both ways. He'd need all the money he could get to keep a hold on Haakonstead once he had won it, and the Thing might make him pay some weregild. On the other hand, he didn't take kindly to having a hole punched in his pride by a woman. She should have known better and given in when she saw his ships coming. An Englishwoman had no right to hold a Norse steading for herself, not in the eyes of any right-thinking man, and Sigurd knew the Thing could be persuaded to see it his way. It would do her good to wear a thrall ring for a while to take her pride down a peg or two. Then he could decide, if Erik still wanted her.

The rain lashed down. They had barely made it in time, Sigurd thought comfortably. A good thing they would be able to winter in Haakonstead. He yawned. By morning his men would have the land roads cleared. The men would be wet and surly, but tomorrow night they could all sleep dry again, with Haakon Olesson's ale and women to warm them. That would be the first thing Haakon's Englishwoman would do for him.

The fjord was a froth of storm waves. The wind and the rain lashed them mercilessly as the three ships beat their way upfjord.

"In Thor's name, *row!*" Haakon shouted. He pulled on his oar and tried to see through the driving rain. A spread sail was too dangerous to risk in this weather, and the sails were furled and lashed down tightly. If one came loose to catch the wind, they could all drown in sight of home.

"*Row!*"

They bent their heads into the rain and pulled, while Knut and Hagar the Simple both leaned on the helm to hold the pitching ship steady. The green hills of the fjord side were a blur behind the rain. Haakon couldn't even be sure how far up the fjord they had come, but the fear of what they were going to find drove him harder than the rain. Slowly the fjord side rose to a familiar curve.

"Ships, jarl!" Hagar bellowed. "On the shore!" The wind caught his words and flung them away into the storm.

Haakon squinted through the rain. There was something familiar about the set of those ships and the long, dragon-necked curve of the prows. They were pulled high on the shore—*his* shore—and lashed down. There was a tent pitched behind them. Someone was very sure he wouldn't have to leave in a hurry, Haakon thought grimly.

"Make shore!" *Gray Goose* ran hard onto the sand, and as she beached Haakon was over the side with Wulf behind him.

The invader's standard, a coiled black snake, was painted along the side of his pitched tent.

"Sigurd Njalsson!"

Curlew and *Gull Wing* beached behind him with a shudder. The crews shoved them high enough that the swollen fjord wouldn't take them back again and scrambled after Haakon up the muddy trail. The sounds of fighting came down to them through the storm.

Sigurd Njalsson's men were all around the steading. Haakon's men fell on them from behind.

"Come and fight me, Sigurd Njalsson!" Haakon bellowed. "I'm not dead yet!"

"It's the jarl!" Guthrun shouted.

"Haakon?" Rosamund stumbled to Guthrun through the mud of the steading yard, but she couldn't see anything through the storm and the confusion. On both sides the shield wall wavered under Sigurd's attack, and whenever a man went down, Sigurd's men poured through the gap before it could be closed. They had been fighting for an hour, and Rosamund knew they wouldn't last much longer.

Sigurd Njalsson spun around from the place where he had been hammering at Haakonstead's defenses to find himself face to face with their owner. Jarl Haakon was dripping wet, and he looked like a sea demon come up out of the fjord. The ax in his hand glowed terribly in the storm light, like lightning. Jarl Sigurd flung up his shield just in time, as the ax crashed down and sheared the whole top fourth of it away.

"You thought I was dead, Njalsson, so the carrion birds came for my leavings!" Haakon shouted. "I'll show you how dead I am!"

The ax came down again, and Jarl Sigurd tried vainly to counter with his own ax. His shield was a wreckage of kindling. All around him his men were fighting with Haakon's, caught between the men from the ships and the defenders in the steading, who had realized by now that someone had come to their aid. Haakon's ax bit into Sigurd's arm and crunched on bone. Sigurd yelped and slipped to his knees in the mud.

"You were too early, Njalsson," Haakon shouted furiously. "You should wait till the corpse has been burned!" The ax flashed, and Jarl Sigurd's head bounced off into a puddle.

Haakon swung the ax around his head and cut a path through the storm and Jarl Sigurd's now faltering men to the steading yard. He arrived in time to see his gentle Christian wife put a bloody spear through the throat of a man with a sword.

In another moment Jarl Sigurd's men were on the run. Haakon's men caught some of them before they reached the slope, but he shouted over the storm to let the rest go. They had done no more than follow their chief, and he was dead now. They floundered down the slope to their ships, hacking frantically at the lashings. Haakon kicked Jarl Sigurd's head down the hill after them.

"Go back to your kennels before I set the dogs on you!" he bellowed.

"Haakon!"

Rosamund leaned against him while Wulf leaped around them, barking. Her gown was streaked with blood spreading pinkly down her skirt in the rain, and her hair was wet and tangled as a blackberry hedge. She had a bandage tied around one arm. Haakon held her to him tightly for a moment, then pushed her away and turned her around and back to face him again. He didn't see any more wounds. "Are you all right?"

"Yes, yes, only a cut, and it's no great matter. But so many of our folk...Haakon, I thought you were dead." Her face had gone white now that it was over, and her hands clutched at his wrists.

"My heart, I'm sorry." He held her to him again. "Things were . . . more complicated than we had thought."

"And Harud?" Please God that he was dead, and Haakon wouldn't go looking for him anymore.

"Dead," Haakon said. He didn't seem to want to say more.

"Where is Ragnar?" She straightened up and began to remember that there were others to be concerned about.

"Coming upfjord behind us. He has most of the cargo, and it's heavy going in this weather. We loaded most of ours into his ships to make better time."

"You knew?"

"Not exactly. But it's late in the season, and there's always someone who's too quick to go plundering. I should have thought of Sigurd Njalsson. He always did have thief's eyes."

"He's been here before," Rosamund said wearily. "And King Harald. We traded your shipwright to Harald for a little peace, Gunnar and I, or I think the king would have been here before Jarl Sigurd."

Haakon looked startled. "Yazid? And my ship?"

"No, no, your ship is hidden at Erik's, and safe. And Yazid's service is only for a year." She looked at the wet wreckage of the steading. "I'll tell you more when you have rested, and we have cleaned up."

Haakon let his eyes follow her eyes. Fann was clinging, sobbing, to Donal in the rain, and the newly arrived men were beginning to pick up the wounded and dead. He spun back to Rosamund, his ship forgotten. "The children! Where are the children? Where's my daughter?"

"Oh, good heaven! Guthrun!" Guthrun let go of Gunnar's hand and came toward them. "Send someone for the children!" Rosamund shouted to her. "They're in the sheepherders' shacks," she said to Haakon, "but they'll be half-drowned, poor babes."

Haakonstead settled in to lick its wounds. There were fourteen dead, and three more who wouldn't make it through the night. Of the other wounded, two would be lame for life, and the rest would be fit by spring. Haakon counted up in his mind how much he was going to ask the

Thing in weregild out of Sigurd Njalsson's belongings. He
would leave enough to feed Njalsson's former men through
the winter, he thought grimly, and not a silver piece more.
Rosamund sat by the fire, drying Asa, who seemed to have
taken no harm from her night in the hills. Asa could stand
now, and walk a little as long as she held onto something.
She clung to Rosamund's knees and looked curiously at
her father over her shoulder.

"She doesn't know who I am," Haakon said indignantly.

"She'll come around," Rosamund said. "Seven months is
a long time." She pointed at Haakon. "Da-da."

"Da-da," Asa said experimentally. "Da-da-da-da-da-da."
She buried her head in Rosamund's gown.

"That is enough of that." Haakon waited until Rosamund
had dropped the baby's gown over her head and then he
scooped her up. "I'm your father, young woman, and don't
you be forgetting it." Asa grinned, showing four teeth. She
grabbed his beard. Haakon yelped and detached her. He
sat down with the baby in his lap, beard out of reach. Asa
stuck out a fat hand and grabbed his dagger. Haakon
handed her back to Rosamund. "She's dangerous."

"She's fearless," Rosamund said seriously. "I can't turn
my back on her for a minute." She cradled the baby and
cooed at her. Rosamund's hair was pinned up again in
matronly fashion under her headrail. She didn't look like
the woman Haakon had seen in the steading yard, putting a spear through a man's throat. Haakon had learned a
thing or two about Rosamund, he thought. There was a
reason for those Valkyrie violet eyes. He peered at Asa.
The baby was going to have them too. Haakon remembered Gunnar telling him that old Earl Edmund had eyes
like that. It seemed that Rosamund was not entirely her
mother's daughter.

"And I swear that I have heard the witnesses and that
the marriage between Gunnar Thorsten, steward of my
holdings and sworn man of mine, and Guthrun, free
woman of this steading, is true and lawful." Haakon poured
the blood on the rune-stone in the field where his mother
and Erik the Bald had been married two summers ago.
The folk who were huddled around them in the rain

cheered and then ran with unseemly haste for the hall, the
fire, and Jarl Haakon's bridal ale. Haakon chuckled. It was
getting colder every minute, and the wind was up again.
The bridal couple didn't seem to mind.

Guthrun was dressed in Rosamund's best gown, and
there was a wreath of dried flowers in her gold hair.
Gunnar was looking pleased with himself. Neither had
seemed inclined to wait for spring and the lawspeaker. A
marriage sworn to by the jarl was binding enough. Haakon
thought that it was high time, too. He had offered to do
the same for Donal and Fann, and Donal had seemed
happy enough with the idea, but Fann would have a
Christian priest or none at all. Where she expected to find
a Christian priest in the Trondelag, Haakon didn't know,
and he didn't think she did either. Anyone would think
that the girl didn't want to get married. Privately, Haakon
thought that was Donal's good fortune, but he knew better
than to say so. To all appearances Donal was contenting
himself with writing a song for Gunnar Thorsten's wedding, but Haakon had seen him the night before, slipping
into the dairy with one of Rosamund's servingwomen.
Donal's blood ran too hot to tie himself to a woman who
would probably sleep with him only on feast days when
she couldn't find an excuse. Ah, well, it was all Donal's
business and not Haakon's. Haakon shrugged and started
off across the field after the merrymakers. Gunnar was still
by the rune-stone kissing Guthrun, and his hand was up
under her gown.

"If you don't come to the feast first, Gunnar, they'll drag
you out of bed and make you sing for them!" Haakon
shouted at him over his shoulder.

The bridal feast lasted until the sun came up the next
morning, with Haakon's men, Ragnar's crew, and Erik and
Sigrid's household all jammed into the great hall at
Haakonstead. It was a victory party as well as a bridal, and
there was enough ale to float a longship. Haakon sat and
watched his guests benevolently while they drank it, and
if the jarl himself wasn't drinking, no one noticed but his
wife. The returning sailors settled in to tell the stay-at-
homes the great things that had befallen them on their

way to Mikligard. By the time the tale was finished,
Haakon noted that sea serpents, dragons, and a tribe of
cannibals had been added to their perils. Gunnar sang as
many songs as he was willing to, and when his audience
showed signs of detaining him forcibly, Donal took out his
harp to keep them quiet while Gunnar and Guthrun
slipped away.

A few of the strong of stomach were still celebrating by
morning, Donal among them. They had begun to make
rude rhymes about each other, to the tune of Donal's harp,
when Haakon stood up and left the hall, his ax in his hand.

He is going to talk to that thing, Rosamund thought
sleepily. She should have been in bed long since, but she
had been parted too long from Haakon to leave his side
before she could help it. Now she stood, weaving on her
feet—for once in their married life, she was drunker than
Haakon—and went in search of her bed. She had always
thought that she was probably happier not knowing more
than she did about that ax.

Behind her, Donal finished his verse triumphantly and
fell into Thorfinn Solvisson's lap, while Knut and Kalki
Estridsson cheered him drunkenly. They would pass out
where they sat, Rosamund thought, but she expected the
thralls could clean around them. The thralls were used to
it.

At the foot of the meadow Haakon took a deep breath of
cold air to clear the sleep out of his head. The rain had
stopped, but a fine mist shrouded the trees. The sun was a
watery splotch of pale light above the mountains. Strange
to be sober at daybreak, but probably most unwise not to
have his wits about him when he had further doings with
Thor Odinsson. It was that thought that had kept Haakon's
hand off his ale horn all night. The past week had taught
him two things: First, it was time to do what he had
promised Thor Odinsson; the golden ax had nearly burned
his hand when he had picked it up, and it was never a
good idea to postpone a god's wishes for too long. And
second, if he planned to sail anywhere next season and
have a steading to come home to, he would have to make
his peace with Harald Fairhair.

Haakon Olesson!

The voice came out of the mist, and Haakon spun around, looking for it, feeling foolish. He had often wondered if the god did that to give Haakon a sense of his own smallness in the face of Thor's power.

I have been waiting, Haakon Olesson, while you drank yourself into a stupor at a skald's bridal.

"I did not drink." *And if you knew where I was, then you are knowing that, too.* He didn't say that. "What do you want of me, lord?"

The service you have been marked for from the start. It is time.

"But—" He had served Thor for two years now.

You did not think you were chosen merely to right such small wrongs as an evil betrothal or to save a man from shipwreck? There are too many such things in the world for the gods to take a hand in them all. I am Odin's son, not a country lawspeaker. No, the shipwright was sent you because you will need his ships. Likewise the lady because she is the woman for you. And because she will give you children who will make a mark in the world, beginning with the little one in the cradle now.

"Asa?"

Oh, yes. The god laughed, some unexplained joke. Haakon found that he was wary of Thor's idea of humor.

"Then what is it I am to do, lord?"

The voice sobered suddenly. *You will preside at Ragnarok, I think.*

"I do not understand." The mist suddenly felt chilly, clammy against his shirt.

There is a new age coming, Haakon, with new ways, and new gods. We have always known of it, and now it is nearly here. And we will fade before it, because it is a force that even we must acknowledge. There was a pause, and the wind began to blow cold down the meadow. *But for this new age there will be a new land. It is there in the west, waiting. And it matters greatly that it be found before we, the Aesir, are gone from the world entirely, that we may leave some mark behind us for the benefit of man.*

"I do not understand," Haakon said again. He felt lost, like a child, in the mist. "The gods do not fade. And

Ragnarok is a battle." The final battle that would see the world born anew, so said the stories.

Everything has an ending, even gods such as we. The voice was not sad. It was comforting somehow. *It may be that Ragnarok is not a battle after all, but only a change in the way of things. Not for you, Haakon. You will come to Valhalla as I promised. But you will open a door to the new ways and leave a bit of the old behind you, that men may know us and remember.*

There was nothing more, only silence, no spoken farewell. But Haakon knew that the god was gone and that he was alone in the meadow. He looked at the ax. The gold blade glowed faintly. Not entirely alone, then. He looked out to where the fjord lay veiled in fog. It would snow soon. And somewhere beyond the fog and snow was a new land—waiting, like the islands that Donal said his people had once believed lay beyond the western sea. Maybe they had been right, then.

Haakon stood thinking. The things that Thor Odinsson had said were fearful, but somehow Haakon didn't find himself afraid. For Haakon, for the old gods of the Aesir, there would still be Valhalla. And there was the new land, which, he realized, had already begun to call to him. A foot in both worlds. That was none so bad—Haakon laughed suddenly—and a way to make peace with Harald Fairhair maybe, if Haakon agreed to sail in Harald's name for the glory it would bring him.

He shouldered the ax, whistling. With so much decided, that left only two matters: to think of a way to tell his wife that next spring he was sailing off to look for the edge of the world, and then to somehow convince his men that they would not be eaten by dragons if they came with him. That should keep him busy through the winter. Hjalmar alone would take three months' argument.

Glossary

curragh: small boat made of wickerwood and covered with hide.

forswear: to renounce an oath or to swear falsely.

Hel: in Scandinavian mythology, the underworld region where spirits of men who had died in their beds resided, as distinguished from Valhalla, the abode of heroes slain in battle.

jarl: tribal chieftain.

knarr: broad-beamed ship, deep in the water, with a high freeboard.

Norns: deities who tended men's destinies.

skald: Norse reciter or singer of heroic epics, a poet.

spaewife: female fortune-teller or witch.

thane: retainer or free servant of a lord.

Thing: northern assembly of free men for law, debate, and matters of regional importance.

thrall: a member of the lowest social class; a slave to a master or lord as a result of capture or an accident of birth.

wadmal: coarse, woolen material used for protective covering and warm clothing.

weregild: a value set by law upon the life of a man, in accordance with a fixed scale. Paid as compensation to kindred or to the lord of a slain person.

Wyrd: fate.

Author's Note

For the reader interested in separating fact from fiction, Haakon and his band are my own creations, but Leo VI, his chief minister Stylian Zautzes, and Symeon, king of the Bulgars, were real people.

Their war, and the intervention of the Magyars and the Pechenegs in it, was real and serves here as the background for a fictional tale of viking adventurers, who are known, in fact, to have traded often in Constantinople. Oleg, prince of Kiev, and Harald Fairhair, king of Norway, are also taken from history.

I owe a debt of gratitude to many for their tireless kindness and help with this book, but primarily to the people at Book Creations, Inc. To Lyle Kenyon Engel, Marla Engel, and George Engel; to Laurie Rosin, an editor of unflagging charm and patience; and to Sandra Pavoni, for her hours spent in gathering the mountains of research material that go into the writing of a historical novel. My love and thanks to them all.

Eric Neilson